THE
GIRL IN THE
CLOCKWORK
COLLAR

THE
GIRL IN THE
CLOCKWORK
COLLAR

Kady Cross

HARLEQUIN® TEEN

 HARLEQUIN®TEEN

ISBN-13: 978-0-373-21053-4

THE GIRL IN THE CLOCKWORK COLLAR

For Kenzie Mae. The world's a little brighter with you in it.

Chapter 1

High above the Atlantic Ocean
July 1897

"What are you doing?"

Finley Jayne smiled in the darkness. She should have known Griffin would come looking for her. Gripping the slender prow with both hands, she glanced over her shoulder and saw him standing just inside the dirigible's softly lighted observation deck. The wind blew strands of hair into her face. "Finding out how it feels to fly," she replied.

"You're over three thousand feet in the air." His gravelly voice carried over the sound of the airship's engines. "Flying might prove fatal."

Finley laughed. That was his way of scolding her for having ignored the signs that warned passengers not to climb out the windows or over the protective railings. Griffin King was the Duke of Greythorne, and sometimes he carried the weight of the entire world on his shoulders. That he was worried about her was…sweet.

"We're going to be landing soon," he called, trying another tactic. "Why don't you come in and make sure you have all your things?"

"I'm packed and ready," she called back. "Why don't you come out here and see how beautiful New York City is at night?"

She didn't expect him to take her up on the dare. It wasn't that he was a coward—he was anything but. However, as a duke and an only child, it would be irresponsible of him to risk his life for no reason but a pretty view, just because she asked. No, Griffin wouldn't be so foolish, but Jack would.

Finley pushed the thought of the notorious criminal Jack Dandy from her mind. Jack was in London, and it wasn't fair of her to compare Griffin to him when neither of the young men had an equal.

There was a faint noise behind her, and the next thing she knew, Griffin was there, sitting with her on this narrow shaft. All that was below them was the ship's figurehead—a robust blonde woman of dubious virtue carved from wood—and thousands of miles of night.

"What are you doing?" Finley demanded, her tone a reflection of what his own had been—only slightly more panicked. She wasn't *that* breakable, but Griffin was. "You shouldn't be out here."

One of his legs brushed the back of hers. Beneath her striped stocking, her skin prickled. "I know, but I hear it's the only way to experience the sensation of flying." She could tell he was smiling without being able to see his handsome face. "It is magnificent, isn't it? Look, there's the Statue of Liberty."

It *was* magnificent, so much so that Finley couldn't find words to reply. Spread out before them—just beyond the ship's lanterns—was a blanket of lights. It looked like stars covered the ground, and set a short distance from it all was the largest lady she'd ever seen, the glow from her torch illuminating from her raised hand to just the top of her crowned head. The lights of the dirigible brought the rest of her into view.

"I asked the pilot to fly by her so we can have a better look," Griff said.

"Asked or told?" she teased. This was Griffin's private airship—the *Helena,* named after his mother. Someone else might fly it for him, but he was the one in charge.

He smiled. "Asked. What do you think of America so far?"

"It's grand." It came out a little more exuberant than she'd planned. She had never been outside England—never been outside London—so this was already the adventure of a lifetime for her. Never mind that only a fortnight ago, she'd been battling for the safety of all the world against a madman. That had been terrible and frightening and not really

a proper adventure at all. But this—soaring above the vast
Atlantic Ocean with the night wind in her hair and Griffin
sitting behind her—was amazing.

She felt close to him, enough that it scared her a little. She
didn't even know who she was inside, and he was a duke who
could bring down buildings from the inside out by controlling the Aether. There could never be anything but friendship
between them, but that didn't stop her from the occasional
daydream. He made her feel like she could do anything she
set her mind to—what girl wouldn't have a bit of a crush?

"Would you like to know how it really feels to fly?" he
asked her.

Finley turned her head. Their perch was precarious at best.
One wrong move, and one, if not both, of them could tumble
to their very death. Part of her was terrified at the thought
and another part was thrilled by the danger. Recently, she'd
started trying to reconcile the two very distinct halves of herself, and with Griffin's help she'd made incredible progress.
But now she was left trying to ascertain just what sort of girl
she was. Was she the sort of girl who truly wanted to know
what it felt like to fly?

"I…"

"Oy!" cried a strange voice from behind. "What in the
blazes is you two up to? You're not allowed out there!"

"Caught." Griffin's voice held a trace of regret. "Let's go
in before Emily and Sam come looking for us."

Finley waited until he'd slid away before inching along the

polished wood. Griffin was waiting for her on the narrow expanse of deck to give her a hand up. Then he helped her through the window before easing his own body through.

A man in uniform stood on the glossy wood of the viewing gallery floor, a frown on his face. The man glared at her, then turned his attention to the young man beside her, who stood tall and lean in a dark gray suit, his reddish-brown hair mussed by the wind. A lopsided smile curved his lips as his stormy blue gaze settled on the officer. The man paled.

"Your Grace." His voice was hoarse.

Griffin's grin broadened. "Apologies, my good man. You were right to scold us. We'll give you no more worry." Then he turned to Finley. "Want to watch the landing?"

He offered her his arm, and she took it, allowing him to draw her toward the large glass window next to the one they'd just crawled through. It was so amazing that he owned all of this.

"You know, if you weren't a duke and this was a public ship, we'd be in a terrible spot of bother right now."

Griff made a scoffing noise. "If I weren't a duke and this were public, we wouldn't have been able to afford passage. Honestly, what they charge for a transatlantic voyage on these contraptions is akin to highway robbery."

"So you thought buying your own was the more economical choice?" She managed to keep a straight face but not the laughter out of her voice.

He shrugged, but she caught the smile he tried to hide.

"They gave me a very good price. Besides, it was the only way I could make Sam fly. He has Emily check the mechanical parts before every voyage."

"Sam's a baby," she remarked, thinking the comparison fit. She didn't mean any insult—well, not much. Sam Morgan was Griff's best friend. He was also part machine, moody and the biggest lout she'd ever met. Still, he had a way of growing on a person, like mold on cheese.

She kind of liked knowing he was afraid of air travel. He was even harder to hurt than she was and wasn't afraid of much.

"Speak of the devil," Griff murmured, looking over the top of her head.

Finley turned and saw Sam and Emily walking toward them, both dressed for dinner. Sam looked uncomfortable in his black-and-white evening attire, though he looked decent enough with his long dark hair smoothed back. There seemed to be nothing that could be done for his perpetual frown. Emily, on the other hand, was like a ray of sunshine. Ropes of copper hair were wound into a loose bun on the back of her head, and her blue-green eyes were brightened by the russet-colored gown she wore. The four of them looked as though they were going to a ball rather than following a suspected murderer to a strange country.

Their friend Jasper Renn had been accused of murder and taken from Griff's house by bounty hunters five days earlier. They would have followed immediately after him if they could have, but despite having his own airship, it took Griffin almost a day to make preparations and get everything ready.

"Been sucking lemons again, Sam?" Finley asked when the other couple joined them.

The big lad arched a dark eyebrow at her but didn't speak. Since she'd saved his life—after him trying to kill her—he had been almost nice to her, which made her try to bait him all the harder.

"We came to watch the landing," Emily told them in her Irish lilt. "We heard that there were a couple of idiots out on the prow. Did you see them?" A slow smile curved her lips.

Finley and Griff laughed in unison, which made Sam's scowl deepen. "Idiots indeed," he said drily.

Emily started to roll her eyes, but then her head whipped toward the window. "Oh! There's the Statue of Liberty! Isn't she grand?"

Her excitement was contagious, and the four of them went to the glass to watch the *Helena* glide by the statue that Griffin had pointed out to her earlier. It was so big. So beautiful. They would set down on the island of Manhattan, on the landing field in Central Park, and from there, on to their hotel. Tomorrow morning they'd begin looking for Jasper. Surely it wouldn't be difficult, given that he'd been brought back to face criminal charges.

Finley couldn't believe Jasper would kill anyone—not in cold blood. There had to be some kind of mistake. Griffin was convinced he could fix this, but this wasn't England, and Americans might not be so impressed by his title and his fortune. And though each of them had their own unique abilities—evolutions, Emily had taken to calling them—they weren't above the law.

What if they couldn't save Jasper?

As far as prisons went, this one wasn't so bad. Jasper had certainly seen worse—been held in worse.

There were bars on the windows, but his understanding was that those were normally employed to keep folks out rather than in, as the case may be. Still, the bed was big and comfortable—an old four-poster monstrosity—and the room was big enough that he could walk around a bit and exercise.

Dalton—the fella in whose house he was now a "guest"—was an old "friend." Jasper fell in with his gang almost two years ago, when he was too young and stupid to know better. Dalton was a couple of years older and had spouted the usual romantic nonsense about being an outlaw, which sounded good to penniless boys.

Obviously Dalton had done well for himself, if this house was any indication. It was nice—nicer than anything Jasper had seen during his time in the gang. Did Dalton think of himself as some kind of gentleman now? Was he rubbin' elbows with the same kind of people from whom he stole? The Bowery neighborhood was close enough to Five Points to give him an in with the criminal set, but removed just enough to have a little respectability.

Respectable, however, Dalton was not. And it was painfully apparent that his old boss hadn't forgiven him for running off. The tender bruises that covered Jasper from face to hip were proof of that. He had a perfect impression of the sole of someone's boot on his left side. Must've been Little Hank—he was the only varmint in Dalton's outfit with feet that big.

If he had some of Miss Emily's salve, he'd be set to rights; but he didn't, and so he had to heal the old-fashioned way instead of letting her "beasties" do it for him.

He thought of his new friends often since he'd been forcibly taken from Griffin's mansion by men claiming they were going to bring him to America to face murder charges.

Jasper went willingly, almost eager to face his past, maybe clear his name in the process. It wasn't until he was on the airship, without any chance of escape, that he discovered the men worked for Dalton.

Once they'd landed, he had tried to run. It had been stupid, but he had to try. They caught him, beat him, trussed him up and brought him here, where'd he'd been for more than twenty-four hours.

Finally there came the sound of a key in the lock. Jasper moved to the dresser, a heavy piece of furniture he could dive behind if someone started shooting.

It was Little Hank's huge form that filled the doorway.

Over six and a half feet tall and as wide as a bull through the chest, Little Hank was Dalton's chief muscle. He was strong and surprisingly fast. Jasper's only advantage came in being faster, but he didn't want Dalton to know just how fast he had gotten.

Little Hank ducked his head into the room. "Boss wants to see you."

"Now's not a good time for me," Jasper replied, words as stiff as his jaw. "Come back later."

The behemoth hesitated, clearly uncertain of what to do. Jasper would have smiled if he thought it wouldn't hurt so much. Then a scowl settled over Hank's heavy-boned face and he glared at him. "Still a jackass."

Jasper shrugged. "Sometimes a fella has to live up to expectations." He moved stiffly toward the door. Dread twisted in his belly, but he refused to let it show.

Little Hank seized him by the back of the neck, practically dragged him out of the room, along the hall and down the scuffed staircase. From there they took a right turn and ended up in a parlor, where Jasper was finally released. He might not exactly like Griff's friend Sam Morgan, but he wished the large fellow was there at the moment. He'd teach Little Hank a lesson in manners.

Then again, Morgan was just as likely to sit back and smile while Jasper was pounded senseless. Miss Finley, then. She'd knock Hank on his gigantic backside. Jasper would have no problem letting a girl rescue him, but Finley was in London.

They thought he'd been taken in by the law and had no idea that it was just the opposite.

Reno Dalton stood at the window, puffing on a cigarillo. He was a little shorter than Jasper's height of six feet. Leaner, too. He was what in a woman might be called pretty, with longish dark brown hair and ice-blue eyes. He wore a perfectly tailored gray suit that made him appear a gentleman.

In truth he was more like a sleeping rattlesnake. There was just as much chance that Dalton would leave you alone as there was that he'd kill you—and with very little thought to, either.

"Ah, Jasper." A cold smile curved Dalton's lips. He was around twenty, but lines fanned out from his eyes—a sign of time spent out of doors. "Looking none the worse for wear, I see."

If Jasper had been wearing his hat he would have tipped it. "I look good in black and blue."

Dalton waved a negligent hand. "The ladies will be back to swooning over you soon enough. Have a seat."

"I'd rather stand."

The smile vanished. Finally the rattler revealed himself. "Sit."

Little Hank shoved him into a nearby chair before Jasper could reply. It was spindly and felt as though it might split apart if he sneezed. He jerked free of Hank's hand—flinching at the pain that followed—and fixed his gaze on the man before him.

"All right, I'm sitting."

Dalton was back to looking pleasant. "Good." His voice had a slight Southern accent. Years of living in San Francisco had almost erased all traces of the poor kid from Virginia Territory. "We have business to discuss, you and I."

Cold—heavy and menacing—settled in Jasper's stomach. He ignored it. "'Fraid I don't know what you're talking about."

Dalton smiled—without any trace of pleasantness this time. Slowly, he moved around the desk to sit behind the large wooden structure. He plucked a plum from a bowl in front of him. "Let's not play this game, Jasper. You know where the device is. You stole it from me, and I want it back."

Jasper yawned. It hurt like blazes, but at least he looked bored. "I stole it when you went back on our deal and tried to kill me rather than pay me for it."

"I paid you for half the job. The way I see it, you got away with my money and my device."

"You can see it however you want. I don't have your money or the machine." There was no point in lying and no point in arguing that Jasper had taken the money as what was rightfully owed to him.

Dalton's eyes narrowed. "Who has it?"

Jasper forced a smile. "No one has it. But I know where it is. Seeing as how it's the only thing keeping you from killing me, I'll keep the location to myself."

To his surprise, the gleam in Dalton's eyes brightened.

"I'm disappointed, Jas. You know I'd never kill you." When Jasper arched a brow, Dalton continued, "I'll kill someone you care about." With that, he flicked a small switch on the side of his desk. A door to Jasper's left swung open.

Jasper's heart stopped when he saw who stood on the other side of that threshold. She was little and pale, with poker-straight, long black hair that fell almost to her waist. She wore a long turquoise silk dress embroidered with Chinese dragons, and she was even prettier than she had been the last time he saw her—when he had kissed her goodbye. The only thing new was the strange necklace she wore—a snug band of what looked like clockwork pieces all around her throat.

She looked as shocked to see him as he was to see her. Her almond-shaped eyes widened. "Jasper?"

"Mei," he whispered. He was dizzy, like he'd spun around and around—fast as he could—and then tried to stand still. He started to get up, but Little Hank pushed him back down with a meaty hand on his shoulder.

Dalton's smile returned. "So you can see, Jasper, you have something I want and I have something you want." He rose to his feet and crossed the carpet to where Mei stood, guarded by another of the outlaw's men. He ran the back of his finger along her cheek, causing her to flinch.

Jasper pushed against Little Hank's hold, but it was as though his posterior was glued to the chair. "If you hurt her…"

Dalton whipped around, coming toward him like a striking rattler. "Hurt her? I don't think you understand me, son. You owe me. If you don't do exactly what I want, I'll damn well *kill* her."

Chapter 2

The combined Waldorf and Astoria hotels on 5th Avenue were the height of opulence and elegance. At seventeen stories, the redbrick structure had only recently been completed by John Jacob Astor IV.

As they climbed out of their hired carriage, Griffin was the least impressed with their lodgings, and even he thought it splendid. He held his beaver hat on his head as he glanced up. "Grand, isn't it? What do you make of it, Finley?"

"It's bloody marvelous," she replied, without taking her eyes off the building.

He grinned at her openmouthed wonder. He had made arrangements to stay at this place, specifically hoping that his friends would love it. That Finley would love it.

Top that, Dandy, he thought to himself. He knew it was foolish to think of the criminal as competition, but Dandy appealed to Finley's dark side. Never mind that the two halves of her personality had already merged; they still fought for dominance, and there was still a part of her that found Dandy fascinating. Griffin had never been one for physical violence, but Finley's attachment to the older fellow made Griffin want to punch someone—*Dandy*—in the nose.

A handful of bellmen and young boys eager to make a few cents came forward to carry luggage and belongings. Griffin noticed with a smile that none of them tried to take possession of Emily's cat—a mechanical life-size panther. They all gasped when she powered it up and it came to life, stretching like the real thing, digging dagger-sharp claws into the sidewalk. It's reticulated joints were well-oiled and moved silently.

"Don't fret, gents," she chirped in her soft Irish brogue. "She's no danger." Not unless one of them tried to hurt Emily. Of course, she had Sam for protection, as well. Griffin would rather take on the cat than his best friend.

They filed into the hotel lobby, which was just as grand as the exterior. Griffin spoke to the man at the desk, who was clearly impressed at having a duke as a guest. America might have separated from England over a century earlier, but a title and a fortune were still cause for celebrity. The man gave him keys for four rooms. Certainly it would have been more economical to share, but they had separate rooms in London, so it seemed only right to have them here, as well—

especially since it was the only way they could escape each other, if they wanted.

They had to take two lifts to their floor—an operator, the four of them and Emily's cat in one, their belongings in the other. Being inside the small box, packed tightly with his friends, made Griff feel as though someone sat upon his chest. He clenched his hands and tilted his head back and closed his eyes, trying to force himself to remain calm. Soon they would be at their floor.

A soft hand curled around his fist, loosening his fingers so they could twine with hers. He lowered his head, opened his eyes and found himself gazing into eyes the color of warm honey, framed by thick, dark lashes.

Finley.

Suddenly, he was breathless for an entirely different reason. She smiled but didn't speak. She simply stood there beside him, holding his hand as they slowly climbed to their destination. Griffin wanted to reach up and touch the streaks of black in her tawny hair. He wanted to wrap his arms around her, pull her close, lower his head and...

The bell chimed. They had reached their floor.

And just in time, too, because he had started to lean toward her.

The operator opened the sliding doors and bid them goodnight. Griffin slipped him a tip for his trouble and was gifted with a grin and doffed hat in return.

After divvying up the keys, each of them went to their room so that their belongings could be taken inside. Griff peeled more notes from his money clip and pressed them into the eager hands of the boys who had brought their luggage.

His room was spacious and as luxurious as he expected, with a plush carpet, large, comfortable-looking bed and heavily draped windows, which afforded a spectacular view of 5th Avenue. He went to one of those windows and gazed out. New York looked like someone had captured the stars and dragged them down to Earth.

It was late, and he wanted to be up early so they could visit the jail and talk to Jasper—or talk to someone about Jasper. He would do whatever he could to help his friend, even buy his freedom, if necessary. There was no way he was going to allow Jasper to hang for a crime Griffin was certain he didn't commit.

It was that worry hanging over him that kept him standing rather than undressing for bed as he ought. Instead he gave in to his restlessness and turned on his heel. Unpacking would wait.

Griffin closed the door behind him and quickly crossed the corridor to knock on the one opposite. He raked a hand through his hair as he waited, then he heard the sharp clunk of the bolt and the heavy wood opened.

"You should have asked who it was," he cautioned. "I could have been anyone."

Finley smiled as she pulled the door fully open. She looked as tired as he felt. Still, she was the prettiest girl he'd ever seen. "I knew it was you. I heard you leave your room."

Of course she had; she had that bloody sensitive hearing of hers. She was more than capable of defending herself, too. He just worried about her. She was far too reckless and confident at times. It would kill him to see her get hurt.

He pushed the thought to the back of his mind as she stepped back to allow him inside. It was set up much like his own, only with a different view, as her windows overlooked 34th Street.

"I thought maybe you might be interested in taking a walk," he said, glancing around the room. She had already opened her luggage and begun unpacking. It was a little disconcerting, seeing her underthings, even though they were stacked in an open drawer. He looked away. "Those are lovely flowers."

Finley glanced at the bouquet of cream tea roses on the dresser. "They were here when I came in. I assumed they were part of the décor."

"I don't have any in my room." He took a closer look. "There's a card." He plucked the folded card stock from the blooms and offered it to her.

Frowning, Finley took it. "Perhaps it will tell us who they belong to." But as soon as she opened the card, Griffin knew the answer. She looked surprised, pleased and perturbed, all at once.

"They're from Dandy, aren't they?" He didn't really need her to respond. Who else would send her flowers? Not him, obviously.

She nodded, clearly bewildered. "How did he even know where to find me?"

Griffin shrugged and tried to look as though he didn't care. "It would be easy to ascertain that we had left and for where. Then all he had to do was contact hotels."

"Still, I don't know why he'd bother wasting the time."

"Don't you?" Griff studied her face closely. "Surely you know he has feelings for you."

Finley blushed. "We're friends."

As he ran one of his fingers along the petal of a rose, Griffin's mouth twisted into a bitter smile. "Perhaps you ought to enlighten Mr. Dandy as to that."

"Do you believe I've led him on?"

He choked on a bark of laughter. "You spent the night at his house. Could you blame him for making assumptions?"

Hands fisted on her hips, Finley glared at him. "And I live with you. What assumptions have *you* made, Your High and Mightiness?"

He should have stayed in his room. "None. I know better then to assume anything where you are concerned."

Instead of placating her, it only made her frown deepen. "What's that supposed to mean?"

Griffin shrugged. He couldn't win. "Nothing, Finley. It means nothing. I'm sorry I bothered you. Good night."

He moved to the exit and had just wrapped his hand around the brass knob when a hand slapped flat against the door. He turned the knob and pulled, but the door refused to budge—she was that strong.

Slowly, Griffin turned his head toward her, his temper and his power rising. The runes tattooed on his neck and shoulders to help him focus his abilities warmed and tingled. Only Finley had the ability to get under his skin like this. She made him think and act like an idiot. "Don't make me blow this thing off its hinges," he said, voice low.

Her eyes sparkled with disbelief, taunting him. "You wouldn't."

"I would. Not like I can't afford to replace it."

"Where would you expect me to sleep in the meanwhile?"

"I'm sure I can think of someplace." Yes, he could. As soon as he said it, he wished he could take it back. Heat crept up his cheeks.

Finley's lips parted on a soft gasp, and he noted with some pleasure that her cheeks darkened, as well. He also noticed that she did not immediately drop her hand from the door.

Her other hand, however, came up to touch his face. Her fingers were cool against his cheek. It took all of his strength, but he wrapped his hand around hers and pulled it away. "I care about you, Fin. More than I should probably admit, but I'm not going to share you or fight for your affection." Then—because he couldn't help himself—he kissed her fingers.

"Good night, Finley." He opened the door and stepped over the threshold. When the door clicked shut behind him, Griffin tried not to be too disappointed that she hadn't tried to stop him.

It was a good thing Dalton's men had taken his guns, because Jasper would have shot the rat between his eyes without much of a thought—he was that angry. Angry and helpless.

He was still angry hours later, standing alone at one of the windows in his "cell." It was well past midnight, but if he went to bed, he'd only stare at the ceiling.

Of all the secrets and weapons his former friend could have used against him, why did it have to be Mei? He knew why—because Dalton knew Mei was the best weapon to use against him, his guarantee that Jasper wouldn't try to escape.

He pressed his forehead against the cool glass of the window and breathed deep through his nose, but it didn't make him any less angry. He hadn't seen Mei since he left San Francisco a year ago. He'd left to protect her. And he had hidden

Dalton's blasted stolen contraption not only to ensure his own life, but to keep Dalton from becoming an even snakier rascal.

He should have known better than to leave her alone.

If he had just washed his hands of the situation, let Dalton have his contraption before escaping to England, he wouldn't be in this mess and Mei would still be safe. He should have taken her with him. But she hadn't wanted to leave.

When he thought of all the things that could have happened to her in Dalton's clutches...

The sound of a key in a lock brought his head up. Slowly, he turned as the hinges creaked and the door eased open.

He expected to see Little Hank, his knuckles wrapped to deliver another beating, but the person who entered was more than a foot shorter than the thug.

"Mei." To say he was surprised to see her was an understatement. "How... What are you doing here?"

She set a finger to her lips, telling him to be quiet as she closed the door. She was dressed as she had been earlier that evening, and the Western style seemed odd on her, even though the fabric was Chinese. He was so used to seeing her in more traditional clothing. When they were shut in, she locked the door once more from the inside. Gracefully, she moved toward him, her hair shining in the lamplight. "I had to come see you," she explained.

"How did you escape your quarters to get the key?"

"The key is on a hook outside the door." Delicate hands

went to the collar around her throat but didn't quite touch it. "This is my prison. I can move about the house however I wish, but if I try to leave, it tightens."

Jasper reached out to touch it. "Can't you just take it off?"

She stepped back, avoiding his hand. "Don't. If anyone else touches it, it sets off the tightening mechanism. It will strangle me, and you will have to ring for Dalton. I do not want him to know I am here."

Damn Dalton. Jasper's jaw tightened. "How long has he had you?"

"Only a few months. He found me in Chinatown. I had gone back to the house."

By "the house," she meant Ms. Cameron's. Donaldina Cameron had been helping girls and women brought over from China for more than twenty years. A lot of the females were sold into domestic slavery or prostitution once they arrived in the city, as they were illegal immigrants. Jasper had worked for Ms. Cameron as a rescuer and, on occasion, a protector. That's how he had first met Mei—when he rescued her from being sold to a merchant.

The same merchant for whose death he was wanted.

Dalton hadn't liked that Jasper helped the house. He thought Jasper should talk Mei into convincing some of the girls to work for him instead. He referred to it as "diversifying his business practices." Jasper had never been above help-

ing relieve a few richies of a little pocket change—he had to
eat—but he drew the line at profiting from another's pain.

"He went to Ms. Donaldina's?" That was ballsy, even for
Dalton.

Mei shook her head, her poker-straight hair sliding about
her shoulders. "I was trying to rescue another girl. He found
me."

Jasper's jaw clenched so hard it hurt. "Did he hurt you?"
He'd kill Dalton with his bare hands if he had to.

Dark eyes widened as Mei gazed at him. "No. He didn't
want me for...that. He only took me because he knew he
could use me to get to you."

And he had been right.

"He put that collar on you to keep both of us in line."

She nodded. "Yes." And then, "It's good to see you, Jasper."

Despite his frustration and anger, Jasper smiled. "It's good
to see you, too."

She turned away, but not before shooting him a glance
that was as coy as it was shy. Mei stood at the dresser and
ran her fingers over his old, battered hat. The Brits called it
his "cowboy" hat, but he had never worked with cattle in
his entire life, though he had once slept in a train car full of
them. Like big dogs, only they stank worse than any hound
ever could.

"Did you miss me at all?" she asked.

"Of course," he replied with a frown. It wasn't the sort of question a fella felt comfortable answering. "Did you miss me?"

Mei tossed a satisfied smile over her shoulder at him before gliding to the bed and leaning against one of the tall posters. "I knew you'd ask."

"You asked first," he reminded her with a shrug. "Figured since I was being honest, maybe you would, too."

"Still as prickly as you always were about your feelings. Yes, I missed you. I missed you very much, Jasper Renn. You left me all alone."

There was just enough bite to her words to get Jasper's backbone up. "I left so the law would think I was guilty. I left to protect you."

"And here we are." She gestured to the collar around her neck. "Maybe I would have been better protected had you stayed."

Her accent was thickening. It always did when she was riled up. It used to get to the point where he didn't understand half of what she was saying, her English would get so bad.

"Mei, you and I both know if I had stayed, they would have hanged me for murder. Is that what you wanted?"

"Of course not!" She glared at him. "How can you ask me such an awful question?"

"Because you're angry at me for protecting you." He would not shout, no matter how much he wanted to.

"For all the good it did!" She threw her arms out to her sides. "Look at where we are!"

Jasper drew a deep breath. It wasn't Mei he was angry at; it was Dalton—and himself. "I'm going to get both of us out of this mess. Promise."

She actually looked surprised. "Us?" She glanced at him as she moved away from the bed, toward the dresser again. "You are going to get Dalton his device?"

Jasper caught sight of himself in the mirror. His light brown hair stood up in all directions. He raked a hand through the mess but it only made it worse. "Yeah—I'm going to get it for him. What other choice do I have?"

She kept her attention fixed on his hat once more, rather than him. "You could try to escape. Run."

"And leave you with him?" He made a scoffing sound. "Blossom, you know me better than that."

The old nickname he'd given her brought color surging to her cheeks.

"You do not owe me anything, Jasper. I do not wish to have the responsibility of your life on my hands."

"Too bad, 'cause I've got yours on mine."

Her full lips thinned, and then she snatched the shaving mug from the top of the dresser and threw it at him. Suddenly, everything around him slowed as Jasper reached out and snatched the mug from the air.

Gone was her frown, replaced by shock. "You've gotten faster."

"And you've gotten crazier," he replied with a grin. "Come here."

He set the mug aside as she came toward him. When he opened his arms, she stepped into the embrace, wrapping her arms around him as though she was a human version of the collar she wore.

"Can we do this?" he asked, softly. "The collar..."

Mei shook her head. "As long as you don't touch it, we are fine. You can touch me."

Jasper pulled her closer and rested his cheek on the top of her head.

"I cannot allow you to put yourself in danger for me," she whispered against his shoulder. "I can help you escape— tonight."

He shook his head, his arms tightening around her. Old feelings came rushing back so hard and fast he felt unsteady on his own feet. He had loved her once, and now he knew he had never stopped.

"Don't talk so loose," he replied. "I'm not leaving you here. I'll fix this. Trust me."

Mei lifted her chin, and Jasper found himself staring into the dark brown of her eyes—so dark they were almost black.

He felt like he was drowning. He lowered his head, and when he pressed his lips to hers, suddenly, there was only the two of them in the world. It was as though they'd never said good-bye—as though a murder hadn't driven them apart.

The building referred to as "the Tombs" might have been stately were it not so...grimy. It was built in the Grecian style with thick pillars out front and shallow steps leading to the front door. But the structure's purpose showed itself in the sorry state of the stone and the many criminals who darkened its doors.

"You really think Renn's in there?" Sam asked from where he stood at Griffin's left.

Griffin glanced at his friend, who was a few inches taller—and many broader—than he. "We're only a few days behind him. This is where he should have been brought."

Sam shrugged. "Unless they hanged him already."

"Eloquent and succinct as always, Samuel," Griff commented, making a face.

"What?" Sam's rugged countenance was all innocence. "I don't wish it on Renn, but if he is a murderer, there's a chance they've done him already."

"Let's hope the American judicial system is as slow as our own and that Jasper is alive and here."

Sam stuffed his hands in his coat pockets as they climbed the worn steps. "I still don't understand what you hope to do here. It's not as though they're going to hand him over to us just because Your Grace doesn't like people interfering in what you consider your business."

"I just want to see him," Griffin replied, pulling open the door. "I want to hear his side of the story." He ignored the other remark—partly because Sam didn't know what he was talking about and partly because the lout was right. Jasper was his friend and someone had taken him. Griffin didn't like that.

"There's a chance you won't like what he says." There was no censure in Sam's tone, only caution.

Griff nodded, his jaw tight. "I know." And that was why he had to see his friend. He had to know the truth before he decided whether to come back one evening and use his abilities to blow a hole through the side of the building to get Jasper out. After what happened during their battle with The Machinist, he was certain he could do it, but only if Jasper was innocent.

And he had no doubt his friends would help—even Finley, whom he hadn't seen since last night's fiasco in her room. He supposed he owed her an apology for his behavior, but he wasn't the least bit sorry for any of it—only that he'd noticed the bloody flowers in the first place. But that wasn't important right now. He pushed all thoughts of Finley aside and concentrated on the matter at hand: Jasper.

The inside of the jail was no more inviting than the outside—less so. It was doubtful that anyone here would be impressed by his title. There were men in shackles or body bonds—bands that clamped both arms tight to a person's side so they couldn't move them. They were accompanied by lawmen, some of whom had automaton companions for extra muscle. Griffin noted that Sam—who had been brutally attacked by a machine—didn't seem overly bothered for once by the metal men.

Griffin approached the counter and the tired-looking man behind it. "I beg your pardon, but I'm looking for a friend of mine."

The man raised a gray brow and stared at Griff with tired eyes. "And who would that be, Your Highness, the Queen of Sheba?" Then over his shoulder, "Hey, Ernest. You seen the Queen of Sheba?"

A portly man with thick mutton sideburns chuckled as he turned a wheel on the wall, closing a heavy iron gate beyond the counter. "Not recently, George."

It took all of Griffin's will not to roll his eyes. Sam, however, was not so amused. "Watch your tongue, troll. Do you know who you're talking to?"

"Sam…" Griffin warned.

George's expression of wary amusement faded, replaced by a scowl Griffin recognized as the offended pride of a little man with too much power. "No, I don't know, and I don't care. But you watch *your* tongue, mister, or I'll lock you up."

Hands curled into fists, Sam took a step forward, violence promised in his posture and expression. Griffin stopped him with a hand on his arm, his gaze directed at the man behind the counter. "Excuse us." He pulled Sam aside. "What the devil is the matter with you?"

Sam glared at him. "He can't talk to you like that."

"My title is worth very little here, Sam. He doesn't care who I am, and he can speak to me however he likes. You getting angry is just going to make him all the more obnoxious or, worse, get you locked up, as well."

"I'd like to see the bounder try." There was a gleam in Sam's dark eyes that usually meant trouble.

Exasperated, Griffin let go of the larger boy's arm. "That would be a great plan if we knew for certain Jasper was here—and that he was innocent. But if you want to get arrested, go ahead. I'll go back to the hotel and explain it all to Emily."

That took the fight out of Sam's expression. "Right. We'll do it your way, then."

Griffin clapped him on the back. "Good man." He turned back toward the desk and discovered that his place had been taken by a man in a long duster coat and a hat much like the one Jasper usually wore. The sight of him made Griffin reluctant to make his presence known to the guard once more. He didn't think cowboys were much more common in New York than they were in London.

Sam stopped, as well, and the two of them shared a glance

before turning their attention to the stranger and what he was saying.

"Excuse me, friend, but I wonder if you might be able to give me some information."

Griffin watched out of the corner of his eye as the cowboy offered George what appeared to be several dollars.

The guard took the money and gave the man a gap-toothed smile as he tucked the bills in his pocket. "Happy to do what I can, sir. What can I do for you?"

"I'm looking for a young fella by the name of Jasper Renn. Is he here?"

Sam and Griff exchanged another look as George flipped through the sheaths of papers in front of him. After what seemed like an eternity, he lifted his head. "Nothing. Nobody by the name Renn here."

"You're certain?" Even though Griffin couldn't see the man's face, he knew he was frowning. "I heard he was being transported to New York City from London."

George shrugged. "He wasn't brought here."

Griffin swore under his breath. "This is bloody marvelous," he muttered, turning so the man wouldn't hear.

"You think maybe he changed his name?" Sam whispered.

Griffin shook his head. "Jasper Renn's his real name. That's the one the men who came after him used—the name that was on the poster." Maybe it was an alias, but it was the name the men would have used to lock him up.

"Then where the devil is he?"

He raked a hand through his hair. "I have no bloody idea."

The cowboy was talking again, so Griffin turned his attention back to him and the helpful George.

A tanned, slightly callused hand thrust a card toward the guard. "Name's Whip Kirby. I'm a marshal from San Francisco." His voice was strong, as though he wanted to be heard.

That was where Jasper was from. A marshal. So he was a lawman, then. Had he been sent to pick up Jasper and perhaps take him west? If so, where was Jasper?

"I'm not sure I can offer any further assistance, Marshal." George's tone and expression were wary now—as though he thought Kirby might ask a favor.

"Probably not, friend," the lawman drawled. "But if Renn should happen to show up, perhaps you'd be so kind as to send word to me at this address." He slid a card across the desk on top of more bills. "I'd be mightily obliged."

George's eyes lit up at the prospect of perhaps relieving the marshal of yet more money. "I'll keep an eye out for him, sir."

Kirby tipped his hat. "Thank you." He turned to leave.

"Say," George said, stopping him. "What's this Renn done, anyway?"

The lawman paused. "I want to talk to him about a murder that took place a couple years ago in San Francisco."

Sam's elbow struck him hard in the ribs, and Griffin had

to swallow his pain rather than voice it aloud. He shot his
friend a dirty look, to which Sam managed to look passably
apologetic.

"Who was killed?" George asked with obvious interest.

"Businessman. Important fella with a family and friends
who want his killer brought to justice." He rocked back on
his heels. "While we're talking, I don't suppose you've heard
of a fellow by the name of Reno Dalton?"

George shook his head. "Can't say that I have. He in ca-
hoots with your guy?"

"Might be," the marshal replied with a slight smile. He
tapped his finger against the card on the desk. "You hear
anything about either one of them, you let me know, won't
you? One lawman to another?"

George grinned. "Sure thing, Marshal."

Kirby turned on his heel. What the still-smiling George
couldn't see was that the tall man's smile vanished in a blink,
replaced by an expression that Griffin could only describe as
annoyed distaste.

"He was much more effective with Georgie Porgie than
you were," Sam commented when Kirby was well out of ear-
shot. "You should have offered the git money."

"I might have," Griffin informed him with a scowl, "if you
hadn't slipped several notches down the evolutionary ladder
with him. Thump your chest for me, and I could sell you to
the zoo I've heard they're building in the Bronx."

Sam opened his mouth to respond, but Griffin didn't wait for his reply. He turned on his heel and strode toward the exit. "Coming?" he called over his shoulder.

Scowling, Sam followed after him.

Outside, the sun was warming the morning air. It was going to be a hot day. A metal horse—frame oxidized but rust-free—stood just past the steps near the sidewalk. It wasn't an expensive model—its gears and inner workings were partially exposed—but it was a remarkable likeness that the craftsman must have labored over.

"Wonder if that's Kirby's?" Sam asked, examining the metal beast with great interest. "Did you notice if he wore spurs? I didn't see any."

Griffin shrugged. He didn't share his friend's fascination with the American West. "Sorry, I didn't look." He walked toward the hired steam carriage that waited for them just a few feet away.

Sam fell into step beside him. "You still want to look for Jasper? Or are we going home?"

"We came here to find Jasper, and that's what I intend to do." Griffin stepped up into the carriage and instructed the driver to take them back to the hotel. The girls would no doubt want to hear what they had learned. "Since we've had no luck finding him, and we're not the only ones looking, I reckon we need to change tactics a bit."

"What do you have in mind?" his friend inquired, as the

carriage jerked into motion, its engine filling the air with moist steam.

Griffin leaned back against the seat and surveyed the bustling city before him. "I think we need to look for this Reno Dalton fellow. I think he's connected to Jasper."

"Don't you think Kirby's already looked for him?"

"Kirby's a lawman." Griffin ran a hand through his hair. "I doubt he'll have better luck than we will."

"How's that? You think a duke will have better luck?"

"No, but I think a chest-thumping lout will," Griffin informed him.

Sam grinned—and yet somehow managed to maintain a furrowed brow. "Finally. A bit of fun."

Griffin sighed and shook his head. He had no doubt that he could blugg or bribe his way around Five Points—the logical place for anyone of a criminal ilk to hide. He needed information on Dalton and on Kirby. But more importantly, he needed to know whether or not the man he considered his friend was a cold-blooded killer.

Chapter 3

Jasper woke to the feel of tepid water hitting his face.

At least he hoped it was water. He sniffed. Yep.

Swearing, he wiped his face with the back of his hand as he sat up. He blinked furiously as the curtains were torn back to reveal the bright morning sun. He never thought he'd miss overcast London, but Mei hadn't left his room until dawn, and judging from the angle at which the sun glared at him, it couldn't be much later than nine.

"Dalton wants to see you," growled Little Hank. "Get dressed."

Jasper squinted up at him, water dripping from his chin. "Good morning to you too, sunshine."

The hulking brute sneered at him and stomped from the room. Jasper never thought he'd miss Sam Morgan, either, but at least he'd make a little conversation between grunts.

Sighing, he tossed back the blankets and crawled out of bed. There was a little water left in the pitcher on the nearby stand—Hank hadn't dumped all of it on him—so he poured it into the basin and washed up as best he could. Then he dressed in a fresh shirt and trousers—he supposed he had Dalton to thank for those—and pulled on his boots before leaving the room.

Hank was waiting for him in the corridor.

"Walk," he commanded, pointing toward the staircase that led down to the foyer.

Jasper did. He didn't bother to ask what this was all about. He knew why he was there, just as he had known this day would come. He just hadn't thought it would arrive so dang soon.

Little Hank led him to the dining room where Dalton sat at a long, polished table, breakfasting on steak and eggs. The smell of it made Jasper's stomach growl. Were those…flapjacks? And there were biscuits, too—not cookies, like the English used the word but proper soft, fluffy biscuits—just begging to be smothered in butter.

Dalton glanced up at his arrival. "Ah, Jasper. There you are. Come, eat."

At that moment, it wouldn't have mattered if Dalton held Jasper's own mother prisoner—pride did not fill a belly. Dalton sat at the head of the table, so he took the chair at his right and began piling a plate full of hot, delicious-smelling food.

"Did you sleep well?" Dalton asked, not bothering to look at him as he sliced into his steak.

Jasper didn't pause as he slathered butter on a warm biscuit. "All right."

"Really? I thought you were up rather late."

Now he froze, slowly turning his head to meet the other man's gaze. "Oh?"

His former friend grinned. Jasper reckoned even Satan never looked so diabolical. Those bright, clear blue eyes of his were unsettling. "Don't look so suspicious. I have no problem with you and Mei renewing your…acquaintance, so long as I get what's mine."

No. He wouldn't have a problem at all. In fact, Jasper wouldn't be surprised if last night had happened exactly as Dalton hoped—planned, even. He had to know Mei would want to talk to Jasper, and that Jasper would do whatever Dalton demanded.

He nodded—slowly. "You'll get it." What choice did he have?

"Excellent. I know I don't have to tell you what will happen if you cross me, but just in case the thought trickled through that block you like to call a brain, Mei's not my only insurance. It would be a real sin if your brother Nate broke his pistol hand and had to leave the Regulators."

Jasper stilled. The biscuit tasted like dirt in his mouth, but he chewed and swallowed regardless. His oldest brother had a good career ahead of him in the law. The Regulators took their name from the Lincoln County War, which had happened years ago. The only thing they had in common with that band of deputized outlaws was their name. They were a posse that provided protection—the lawful kind—to towns and individuals who couldn't protect themselves. Nate had wanted to be one since he was ten years old.

He'd been stupid. Jasper knew that now. He thought taking the device and hiding it would protect himself, Mei and his family. What he was just realizing was that he had crossed the wrong man. And now the people he cared about were the ones at risk. One telegram from Dalton, and Nate could get ambushed. Or his younger brother, Adam, could have an "accident." God only knew what might happen to his older sister, Ellen.

"You can stand down, Dalton," he said quietly, reaching for his cup of coffee to wash down the biscuit stuck in his throat. "I hear you."

The other fellow smiled and gestured with his knife. "Try the maple syrup. It's from Vermont."

This was quite possibly the most surreal experience Jasper had ever had—the threat of violence delivered in such a friendly manner. Still, he wasn't lily-livered nor was he stupid, so he ate Dalton's food and drank Dalton's coffee and waited.

Once Dalton had finished his own food, he set his silverware on the plate and leaned back in his chair, his fingers lazily curled around his cup of coffee.

"My men found you at the Duke of Greythorne's home."

Jasper shrugged. "So?"

A sharp, dark brow arched. "Would you say you and he are...friends?"

He forced a bark of disbelieving laughter from his throat. The last thing he wanted was to involve Griffin in this mess. "Me and a duke, all friendly-like? Those Limeys would lynch you for suggesting such a thing. Naw, I took care of a delicate situation for him, that's all."

"So it's just a coincidence that His Grace has come to town?"

The bottom of Jasper's stomach fell, but he kept his poker face—and his breakfast. "Reckon so. I can't imagine that arrogant dandy coming all this way for a fellow he wouldn't let enter his house through the front door." That was a lie, of course, and he felt dirty saying it, even though it was to protect Griff.

Dalton's eyes narrowed. "You're lying to me, Jasper. The duke was at the Tombs earlier this morning."

Tarnation. He shrugged. "Could be he noticed a knick-knack or two that might have been liberated from his household."

"Such as?"

He seized the first things that came to mind. "Couple of silver candlesticks. A gold snuffbox. I reckon it's the ring he's after, though. Coulda saved him the trouble of coming all this way. I pawned it in Whitechapel."

Dalton stared at him for a moment, his icy gaze searching Jasper's face for any sign of a lie. But Jasper was a good liar when he needed to be—a trait he'd never been proud of until now. The other man laughed. "No wonder he's here. I'd hunt you down myself."

Jasper's smile was thin. "You already did."

More laughter. Then Dalton gazed at him with something that looked like respect. "It is good to have you back."

"Does that mean I get to come and go as I please?"

"Why would you want to do that? When there's no one in the city you'd call a friend?"

And there it was. Dalton wasn't calling him a prisoner, but they both knew there was no reason for him to wander about the city unless he planned to visit someone—such as the Duke of Greythorne. One wrong move on Jasper's part and Mei would be dead faster than he could blink.

Dalton continued, "You'll collect my device today. Do this and perhaps I'll liberate Miss Mei."

"It's impossible to get it in one day," Jasper informed him. "It's not in just one spot."

Dalton scowled. "You took it apart?"

"In case anyone found it—they wouldn't know what it was." Jasper didn't even know what it was, but he knew it was dangerous, otherwise Dalton wouldn't want it. He'd also known that breaking the thing down would buy him more time if Dalton ever caught up to him.

Too bad he hadn't thought that all the way through.

Dalton considered this. "I'm not sure whether I should commend your intelligence or put a bullet in your brainpan."

As he scooped up yolk with a bite of steak, Jasper shrugged. "At least no one else has gotten their hands on *your* device." No one that he knew of, at any rate.

That cold blue gaze pinned him to his chair. "Where is the first piece?"

"O'Dooley's," he replied. It was a sporting club on the barest fringe of the underworld—a place where working-men and fancy gents could enjoy an evening of bloodshed and brute violence.

He could see that Dalton approved of his choice. "There's a fight tonight. We'll take in some entertainment, and you'll collect what's there. Where's the rest of it?"

Jasper shook his head. "The only guarantee I have that you won't hurt Mei is the fact that I'm the only one who knows where the pieces are."

Dalton leaned forward, all traces of goodwill gone from his features. "I could kill her just for spite."

The thought made Jasper's stomach turn over on itself. "You could, but then you'd never get your gadget back."

"I could make you tell me."

"No," Jasper assured him. "You couldn't." Because Dalton would be dead if he hurt Mei.

Dalton opened his mouth, but Jasper cut him off. "There's

no negotiating to be done. I get your machine back, and you let me, Mei and my family alone. Give me your word or shoot me now." His heart punched hard against his ribs as he waited for his former friend, now his enemy, to respond.

"Fine." Dalton offered his hand. "But for the duration it takes you to get the device, you're part of my gang and you do whatever I tell you to. Idle hands do the devil's work, after all. You try to burn me again, and I'll slit her throat myself."

Jasper swallowed the rage threatening to send him over the edge and accepted the handshake, sealing the bargain. He could drive a fork into Dalton's neck before the screw drew his next breath, but then he'd just bring more trouble down on himself. No, he had to do this right if he wanted Dalton out of his life for good.

And now Griffin was in town. The thought both worried him and gave him hope. If Griffin was here, it meant he was still his friend. But he didn't want to risk Griffin's safety, especially if Sam, Miss Finley and that pretty little Miss Emily were with him. Then there was the fact that if they tried to help him they might very well get themselves killed. Still, if anyone could help him get out of this mess and save Mei, it was Griffin King and his friends.

"Relax," he heard himself say as he reached for another biscuit. "You're in charge here. I'm not going to burn you."

But if he could find a way to save his loved ones and destroy Reno Dalton, he'd do it. Even if it cost his own life.

* * *

"You know Griffin is going to pitch a fit when he finds out what you've done." Emily chewed on a fingernail as she spoke.

Finley shrugged before taking hold of her friend's hand and pulling it away from her mouth. "Not if we bring back information on this Dalton fellow, which is exactly what we're going to do."

"Did we have to go to the worst part of the city to get it?"

She'd shrug again, but that might seem facetious, as though she didn't take Emily's fears to heart. They were in the worst part of town—Five Points was a lot like the slum areas of London, but with a tad more pride—looking for information on a criminal. There were bound to be those who took offense to their snooping about.

Finley was fairly certain she and Emily could look after themselves, and if Griffin was angry that they had taken matters into their own hands, that was his problem. She was still a little angry at him for last night—more because he hadn't kissed her—and he hadn't spoken to her since. How was she supposed to react to that? How was she to know when he acted all interested one moment and then walked out on her the next?

It wasn't her fault Jack had sent her flowers. She hadn't asked for them. In fact, the prat had probably sent them knowing it would irk Griffin.

It was enough to make a girl wonder if there was something wrong with her—and Finley had had quite enough of that already, thank you. So if Griffin wouldn't acknowledge her on his own, she'd make him.

People stopped to stare at the two of them as they strolled down the dusty sidewalk, putting Finley on her guard. It was a sunny day with a light breeze, which unfortunately carried the smells of this part of the city on it. Behind run-down buildings, clothing fluttered on battered lines. Some of those items were so grimy they barely looked washed at all.

Someone here had to know how to find this Dalton fellow, who was apparently a friend of Jasper's. When Griffin had returned from the Tombs that morning, he'd said he'd run into a lawman who'd claimed that Jasper may have returned to his former lawless ways. That Jasper might have been responsible for a man's death in California. Finley didn't believe it. Oh, she had no doubt Jasper had his own sense of right and wrong—just as she often did—but he wasn't a killer. Not without reason. If Griffin was going to give up just because of a murder suspicion, then he should have tossed her out when Scotland Yard believed she killed Lord Felix, a fellow who had attacked her.

Finley and Emily defended Jasper, much to Sam's chagrin. It was no secret Sam was jealous of how the cowboy flirted with Emily. Couldn't the brute see how much Emily adored him? Finley didn't understand it, but it was obvious to everyone but Sam that Emily loved him.

Regardless, when Griffin had said that he and Sam were

going to see what they could find out about Dalton, Finley had taken his attitude and the fact that he'd refused to make eye contact with her to heart and decided to do a little detective work of her own. Emily, of course, had refused to let her go alone.

"Do you think the lads are here, as well?" Emily asked, glancing about.

Finley was busy trying to catalog everyone watching them. "Dunno. I'm more concerned with us at the moment, Em."

Her friend glanced at her, face even paler beneath her freckles. "Do you think we're in danger?"

"I think we'd be idiots to assume otherwise," she replied, oddly calm. This was one of the things she had to accept when Griffin began the process of helping her merge the two aspects of her personality. She thought things now, did things that she wouldn't have before. So being cocky yet anxious in the face of potential danger was new to her—and most inconvenient.

Slowly, she nudged her small friend toward the center of the square. She'd rather be out in the open than risk being hauled into a building or alley. These people weren't the sort to shoot someone in cold blood; they were fist-and-blade sort of people—the kind that took killing personally. There was more honor in meeting a foe toe-to-toe than picking them off from a distance.

She could respect that. She was also thankful for it.

"You girls don't belong here" came a thick Irish brogue.

Both Finley and Emily turned toward the voice. It belonged to a young man, not much older than themselves. He was tall and thin, his dark auburn hair glinting in the sun. His shirt and brown trousers had been washed so many times they were both a muddy color and mended in several spots. Still, he stood there like he owned the place.

Cheeky bloke, Finley thought. "We're looking for someone," she told him.

His eyebrow jumped at her voice. "There be no one you want here, English," he informed her in a mocking tone.

Finley smiled coolly. "I haven't even told you who it is, *Irish*." She kept her gaze focused on him, but her peripheral vision was filled with the sight of a crowd gathering around them. Damnation.

"Ye're not wanted here" came a female voice from behind. "Why don't ye just go back from where ye come." It wasn't a question but a command.

Finley turned. The girl was about her own height—a little heavier built—with dark hair and bright blue eyes. Black Irish, they called it. Behind her was another girl with dusky skin and an exotic prettiness, which was heightened by the emptiness of her lavender, catlike eyes. She was the real danger here, not the mouthpiece in front of her. Still, Finley didn't reckon they were in any immediate danger from cat-girl.

"Gladly," she replied. "As soon as someone tells us where I can find Reno Dalton, we'll be on our way."

"Dalton?" It was the dark girl—the one with the catlike eyes that asked. Her voice was low and smooth, with no trace of hostility, yet Finley felt it in the base of her spine. "What do you want with him?"

"No offense," Finley replied, "but that's personal." She wasn't about to give Jasper's name and have that get back to Dalton.

The girl nodded. "Fair enough."

"She's probably knocked up with his brat," the auburn-haired boy sneered, his gaze raking over Finley like a pair of dirty hands.

The blue-eyed girl stepped forward, flanked by two more who had reddish-brown hair. One of them carried a cricket bat. "We don't appreciate strangers comin' into our home, bringin' their trouble with 'em."

Finley stood her ground. She turned her face but not her gaze toward Emily. "Get out of here," she commanded. "Now."

She didn't have time to see if her friend listened to her or not. A fist came flying out of nowhere. She dodged it but got smacked with the bat for her trouble. Pain exploded in her skull. It also woke up that part of her that wasn't used to being welcomed just yet. When the next blow came, she deflected it and countered with one of her own, her fist connecting with a jaw. She struck again and again, but for every one she knocked down, there seemed to be two to take their place.

Fast as she was, she couldn't escape them all, and if they got her to the ground she'd be in serious trouble.

Suddenly, two of her attackers—one of whom had just hit her hard enough in the mouth to make her bleed—jerked back, their bodies spasming as though they were having some sort of fit. Then two more did the same. What was left of the gang around her stopped their assault on her to step back.

Finley shook her head to clear the ringing in it and lifted her hand to her mouth before raising her gaze. What she saw was enough to make her grin—despite her split lip.

Emily stood but a few feet away, hands out from her sides. She wore gloves with metal fingertips, which sparked and crackled in the sudden silence.

"Back off," she snarled. "Or I'll give a bit of this to the rest of ye."

Finley could have hugged her—if she didn't think she'd end up like the droolers in the street. Plus, Emily looked mad—really mad.

"The lot of ye ought to be ashamed of yourselves." Her voice was strong and clear, despite a tremor of emotion, her accent strong. "Look at you. You left Ireland to escape the violence and troubles there, and now see what you've become—bullies who'd gang up on a girl only looking for information. Cowards who think with their fists rather than the minds God gave 'em. If your ancestors could see what you've done to the name and pride of Ireland on this land, they'd weep in their graves."

A wave of shame washed over Finley, and there wasn't even a drop of Irish blood in her veins. She glanced around at those who would have beaten her to death just a few moments ago and saw the guilt in their faces.

Emily glared at them; her eyes, which could never seem to decide if they were blue or green, sparkled with anger. "I've never been more ashamed than I am right now. You disgrace our homeland."

Not even the formidable Miss Clarke—a governess Finley had once punched in the mouth—had ever reduced people to such a glum, self-loathing mass as Emily just had, with her impassioned words and sparking fingers.

"Dalton likes to watch the fights at O'Dooley's," the dark girl told them, as she stepped forward to stand between the girls and the crowd. She directed her attention at Finley, despite Emily's laying low of the mob. "There's one tonight. That's where you'll find him. But take care, there's been a high-and-mighty feller sniffin' around after him, as well. He'll be well protected."

Finley didn't glance at Emily for fear of tipping anyone off that they were well acquainted with this "high-and-mighty feller." It had to be Griffin.

Feline eyes raked over her. "Word is Dalton likes rough girls."

Finley grinned, well aware that there was blood in her mouth. "Then he ought to love me."

★ ★ ★

When they were back at the hotel—having snuck in through the back entrance so Finley didn't have to walk through the foyer in her ripped and bloodstained clothes— Finley made Emily promise not to breathe a word of what had happened in Five Points to Griffin, if their paths crossed. Especially not about the fight that evening.

"You'll tell him, right?" the redhead asked once they reached their floor. She followed Finley to her room.

Finley glanced at her out of the corner of her eye as she slipped her key into the lock. "Sure. Nice work with those conductive gloves."

"People think they can hurt me because I'm small. I'm not going to let anyone hurt me again." There was something in her eyes that made Finley want to hug her, but think better of it.

"Fair enough." She knew better than to ask. Emily would share her secrets when and if she was ready.

"*When* are you going to tell him?" Emily demanded, changing the subject as Finley opened the door.

"Maybe when he barges in here and announces that he and Sam are attending a fight tonight and that it's no place for girls." She knew better than to hope that Griffin hadn't found out about O'Dooley's.

Emily scowled, wrinkling her little, freckled nose. "But he knows you can look after yourself."

"Mmm, but he's miffed at me right now." Her own ire

rose. "Maybe I won't tell him at all. Won't that stick a bee in his bonnet if you and I show up and do what he and Sam can't?" She flashed a grin at the other girl.

Emily raised a brow—a wealth of warning in that simple gesture. "This is about helping Jasper, not you sticking it to Griffin. Why's he all scurvy with you, anyway?"

Finley gestured toward the dresser and the vase of flowers there. "They're from Jack."

"Oh." Emily's big eyes widened even more as she studied the arrangement of roses. "They're beautiful. How did he know where to send them?"

Finley chuckled, even though the situation really wasn't that funny. "Griffin assumes he went through all manner of trouble tracking me down. Knowing Jack he simply grinned at one of the housemaids. He probably wanted to needle Griff. Regardless, it wasn't meant as a romantic gesture."

"They look pretty romantic to me," Emily replied, slightly awed as she lowered her face to smell the beautiful blooms.

"If Jack Dandy wanted to woo me, that arrangement would have a personality of its own—one that complemented mine. Roses are just his way of saying hello."

Emily sighed. "I wish someone would say hello to me."

Finley crossed the carpet to the dresser and plucked the most perfect rose from the bouquet. She offered it to her friend. "Hullo, Em."

Her friend—it still felt wonderfully odd to call her that—beamed. Pale arms wrapped around Finley's torso. "Thank you." Like most Irish, she dropped the *h,* and it came out "tank."

Finley gave her a squeeze before releasing her. Smoothing her hands over her violet corset—thankfully none the worse for wear—she turned her mind once again to Jasper, pushing all thoughts of Jack, and especially Griffin, away.

"I'm going to need my steel corset, and we're going to need to rough you up a bit so you look like you could fit in with the Irish gangs. Though, you certainly made an impression on them today."

Emily's spine stiffened. "Don't you worry about me, Finley Jayne. I'll look the part. I've got the earbuds, so we can communicate with each other. I just wish I had time to graft metal to your knuckles. It would make you hit that much harder."

The idea of Emily cutting open her hands and brass plating her bones made Finley vaguely queasy—never mind that she had witnessed the girl cracking open Sam's chest cavity like an oyster.

"I'll wrap my hands the way Jasper taught me," she said. A silence fell between them as they both thought of him.

"He's not a killer," Emily insisted. "No more than you or I are."

"Anyone can kill for the right reason," Finley remarked absently as she picked up the newspaper Emily had brought in with her. A photograph of a man named Nikola Tesla stared up from the page. She'd heard Emily talk about him before. Apparently he had a laboratory here in New York.

"There's a right reason to kill someone?" The smaller girl's tone was incredulous at best.

Finley dropped the newspaper onto the dresser once again. "If someone tried to kill you, wouldn't you fight back?"

"Of course!"

"You might kill him. Saving yourself is a good reason. Saving someone else is an even better one."

Bright eyes narrowed. "Do ye think Jasper might have been protecting someone, then?"

"Dunno." Finley leaned her head to one side, sighing as a loud popping noise filled the room. Then she repeated with the other side. "But Jasper's not the type to kill for no good reason."

Emily gave a quick, determined nod. "We need to find out the truth about what happened. And stop doing that. It turns my stomach every time some part of you pops and snaps."

"We'll find the truth." Finley's stomach growled. "Good Lord, I'm starving. I'm going to ring the kitchen for some food. You want something, too, or is your delicate stomach still suffering from my pops and snaps?"

Emily made a face at her, but it was obvious the jest didn't really bother her. They decided to order tea, sandwiches, fruit and cakes. For once Finley didn't feel the least bit guilty knowing that Griffin would be paying for their indulgence. He had been perfectly awful to her last night. Worse, he'd hurt her feelings when he told her that he wouldn't fight for her affection. Why ever not? Isn't that what heroes did when faced with the notion of losing their heroine?

She'd fight for him. Wouldn't she? Honestly, she didn't know. She would never stand by and allow someone to hurt him, but to fight for his affection... Well, once again she needed to remind herself that nothing could come of a relationship between the two of them. She could argue against it until she was blue in the face, but the simple fact remained that she liked him—enough that she had taken to researching for information on couples from different social spheres. Cinderella and her prince didn't count, but that story had started somewhere and gave hope to every poor little girl who had ever heard it.

So if Griffin King thought he could ignore her—and the fact that he had practically propositioned her—he was wrong. That he treated her like that hurt. It was demeaning, and she didn't know if she could forgive him for it. Did he think he could talk to her like that just because she didn't behave as he thought girls should?

A few weeks ago, she never would have dreamed of doing something dangerous just to get a fellow's attention. In fact, she would have mocked any girl who behaved so stupidly, and yet here she was, hatching a plan that would hopefully help Jasper and stick in Griffin's craw. Not just to get his attention, but to rub his face in the fact that she was who she was—and he had helped make her this way by setting her on the path to amalgamating the two sides of her personality.

"Are you certain I can't talk you out of this foolishness?" Emily asked a little later as they sat at the table near the window and ate their splendid meal.

"I am. Word's now gotten back to Dalton that the Duke of Greythorne is in the city and asking about him. Dalton won't expect Griff to keep company with a girl like me—not for long, at any rate."

Emily made a face at her crude talk, but it was true, and Emily knew it just as Finley did. "I still don't like it. We really don't know anything about this Dalton character other than what little you and Griffin found out—and all you discovered was that he has a fondness for tough girls."

Finley took a bite out of a cucumber sandwich. She chewed and swallowed before saying, "That's all I need to know right now. I'll find out the rest when I get inside. I'll have my portable telegraph device if I need to contact you."

"You will contact me. I want to hear from you every three hours if this fool plan works."

She put on her best placating expression. "That might not be possible, Em."

A pale finger jabbed the air in front of her. "You listen to me, Miss Finley Jayne. You make it possible, or I'm coming to get you."

Finley couldn't help but grin. She loved having a friend, especially one that cared so much for her welfare. "All right, fine. But save your worrying for when I catch Dalton's attention. He won't bring me into his gang immediately. So why don't we concentrate on the fight tonight, and you can worry about me being in Dalton's clutches when the time comes? You do know I can pound most grown men senseless, right? I mean, I can fight." In fact, she liked it. It had been part of her darker nature before, but now that she had brought the two halves together—though she still had a lot of work to do on sorting herself out—it was simply part of her.

"I just hope Dalton doesn't have any abilities of his own." Emily chewed on her thumbnail. "I'd rather we not have any surprises."

Finley had thought of that herself. "If I think it's too dangerous, I'll run. I promise. Now can we talk about tonight? I have to win a fight, and then I have to deal with Griffin's wrath." She grinned. "It is a good plan, isn't it? Dalton's bound to notice me, and if I can get into his gang, I can get to Jasper. You know Griffin and Sam will hate the fact that we managed to do what they couldn't."

It was obvious that Emily tried to fight her smile, even though it was futile. Her pink lips parted, flashing straight white teeth. "They will at that, lass. They will at that."

Jasper expected that Dalton might put a watchdog on him when he went to collect the first piece of the disassembled device. What he hadn't expected was that Mei would be that watchdog.

He was certain Dalton had sent her to taunt him—to taunt them both. They were alone, and in any other circumstances, they could escape to safety. But Dalton could kill her with that damn collar, and there was nothing Jasper could do to help her. Wasn't as though he could shoot the thing off her, even if he had his guns.

If only he could find Miss Emily. She'd know what to do. But if she'd heard the rumors about him, she was just as likely to tell him to bugger off.

"Exactly what does this device do?" Mei asked as they navigated the darkness, which was the cellar at O'Dooley's, with only a feeble hand torch to light their way.

"Danged if I know," he replied, mentally counting out in measured footsteps to the correct spot. "But it's important enough that Dalton hunted me down to find it."

Not for the first time, he cursed himself for taking the blasted thing at all. He had deliberately broken it down into components to buy himself time if this sort of situation ever arose, though he really hadn't thought it through. It was only because Dalton didn't want to draw attention to himself that he didn't send Jasper after the entire device in one night. Some of the locations were going to require stealth, as well as unlawful entry. Jasper had to remember exact locations—it wasn't as though he'd drawn a map. He was relying on memory.

But Dalton wasn't stupid. He wasn't going to sit back and let Jasper be lazy about it, and he wouldn't put it past the outlaw to punish Mei over every delay.

He counted out the right steps, pivoted on his heel and faced the rough brick wall. As soon as he saw the patch, he knew exactly where to use the mallet and chisel he'd brought with him for this bit of business.

When they'd first stolen the thing, Dalton had been as excited as a kid let loose in a sweetshop. That was how Jasper had known how important the device was.

Obviously he had overestimated his own importance where Dalton was concerned. Dalton hadn't cared if Jasper bolted or not. What he cared about, apparently, was the device. And now Mei was paying the price for Jasper's mistake.

If he got them both out of this mess alive it would be a miracle.

"Hold this, please." He handed the torch to Mei. She took it and immediately held it at exactly the right angle for him to work. But then, it always seemed as though she had a knack for knowing what people needed. He didn't know if it was a "talent" exactly, but she just seemed to intuit the right thing, all the time.

Crouching, Jasper applied the chisel to a seam between two bricks and gave it a hard tap with the hammer. Bits of mortar crumbled and fell to the dirt floor. When he'd hidden the piece in this wall, he hadn't had the time nor the inclination to put it back exactly the way he found it. He'd patched it up so that it could be easily accessed if he ever needed it but stand up to scrutiny at the same time.

It took a few minutes to chisel a hole big enough to stick his hand in and draw the part out. He had packed it in a small box to protect it from dust and rodents. As he pulled the rough wooden box from the wall, he could hear the dull roar of the crowd above—a bunch of bloodthirsty men and women feeding off each other's aggression. Were Griffin and Sam there yet? He knew they would come. Would they think the worst of him when they saw him? He knew better than to hope that somehow they wouldn't notice him.

God, he hoped Emily and Finley weren't with them. He had a soft spot for each girl—especially Emily—and the idea of being less in their estimation… Well, it hurt.

He opened the box and unwrapped the paper inside. This particular section of the device—which looked like a crown of tuning forks—was exactly as he remembered. In the back of his mind, he realized he'd been hoping to find it destroyed, so Dalton wouldn't be able to use it.

"Is that it?" Mei asked, leaning over him with the lantern.

She smelled of cherry blossoms, he thought. He could close his eyes—just for a moment—and pretend they were somewhere else. Instead, he nodded, shoved the "crown" back into the box and rose to his feet. "Part of it. Do you have the sack?"

He could feel her confused gaze on him as she gave him the leather pouch. No doubt she wondered why he didn't look at her, why he was so curt. But if she did have a talent for knowing what people needed, she'd know that right now he needed to put some distance between them, because the last thing he needed was to fall in love again when both their lives hung in the balance. Love was what had gotten him into this mess to begin with.

With their bounty in the sack, Jasper gestured for her to walk in front. There was nothing he could do about the bricks and mortar dust on the floor—that would be someone else's mess to clean up.

No one was around to see them as they slipped out of the cellar opening. The crowd was louder up here—the fights being held in a nearby room. They exited into the vestibule, where spectators waited like a herd of cattle to be allowed inside. Little Hank was waiting for them by the door and corralled them toward the main hall. Apparently Dalton wanted them to stay for the fight, as well. Tarnation, there went any hope of Griffin not seeing him.

There was a bit of a commotion as the night's fighters were brought in. These brave—or insane, however you wanted to look at it—scrappers would be put in a ring against each other and machines in a "last man standing" sort of event. Killing your opponent wasn't encouraged, but it wasn't against the rules, either. The only rule was that to win, you had to be the only fighter left alive and conscious. It was nasty and brutal and not at all the sort of thing Mei should see—never mind that she had been the one to teach Jasper the Chinese martial arts.

He turned his head to watch the parade of fighters, because it was less painful than looking at Mei's pale but pretty face. Tonight's contenders were a hard-looking lot of criminals and thugs…

"Good God!" He exclaimed.

Mei's head whipped around. "What?"

His heart was beating hard against his ribs, and his breath seemed to have caught in his throat. One of the fighters had looked straight at him and *winked.*

"Jasper, do you know that girl?" She sounded jealous.

He shook his head, watching in horror as Finley walked into the hall with the rest of the fighters—her opponents. What the tarnation was she up to? She had to be there to get close to Dalton—that was the only explanation.

This night couldn't get much worse. If he thought Griffin would never look at him the same now, it was going to be even worse if Miss Finley got herself killed.

Chapter 4

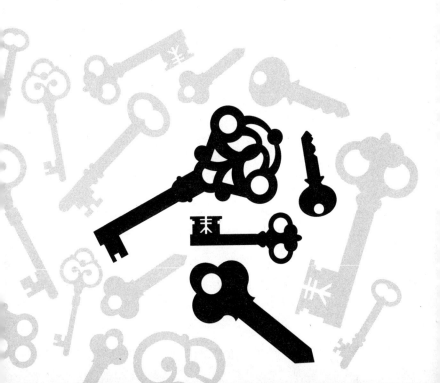

No one had told Finley that this was an ongoing night of continuous fighting, weeding out the opponents until you were the last one left. The first time one of the fighters injured another so badly the results surely had to be fatal, she almost heaved the contents of her stomach all over the rough-hewn floor.

Emily was with her, watching the violence from the sidelines, dressed in a white shirt, vest and striped green trousers with high thick-soled boots. Her ropes of hair were pinned up on the top of her head, and she sported a silver hoop through the right side of her nose. It didn't really pierce her skin, but clamped on in order to appear as though it did. The hoop and the trousers were gang related. Apparently there was some kind of Irish gang in the city who wore the same jewelry and trousers. They were known as fighters—either being tough themselves or handling fighters who were tougher.

It was a good disguise. Emily wasn't as tall and muscular as Finley, so the kit provided some protection. No one would mess with a member of the *Uisce Beatha* gang. *Ish-ge Bah-hah,* Emily pronounced it. It meant *whiskey* in Irish.

"Right," Finley said when another man was carried—groaning in agony—from the ring. "I'm going to knock 'em out as soon as I can, Em. Do as little and take as little damage as I can."

"A sound notion," her friend replied in a strained voice. "Just be careful, Finley. I'm not certain this was such a grand idea after all."

Finley's smile pulled tight. "It's not, but it's the best I have, unless you think me throwing myself at Dalton would be better?"

"He is lovely to look upon, but I reckon that's not the way to win his trust and respect. Plenty o' women have been practically swooning over him all evening."

Emily was right. The criminal was possessed of an uncommonly fine face. They'd spotted him shortly after their arrival, because he had Jasper with him. Dalton was almost too handsome with his silky brown hair, blue eyes and high cheekbones. It bothered her to look at him for too long.

Griffin, on the other hand, was a bit more rugged-looking, not quite so perfectly put together. He wasn't as overtly chiseled, but she could look at him for days and not get bored.

She glanced at Jasper. From where they stood, they could see him fairly clearly, though she doubted he could see them, shrouded in shadows as they were. Jasper did not look like the carefree, smooth-talking cowboy she'd met in London. He looked weary, guarded and strangely dangerous—as though he was a man on the verge of violence.

"Jasper doesn't look as though he's enjoying himself," she remarked, not taking her attention off of him as Emily wrapped her hands.

"No," Emily agreed. "I think he must be with Dalton against his will. Who do you suppose the girl is?"

Ah, Finley had wondered when that would come up. "No idea. They appear to know each other quite well."

"Quite." There could be no mistaking the jealous tone of Emily's voice.

"I thought you'd set your cap at Sam." She turned her head to look at her friend. "Has that changed?"

Crimson splotches bloomed on pale cheeks. "No. Although, I'm not sure what it says about me that, even though I prefer Sam's attentions to Jasper's, I still do not like Jasper turning that attention elsewhere."

Finley chuckled at her honesty. "I don't know a girl who would." She paused. "You saw that Sam is here?" She hadn't been surprised to see the big lad at the fight, but she had been surprised to see he was a contender. She should have known Griffin would come up with a similar plan, blast it all.

"Yes," Emily replied, expression grim. "Don't you hurt him."

The warning in her friend's tone startled her, but she heeded it all the same. Emily's bad side was not a place she wanted to be. "I won't."

"Up next," boomed the announcer's voice, "Harpy O'Malley versus Finley Bennet."

Her stomach felt as though it had dropped between her ankles. She'd given them an alias she had used before, in case anyone started asking questions—no way to link her name to Griffin's. "I'm nervous," she admitted.

"Harpy's not intimidating," Emily informed her, giving her a gentle shove. "Bird woman. You can defeat a bird woman. Off with ye now, before we attract even more attention. And be careful."

There was no turning back. One look at Jasper, and Finley knew she couldn't walk away. Besides, she wasn't a coward. She simply wasn't used to walking into a fight without aggression already driving her. She wasn't going up against an enemy, just another person.

Another person willing to kill her to win. That realization drove the importance of the evening home. Calm settled over her. Calm determination. She had not come here to lose.

She stepped out of the shadows and walked the short distance to the raised platform where the ring sat. Slipping between the ropes, she forced herself to think of one thing and one thing only: survival.

"Harpy" turned out to be a strapping woman of Irish descent. She had long ginger hair, which she wore in thick braids on either side of her head, and arms the size of Finley's legs. Some might have called her heavy or sturdy but there wasn't an inch that wasn't muscle. She wouldn't go down easy, but when she did, she'd stay there.

Finley smiled and flexed her wrapped hands. She almost regretted the fact that she wouldn't be able to cut her knuckles on Harpy's teeth. Oh, yes. Her fighting side had shown up in full force. The runes Griff had tattooed on her back tingled so slightly it might have been her imagination.

The Irishwoman came at her fast and furious, swinging her meat-hook-like hands with such force they created a breeze. Finley avoided one swipe but took another on the chin. It felt as though her teeth had been driven up into her brain, it hurt so bad. But as she'd learned in the past, pain was often a trigger for her particular "talents," and this was no different. She managed to avoid another couple of swings by dodging out of the way. Once her head cleared, she could concentrate on the anger that being hit brought out in her—and the single-minded determination to not feel that pain again.

Harpy was already panting, having exhausted herself with all that constant exertion. Her movements had slowed, and that was all the enticement Finley needed. She whirled around in a move Jasper had shown her, pivoted her body down toward her left leg and brought her right up, connecting with her opponent's head with a solid kick. She was right—Harpy went down hard.

As the woman's unconscious body was lugged out of the ring, Finley caught Dalton's appreciative gaze. She'd grabbed his interest; now to see if she could keep it. She waggled her fingers at him in a way she hoped made her appear flirtatious, rather than deranged, and was rewarded with a lopsided grin.

"Get out of the ring" came a stern male voice from behind her. "We got another fight comin'."

Finley did as she was told. Her victory guaranteed that she'd be back in the ring later, so she could continue to work on Dalton then.

As she approached the shadows where Emily stood waiting for her, grinning like an idiot, Finley glanced out into the audience. Her gaze locked with another—one the color of a stormy sky and every bit as volatile.

It was Griffin. And he wasn't nearly as impressed with her as Emily was.

Finley's last fight was against Sam.

It was ironic that her former nemesis be her final fight. She wasn't surprised that it had come down to the two of them. If she had to fight all comers till the end of the world, it would still end up just her and Sam, squared off.

"What are you doing here?" he growled as they stood face-to-face.

"Same thing you are—trying to fight my way into Dalton's gang."

"You're mad."

"And you've been seen with the Duke of Greythorne." That drew him up straight. "Sam, Dalton's already noticed me. He likes girls that fight. Stay with Griffin and Emily. Protect them. Let me have Dalton."

"What are you waitin' for?" A voice from the crowd shouted. "Fight!"

A roar rose up in the crowded room, reverberating off the walls, trembling through the floorboards.

Sam raised his fists. "Let's do this."

Finley adopted a fighting stance. "Are you going to take a fall?"

He nodded, jaw clenched. It would be a blow to his pride, she knew it. "But I'm going to make you work for it."

And she did work for it. By the time Sam finally hit the floor, she had the bruised—at least she hoped they were only bruised—ribs, sore jaw, split lip and assorted other injuries to prove just how he'd made her work. She stood in the center of the ring, battered and bloody, exhausted and exhilarated, and reveled in the roar of the frenzied crowd.

She hadn't seriously injured anyone, and she was proud of herself for that, because other fighters hadn't been nearly so considerate. She'd taken pleasure in knocking out those who had such little regard for human life. In fact, she'd toyed with them like a cat with a mouse—taking her time in putting them down. Perhaps that didn't say much for her character, but in the moment, she hadn't cared.

She had achieved what she wanted: she had Dalton's attention. He tipped his hat to her when her gaze settled on him, and she smiled in return before looking away. It wouldn't be good to appear too eager.

With her one good eye—the other was swollen shut—she turned so that she could see Griffin. She didn't make direct eye contact with him, because she knew Dalton was watching her, but she had to look.

Griffin stood now, as did all the other spectators, only they cheered for her—or booed her. The Duke of Greythorne just stood there, stoic and expressionless. Then he said something to Sam and turned away. Sam flashed her a quick, almost apologetic glance and followed after him. The crowd swallowed them wholly and quickly.

Finley looked away, refusing to hunt him down with her gaze. The sudden ache in her chest rivaled any of the injuries she'd suffered at the hands of her opponents. She knew he couldn't come to her, couldn't show any emotion because of Dalton, but she would have liked to see a little anger in his gaze, perhaps a little pride. She'd done good.

She pushed thoughts of Griffin aside as Emily joined her, supporting her physically and emotionally as Finley acknowledged the crowd with a cocky grin. Together, they made their way to the place where all the fighters had waited for their turn. Emily had to hold the ropes as far apart as she could for Finley to slip through. As it was, her ribs cried out in protest.

Bloody hell, she needed a hot bath and bed. And maybe some laudanum for the discomfort until the Organites did their work. She didn't care if people noticed how fast she healed. She wasn't allowing this pain to linger. The little "beasties" from far below the earth—supposedly the ooze from which life began—would fix her up in no time.

Those dreams were dashed when a behemoth of a man stepped in front of them. Finley looked up—way up. The man was bigger than Sam. A giant. Emily stiffened at the sight of him.

"Mr. Dalton wants to meet you," he said in a voice that sounded as though it came from his toes.

Finley scowled at him. This is what she had hoped to achieve, and now that she had, she was annoyed. "Mr. Dalton can wait."

The man straightened, making himself even taller. "Mr. Dalton doesn't wait."

A sharp glare wrinkled Emily's brow. "Look, you…gargantuan, she's hurt, and she's not running off to meet your master until I've addressed her injuries. Is that understood?"

Surprise lit his large face. He nodded. "Yes, ma'am. I'll wait here."

As they walked away, Finley turned her head to look at her friend, admiration taking the sting out of her wounds. "You're a fierce one, Emily O'Brien."

"I don't like being ordered about or bullied" was all the explanation she offered. For the second time that day, Finley had violent feelings toward whoever had hurt her friend in the past.

"I'll clean your wounds and apply some cosmetics so no one notices that you heal faster than regular folk, but I'm going to inject beasties into your ribs to mend them—and remedy any chance of internal injury."

Finley assumed her insides would heal just like everything else, but serious internal injuries could kill her faster than she could repair herself. She knew this because she had once injured Sam and almost killed him. She nodded in acquiescence.

They found a bench toward the back of the hall, and Finley gingerly sat down. Emily rummaged through her bag and removed a metal syringe, which she filled with an earthy-smelling substance Finley recognized as Organites. Griffin's grandfather had discovered it on his property years ago. It was also believed to be the cause of these "evolutions" she and the others had gone through. Her father had experimented with the stuff, and so she had been born with her abilities, but Emily, Sam and Griffin had developed theirs over the years. Sam was part machine and wickedly strong. Griffin could harness the Aether—a dimensional energy unnoticed by most of the living. And Emily could talk to machines.

Organites were everywhere—part of the earth. Who knew who else had been affected around the world? Jasper had developed abilities while living in California, though they'd increased after using some of Emily's healing salve.

"This may hurt," Emily warned as she positioned the needle between the plates of Finley's steel corset. The sharp point went through her shirt to pierce her skin. Finley hissed as it struck one of her abused ribs, but she remained still. The last thing she needed was for Emily to puncture her lung.

"Sorry," her friend whispered. "There, done." The needle slid out.

Almost instantly, Finley felt the Organites go to work. There was a tingling sensation, almost like a tickle, and then the pain in her torso began to ease. It would take a little while to heal completely, but at least it didn't hurt so much.

Then Emily cleaned the blood from her face while Finley unwrapped the damp and soiled bandages from around her hands. She flexed her fingers. Her knuckles were sore, but none were broken.

"Ready?" Emily asked when she was done.

Finley nodded. "Em, maybe you should go back to the hotel with Sam and Griffin."

A dark flush rose in the other girl's cheeks at the suggestion. "And leave you to face that giant and Dalton alone? I don't think so, lass."

Perhaps not, but all Finley could think of at that moment was how badly hurt Emily had been when they went up against The Machinist and his automatons. She would never forgive herself if anything happened to her friend while she was with her.

"Em…"

"You just shut your mouth. I am not letting you do this alone, so you can either let me go with you, or I can march out there and tell that mountain of a man that you're the Duke of Greythorne's girlfriend."

Finley's jaw dropped. "You wouldn't do that."

Movements stiff, Emily crammed her supplies back into her satchel. "Don't push me. I'm all for bravery, but there's a fine line between that and buffoonery. You're quickly siding on the latter." She hoisted the bag, face impassive, and jerked her head toward the entrance. "Let's go."

Gingerly, Finley rose to her feet. It didn't hurt as much as she expected. She was able to walk by herself as they made their way to where their "escort" waited.

"Right, then," Finley said to the giant as they approached. "Lead on."

He pointed at Emily. "Not her."

Emily opened her mouth, but Finley cut her off. "Sorry, mate. She goes where I go." She had to stop herself from putting on an accent as atrocious as Jack's butchered English. She wanted to sound a little lower class than she actually was, but not so much that Dalton felt too superior.

The big man didn't like this change of plans, but he didn't argue with her. "Fine. Follow me."

Finley had to walk faster than she wanted, to match his

long stride. Poor Emily practically jogged beside her. Some-how they managed to keep up as he led them from the fight-ing area to a small parlor—for lack of a better term—just off the main vestibule.

The room was sparse and in need of fresh paint and paper. The furniture was aged but sturdy. Dalton sat on a small blue sofa, while Jasper and the Chinese girl were seated to his left on a red love seat. Three armed men, looking as though they'd just stepped off the cover of a cowboy dime novel, stood behind Dalton.

Finley stopped in the center of the room, trying not to look at Jasper, who had been a gentleman and stood when they came in. He was supposed to be a stranger, after all. Hope-fully Emily remembered that, as well.

"Hello," Dalton said. He stood, too. "I'm Reno Dalton. And you are Finley...Bennet, is it?"

She almost snorted. She'd wager ten quid he knew exactly what her name was—or rather what she pretended it was. In-stead, she smiled. "That's right. Your man said you wanted to see me, so what do you want?"

Emily shot her a startled glance at her abrupt tone, but Fin-ley ignored it. She'd known entirely too many young men like Dalton, and she'd knocked out over half of them. She knew just how to get their interest—by being disinterested in them.

Dalton arched a brow. "Blunt little thing, aren't you?"

She shrugged. "In my experience people only want to talk

to me when they think I can be useful to them. I'm assuming there's something you think I can do for you, so let's not beat around the bush, eh? I'm hungry." She was, too. Fighting burned a lot of energy.

Dalton walked toward her. The closer he came the more she realized just how utterly beautiful he was. Really, it was a wonder he didn't leave a trail of swooning women in his wake. Then he smiled, and Finley felt like she was facing a shark—one that smelled blood. Dalton was bad news, and part of her liked it. Not him, but *something* about him.

"Forgive my manners, Miss Bennet. We tend to do things differently in America than in England. I understand that you must be sore and tired and understandably hungry. Perhaps you would care to meet me for dinner tomorrow night? I have a business opportunity I would like to discuss with you." His pale gaze traveled over her. "You like money, don't you?"

Finley took a step toward him and peered up at him with a smirk. "As much as the next girl. When and where?"

"My driver can fetch you."

"I'll fetch myself, thanks." She couldn't very well tell him to collect her at the Waldorf-bloody-Astoria, could she?

Dalton inclined his head, curiosity lighting his already bright eyes. "Very well." He withdrew a card from inside his gray coat. There was an address on it. "This is where I'm staying while I'm in the city. Come around seven."

Finley nodded as she slipped the card inside the top of her corset, between the garment and her shirt. It wasn't completely risqué, but she could tell Dalton appreciated the action. "Seven it is." Then she turned to Emily. "Come along, ducks. I've a craving for pudding."

Dalton bid them good-night, and Finley returned the sentiment. She managed to sweep out of the room without directing the barest glance at Jasper. Hopefully he was the stand-up sort she believed him to be and wouldn't give away her true identity to Dalton.

It would be a shame if she got all dolled up for dinner only to get herself killed.

"Do you know her?"

Jasper looked up when Dalton spoke to him. "Who?" he asked, playing dumb.

Blue eyes rolled heavenward. "The Queen. Who do you think? The scrappy girl."

Finley hadn't even left five minutes ago, and already, Dalton was asking questions. She must have made an impression.

"Uh, England might not be as big as the States or even Texas, but it's still a country with lots of people living in it. Just 'cause I've been there doesn't mean I met them all. Though I did hear stories about a girl linked to Jack Dandy who was incredibly fast and strong." If he was right, and Finley was trying to get into Dalton's gang, she would need the worst reputation she could get. "She was suspected in the death of an aristocrat, but nothing was ever proven."

Dalton's expression was all curiosity. "Really? She does

sound like an intriguing female." He paused. "How many more pieces are there to retrieve?"

"Half a dozen," Jasper replied. "Give or take."

The other man's expression turned hard. "You better hope you remember where you hid them all."

Jasper nodded. "I remember."

Slapping his thighs, Dalton replied, "Good. You'll get the second one tomorrow. Now let's get out of here. This place smells like sweat and blood."

It did at that, and Jasper wasn't sorry to leave it. The ride back to Dalton's rented house was quiet. Not even Mei spoke, though Jasper caught her glaring at Dalton once or twice. The cad only smiled at her in return.

Jasper's mind whirled. If Finley was trying to infiltrate the gang, then surely she and the others believed in his innocence. He didn't know whether he loved them for it or wanted to cuff 'em upside their fool heads. He was touched that they came for him but terrified one or more of them would be hurt—or worse—because of him. It seemed he couldn't get close to anyone without putting them at risk.

At the house, Little Hank practically shoved him all the way to his room and tossed him inside without a word. Jasper kicked off his boots and tossed his hat and coat on a chair before dropping onto the bed. He stared up at the ceiling. He had only just started ruminating on a way out of this mess when he heard the key turn in the lock.

Mei.

She came into the room in a bright blue silk dressing gown, carrying a medium-size polished oak box, which appeared to be heavy. Jasper got up and took the burden from her.

"Set it on the desk," she instructed, and he did, noticing that it wasn't really a box at all, but some kind of auditory device. Set into one side of it was a brass funnel—like one would find on a Victrola.

"What is this contraption?" he asked.

Mei smiled as she opened the lid, revealing a panel of knobs and switches and a place to insert punch cards. "Dalton calls it a portable phonograph. It runs on a power cell made in England." Jasper didn't tell her Griffin's grandfather had discovered the ore that made the power cell possible. It was a modern marvel, but a good part of the world still depended on, or preferred, gaslight or even candles and lamps.

"Where did it come from?" he asked.

"I believe Dalton stole it from someone named Edison."

"Thomas Edison?" Jasper asked, dumbfounded.

Mei nodded. "That's it."

Was the machine Jasper had hidden something of Edison's, as well? If so, no wonder Dalton wanted it back. It could be a terrible thing—after all, Edison was the man who had electrocuted animals to prove electricity could also be used to execute criminals.

She flicked a switch, adjusted two of the knobs and then inserted a punch card. Music wafted from the funnel, clear and sweet. Mei adjusted the volume so that the music would only be heard in that room and then took him by the hand with a gentle smile.

"Come," she said. "Talk to me."

They lay down on the bed, where they could be comfortable. Jasper held her in his arms, against his chest, and breathed in the sweet, flowery scent of her. In that moment, he could forget just what a dang mess he'd made of things.

"You really didn't know those girls tonight?" she asked.

He hesitated. He wanted to tell her who the girls were, that he had friends who would do their best to help Mei and him, but if she didn't know, then she wouldn't have to lie to Dalton. She wouldn't be in danger.

"No," he said. "I don't know them. That one with the black in her hair sure is tough, though, ain't she?"

"Very," she replied, clearly impressed. "And she knows Eastern fighting techniques."

"They're becoming all the rage in London now," he responded. She'd sounded slightly suspicious. "Especially among the suffragettes."

"Warrior women," she mused with a smile. "I like that. I...noticed you looking at the red-haired girl. Do you think she's pretty?"

Asking if Miss Emily was pretty was sort of like asking if the sun was warm. She brightened any room she was in, as fresh and light as Mei was dark and exotic. There was no way he could compare the two of them, and that's what she was asking him to do. What she really wanted to know was if he thought Emily was prettier than her.

"She's all right." He squeezed her against his chest. "She's not you, though." That was the most diplomatic reply he could think of.

Clearly it worked, because Mei smiled and cuddled against him. When she lifted her face for a kiss, Jasper paused again. A soft ticking noise captured his attention—it was coming from her. "That collar. Does it hurt?"

Mei raised slender fingers to the clockwork device around her neck. "It's a little tight when Dalton winds it, but I've gotten so accustomed to it, I barely notice anymore."

"So he doesn't tighten it to punish you?"

"He did in the beginning—when I tried to escape. That's how I know that it actually works. I don't know how, but he knows when I try to leave. But tonight, at the fight, I was fine."

Jasper's jaw clenched. He could kill Dalton. "It probably transmits through the Aether." He didn't know much about the "energy" but he had seen machines that could harness the power—it was like they could work without wires or connections. Mei had been fine, because she'd been close to Dalton. "It's a big risk you're taking, sneaking in here to see me like this." If Dalton found her not in her room, he might tighten the collar just to remind her of her place.

She stroked his cheek with her delicate fingers, eyes sparkling up at him. "It's a risk I'm willing to take."

"What if Dalton finds out?" He couldn't stand it if she got into any more trouble because of him.

Mei inched closer, bringing her face to his. "I don't care," she whispered, resolute.

The second her lips touched his, all of Jasper's misgivings evaporated, and he realized that—at that precise moment— he didn't care about Dalton, either.

Chapter 5

Griffin knew the exact moment Finley returned to the hotel. He knew because he was waiting for her in her room. He sat in a chair playing with a little clockwork owl he had bought for her earlier that day—thinking it might help make up for being such a git to her the other night. When wound up, it turned its head, blinked its big eyes and fluttered its delicate brass wings.

Perhaps it would be petulant of him, but he was tempted to crush it beneath his boot.

He was so angry at her. She could have gotten herself seriously hurt. She could have gotten herself *killed*.

He had lost his parents. He'd almost lost Sam. He would not lose her. Emotion seethed inside him, churning his insides until it felt as though all of his organs had been displaced.

Unfortunately, heightened emotion tended to trigger a defense response from his abilities, which was never good.

Griffin was connected to the Aether, which, simply put, was energy. It came from all living matter and made up the realm of the dead. Most people went their entire lives without ever touching it. Some people could harness it to speak to the dead, see ghosts. Griffin could literally cross over into it. He could wield it as power, but sometimes, if he wasn't careful, the Aether used him. He had runic tattoos, similar to the ones he'd given Finley, that helped him focus and channel his power, but there was only so much symbols could do. Even those made from Organite ink.

That raw power closed around him, thinning the veil between this world and the next, filling him with restless energy. He had to calm down before it was too late.

Slowly, he drew a deep breath and exhaled it. Then again. In his hand, the little owl fluttered, going through its repertoire of motions as he allowed bits of Aetheric energy to flow into it.

Never before had anyone inspired such turbulence within him. Finley Jayne had been trouble from the night he literally ran into her, and yet, he could not bring himself to let her go. He wanted to trust her as deeply as he wanted her to trust him, but at this rate, they would never get there.

When he heard the sound of a key turning in the lock, he stilled—and so did the owl. He focused his attention on the door; for a moment, he thought the heavy wood bowed ever so slightly on its hinges, pulling toward him.

Another breath. In. Out. Calm.

The moment she crossed the threshold, his heart punched his ribs as though it was fighting for life—so hard it was painful. Her black-streaked, honey-colored hair was a mess, tendrils escaping from sticks she used to secure the thick knot on the back of her head. Her knuckles and corset sported rusty smears—dried blood. Her pretty face hosted similar blooms of color along with violent-looking bruises, which smeared across her skin.

Smeared?

Griffin's eyes narrowed. Not bruises—not anymore. The smears were from cosmetics, no doubt employed to keep Dalton from noticing that she had healed faster than she should. To be honest, he would think her healing abilities would only serve to make her more attractive to the criminal. Should he mention that or simply be grateful she hadn't been eager to give away all her secrets?

Emily was with her, laughing at something Finley said as they entered the room. It was Emily who first noticed him, laughter dying as she saw him. Whatever she saw when her gaze locked with his made the cute little redhead blanch.

"Evening, lad," she said, voice slightly strained.

Griffin rose to his feet—it was what a gentleman did when ladies entered the room. "Good evening, Em. Finley."

Finley didn't pale when she met his gaze, although it would

be hard to tell with the amount of dried blood and cosmetics on her face. Her chin came up defiantly, however. She expected a fight. He wasn't surprised, as a fight was exactly what he suspected she wanted. She'd taken and delivered over an hour's worth of violence during the fights that night and still had a little steel left in her spine.

He had told her he wouldn't fight for her affection, but that had been a lie. He would fight. Only, he hadn't thought that she would be his opponent.

"I'm really tired," Emily announced out of the blue. "I think I'll trundle myself off to bed. Good night!" She was gone before either Griffin or Finley could respond, the door clicking shut behind her.

The air seemed to thicken now that just the two of them were left in the room. The temperature seemed higher, as well, as though their mutual anger set the water in the radiator to boil.

Finley crossed her arms over her chest and stood with legs braced, as though ready for battle. Griffin kept his own hands at his sides, the thumb of his left stroking the owl.

"You put Emily at risk tonight," he accused, because he couldn't think of how to put his feelings into words. He was too afraid of making an idiot of himself. It was better to be harsh than vulnerable.

A deep scowl furrowed between her arched brows. "I didn't make her come along. You ever try to talk her out of something once she's made up her mind? Besides, she can take care of herself. You and Sam treat her like a china doll rather than a capable female."

Perhaps he and Sam were guilty of behaving *too* protectively toward Emily, but it was how they had both been raised to treat women—even ones as capable as Emily and Finley. He tried to remember that they could fend for themselves quite nicely, and most of the time he succeeded, but his natural tendency was to play the gentleman.

"Is that what this was about?" he asked in a deceptively calm tone. "To prove just how *capable* you and Em are?"

Bright amber eyes narrowed thoughtfully. "What are you really angry about? That I entered the fight or that someone other than you came up with a plan that worked? Dalton wants to meet with me."

Her words stung like a slap, and Griffin winced accordingly. Is that what she thought of him? "You may have noticed I came up with a similar plan, which you would have known, had you talked to me."

She snorted. "Dalton'd see through you and Sam in a second. You're too fine. Too good."

"Perhaps I'm concerned about the fact that you have developed a penchant for unsavory company," he replied, making a dig of his own. "Perhaps I'm angry because we're supposed to work together, and you went behind my back." He should have known she was up to something. She probably did this just to rub his face in it.

She shrugged. "You would have tried to stop me." She

didn't say a word about the kind of company she preferred, which stuck the thorn in Griff's pride just a little further.

"You're bloody right I would have!" He squeezed the mechanical owl so hard the beak cut into his palm. "And then you could have persuaded me to your side. You could have made me see that your plan was our best option." He raked a hand through his hair. "But you didn't trust me, and you came up with your plan just to spite me, and *that* is what makes me so damn angry."

Finley stared at him, eyes wide, mouth wide. "Griffin—"

He cut her off. "I had to sit there—helpless—and watch as you took beating after beating tonight, and I couldn't show any emotion. I couldn't cheer when you won or show my fear when you got hurt. I couldn't do anything."

Bloody hell, he was not used to feeling helpless.

"You didn't need to do anything!" She threw her hands in the air. "The rest of us are capable people, Griffin. You're not the only one who can take charge of a situation."

She was right, but it was his crew and he felt responsible for them. He set the little brass owl—warm from his hands—on the polished top of the dresser. "Reno Dalton is not Jack Dandy, Finley. He'll kill you if he suspects you're playing him. Is that a risk you're willing to take?"

Finley nodded curtly. "If it will help Jasper."

"All right, then." He kept his opinions tucked inside. "If it's not too much trouble, I would like to hear the rest of your plan tomorrow morning when we're all together. That way, there will be no more surprises, and we'll all know our parts."

She said something, but Griffin wasn't listening. He was suddenly so exhausted that all he wanted was his bed. There was no point in discussing this further. Finley wanted to help Jasper, and he couldn't fault her for that. He might not like how she went about it, but she'd gotten closer to Dalton than he had. If he was jealous of how she looked at Dalton, that was his problem alone. He would either trust her not to get involved with the criminal or he would not. It was entirely possible that Dalton would win her over and she would fully give in to her darker nature.

He met her gaze steadily—unemotionally. "I stood by you when you were questioned about Lord Felix's murder. I've done everything I can to help you, and in return you—" He stopped and shook his head. "This isn't about me. Either you want to be part of this team, or you don't. That's your decision."

Her eyes narrowed. "You've given me a lot of ultimatums recently, Your Grace."

"Not ultimatums, choices. You're no longer two sides of a whole, Finley. You are one person—singular. That means choosing who you want to be—*where* you want to be."

"Let me guess," she began bitterly. "If I decide to be part of the group, that means I have to tell you everything I do."

"Of course not. If you decide to stay, it means you don't run off on your own. It means you have respect for the people who have accepted you as a friend. I saw how you looked at Dalton—how he looked at you. You're attracted to the danger he offers."

A smirk twisted her lips. "Is this the part where you remind me of how 'dangerous' you can be?"

She was mocking him. Mocking *him*. Deep inside his chest it felt as though someone flicked a switch—or punched a hole.

The lights flashed—not just in this room but also in the buildings visible through the window. The little owl began to hop around the dresser. The portable telegraph machine in his pocket began to hum, as did the one on Finley's nightstand. And somewhere in the building a boiler fired up—he could hear the echo of it in the pipes.

"Griffin."

The bulb in the lamp beside the bed blew, throwing glass everywhere. Finley cried out. "Griffin!"

It took all of his strength, but somehow he managed to regain control. The lights returned to normal. The little owl and the telegraphs quieted.

Finley stared at him as though she didn't recognize him— as though he frightened her.

Pivoting on his heel, he tore open the door and stepped into the hall. The door to Emily's room opened, and she stuck her head out. "The cat just powered up all by itself. Any idea… Oh, dear God."

Griffin glanced at her. He could only imagine how he appeared to her—sweat dripping down his brow, eyes wide and crazed. No doubt he was pale. Lord, it felt as though electricity danced between his fingers—in his head.

"Get in here, lad," she commanded.

Griffin heard the urgency in her voice and followed her into the room. She grabbed his hand, but he jerked back. His control was too fragile. If she touched him, the Aether would rush through his fingers into hers. He couldn't risk hurting her.

She led him out onto the balcony, the cat clinking behind them. Outside, the summer air was warm but carried a lovely breeze, which helped cool Griffin's fevered head. Still, he had to fight to remain in control as he watched Emily flick switches and push buttons inside the cat's control panel. Suddenly, the metal panther began to shudder, click and whirl. He couldn't quite believe his eyes as the automaton began to reshape itself. The legs disappeared, as did the tail. A long vertical rod extended from the inside, opening to resemble a double row of long fan blades—a propeller.

When it was done, the cat had completely metamorphosed into something Griffin couldn't identify.

"It's my Icarus construct," Emily explained, guiding him toward the thing that had two belts lying loose on its top. "A flying machine."

"This can't be safe," Griffin remarked as she made him straddle the thing, then sit so she could quickly fasten one of the belts around him.

He thought he heard her mutter, "We're about to find out,"

but he prayed that wasn't true as she climbed on in front and fastened the other belt around her hips. She pulled goggles over her eyes. "Hang on, lad!"

The propeller above his head began to whirl and sputter. Griffin wrapped his hands around the post for support—and to let a little of his power crawl along the metal. If he could make things power on, then it stood to reason he could give them a boost, as well. Maybe the slight drain would keep him from losing control too quickly.

The propeller whirled so fast it seemed one singular piece. The machine lifted off the balcony and lurched forward.

Griffin glanced down as his feet dangled over empty night air. The lights of Manhattan Island twinkled around them—below them. The wind whipped through his hair and brought water to his eyes, so that soon, it was difficult to see anything at all. He would have to get Emily to take him out again when he could actually enjoy the sensation of flying.

The wind cooled a short while later as they flew over water. Bedloe's Island was where they were headed—the place where the Statue of Liberty stood.

Emily flew them as close to the torch as she could. "You're going to have to jump," she shouted. "Grab the light and let go!"

Griffin unbuckled the belt and let himself slip to the terrace below—the rim of the lit torch. It was so bright it was almost blinding, intensifying the growing ache behind his eyes. He didn't know why Emily hadn't taken him to the water below. Perhaps she thought he might drown. He was only glad to be so far away from people.

He waited until the sound of the propeller faded away—Emily knew to get as far away as she could—before placing his hand on the base of the light that made the torch appear to burn. All of his focus went into that torch and its bulb.

And then he let go of all the energy inside him. The release made him throw back his head and scream. For a second, he would have sworn that he saw light come out of his own mouth as he channeled everything into the torch and outward. It always flowed outward, unable to be contained.

Then there was a huge flash, and everything went black.

The next morning, Finley opened her eyes after a fitful night. She'd gotten—at best—four hours sleep. The rest of the time had been spent thinking of Griffin, the awful things they'd said to each other, the fact that she had pushed him so far his power flared.

She shouldn't have mocked him. She hadn't meant to, though she wasn't quite certain what it was she *had* meant to do.

Looking back at the weeks she'd spent with her new friends, there had been several shameful times when she had acted alone. She had snuck off to visit Jack Dandy—which led to a strange, flirtatious friendship. One night, she disappeared and had no recollection of where she had been. Lord Felix, the son of her former employer, died that night. Even she couldn't say with certainty that she hadn't killed him. Fortunately, her name had been cleared. Later, she chased after Sam without alerting anyone else, and the two of them had ended up in a battle with an automaton, which could have killed them both.

Worse, she had contrived to join last night's fights to spite Griffin. To prove to him she could do it. And why? Just because he made her angry and happy and nervous, all at the same time. Never mind that her plan had worked, she should have shared it with the entire group, instead of just Emily. She had put the other girl at risk. She had put them both at risk.

Before, she could have blamed this sort of behavior on her darker half, but that was no longer the case. Griffin had helped her begin to unite her two sides, and now she was no longer one or the other, but both. Now it was up to her to decide what sort of person she wanted to be.

She didn't want to go back to being alone, especially now that she had found friends. Real friends. Family. Especially Griffin. He had done so much for her, and she'd repaid him by being snide and mocking.

But she hadn't wanted him to see that he was the one thing that frightened her. When she'd first met Griffin, he had told her that he would give her his trust, and in return, he would settle for nothing less than hers. She had been treated poorly by fellows of his station before, and part of her mind couldn't let go of that wariness; it was the only protection her heart had.

Because if there was one person in all the world capable of breaking her heart, it was Griffin. Perhaps that was why she ran to Jack whenever she felt cagey. Jack didn't have expectations. Jack would eventually let her down, while she'd be the one to do that to Griffin—if she hadn't already.

This was ridiculous. She threw back the covers and slipped out of her incredibly comfortable bed. She could laze about all day wondering and thinking, but thinking always seemed to get her into trouble. Although, not thinking got her into trouble, too.

Who was she trying to kid? Trouble seemed to find her, no matter what. If trouble was going to come calling, she might as well be clean.

She bathed and dressed in pale pink knee-length trousers with a frill at the bottom, white shirt and her pink-and-black-striped corset. She laced heavy black boots up to the hem of her trousers and wrapped the ends of the laces around each boot once before tying them. Then she brushed her hair and twisted it up onto the back of her head, securing it with two chopsticks.

The bruises on her face had faded to almost nothing overnight. Her ribs were stiff, but she could draw a deep breath without them hurting. A normal girl would be so stiff and sore, she would barely be able to move about. Then again, if she was a "normal" girl, she wouldn't have been in the ring in the first place. This was one of those times that being a freak came in handy.

Her stomach fluttered as she left her room. Odd how she felt so anxious going to meet her friends, when Dalton hadn't inspired half so much fuss. Last night, she'd felt triumphant, but now she felt a little...silly and self-conscious.

She stopped to knock at Emily's door. No answer. They must have gone downstairs already. Finley said hello to the boy operating the lift and spent the rest of the trip wondering if the little box could move any slower. Seriously, she could have jumped over the railing in the stairwell and been there by now.

They were all gathered around the dining room table and looked up at her entrance when she walked in. Sam only glanced at her for a split second before turning his attention back to the mountain of food piled on his plate. Surely eating that many scrambled eggs couldn't be healthy for a body.

"Morning, Finley," he mumbled.

"Good morning, everyone," she replied and winced at the cheer in her voice. Emily smiled at her from her seat beside Sam, but Finley didn't miss the glance her friend shot in Griffin's direction.

Slowly—determinedly—Finley made herself look at him. He sat at his customary spot at the head of the table, but his breakfast was nothing more than coffee and toast. He looked tired and drawn, with dark circles under his storm-blue eyes.

Was she the cause of those dark smudges? The thought

added more guilt to her already heavy shoulders. She tried to smile and found her lips incapable of the movement. "Griffin," she whispered.

"Finley," he echoed with the ghost of a grin. Did he mean to tease or to mock her? "I hope you slept well."

"Tolerably," she replied, sitting down at the place set for her at his right. "You?"

"Once I got there, you could say I slept like the dead." He chuckled drily.

Emily looked at him again, and this time Finley saw concern in the other girl's eyes. What did she know that Finley did not? Had Griffin told her of their conversation?

"Says here there was a 'flash of light, like lightning,' from the Statue of Liberty last night," Sam announced as he perused the front page of the morning *Times*. "Any of you see it?"

Griffin seemed to find this hilarious and began to laugh in that way Finley often did when she hadn't enough sleep.

"Actually..." Emily began, glancing at Griffin as though he'd gone mad.

"It was probably something faulty with the lantern mechanism in the torch," Griffin interrupted, suddenly serious. "I'm surprised it's never happened before."

Sam shrugged. "I suppose so. Call me paranoid, but every time something strange happens now, I expect to find some kind of villain at work."

"You're paranoid," Griffin replied with a grin. "I wager

the torch will be lit again tonight, and no one will give it another thought."

Except for her, Finley thought as she took two pieces of toast from the warming plate in front of her. Whoever invented heated dishes should be knighted. Did they knight people in America? Probably not.

She hadn't missed the startled look Emily shot Griffin when he interrupted her, which meant that both she and Griffin knew what had happened out on that island last night. Why the secrecy?

Then it hit her. It had been Griffin. He'd been on the verge of losing control of his abilities last night—because of her. Somehow he'd gotten out to the statue or had done something that had made that flash.

She stared at him. "I owe you all an apology," she blurted.

Three pairs of eyes turned toward her. Heat seeped into her cheeks, like tea in hot water. "I shouldn't have taken Emily to Five Points to dig up information on Dalton. And I should have told Sam and Griffin about the fights. I'm sorry."

Sam helped himself to more sausage. "I'm the last person who would give you bother about that." It was no secret that he had once taken off on his own a lot, but that seemed to have changed since the fight with The Machinist.

"I had fun," Emily added, a tad defiantly.

"Yeah, about that," Sam began, gesturing at her with his knife. "You need to be careful. This isn't London. Those gangs are dangerous." The fact that he hadn't attempted to lock Emily in her room to keep her safe also showed how different he was. Finley knew it must be hard for him to give up some of his protectiveness.

Emily shot him a glance out of the corner of her eye. "I'm Irish, Sam Morgan. Most of those 'gangs' are my people."

"But the rest aren't," Griffin interjected, rubbing his forehead with the heel of his hand. "And to some of them, the only good Irish is dead Irish, and they *all* hate the English, so there will be no running about alone by any of us. Understood?"

The three of them nodded. Finley knew the remark was mostly directed at her, but she wasn't about to get her knickers in a twist over it. He was right. They weren't in London, and there was danger in this city for all of them.

"Good." He leaned back in his chair and reached for his cup of coffee. "Finley, you have an engagement with Dalton tonight, correct?"

She chewed and swallowed the bite of egg in her mouth. "Yes, though I think dinner is just a formality. I reckon he'll want me to join his enterprise. He's fond of rough girls."

"No doubt he plans to seduce you," Griffin remarked thoughtfully. When Finley's cheeks turned red, he added, "Into his gang, of course. I'm sure he'll waste no time now that he's seen what you can do."

It was as much of a truce as he was probably going to offer, and she was glad for it. In fact, she liked him all the more for not making it too easy for her.

She knew there really wasn't much point in having a crush on Griffin. A duke would be expected to marry someone of his own social sphere—not that Finley wanted to marry him! But he wouldn't make her half so mental if she didn't like him.

Emily perked up. "I'm going to listen to Mr. Tesla give a talk at the New York Repository of Science this evening. I'm so excited!"

"I'm going with her," Sam added. Finley noted with amusement that he did not sound half so enthusiastic as his companion about the evening.

"And I am off to a party," Griffin remarked. "Seems dukes are quite the popular commodity here in Manhattan."

Sam made a face. "I thought the aristocracy was one of the things the Yanks hate about us."

"You can take the American out of England..." Griffin grinned. "It might be fun to be introduced to the Knicker-bocker set."

"Lots of rich heiresses trolling for a title," Sam remarked. "Be careful you don't come back engaged."

Finley's stomach dropped, but then Griffin laughed. "Wouldn't dream of it." Then he turned to her. "Don't worry, Fin—" her eyes widened "—I'll have my P.T. if you run into trouble. So will Sam and Em. We'll be there in a flash if you need us."

Both relieved and annoyed that he hadn't sought to ease her mind as to the heiress issue, Finley was nevertheless comforted by the fact that her friends would come to her rescue if she telegraphed them.

She didn't think she would need them. She was fairly confident in her ability to get and hold Dalton's attention. She was also confident in her own ability to break his arms should he cross any lines.

She could break the arms of any heiresses who thought to catch themselves a duke, as well, but she kept that to herself.

"I need to go do some work," Emily announced suddenly, pushing her chair back from the table. "Come with me, Sam."

The big dark-haired fellow looked down at his plate. A lone sausage lay there. "I'm not done."

"Bring it with you. Come on." She looked impatient. Sam shrugged and obeyed.

Finley barely had time to say goodbye before they disappeared.

Griffin chuckled. "Do you think Emily wanted to leave us alone?"

"Certainly seems that way," she replied, her own smile wry. "Listen, Griffin—"

He held up his hand. "Tell you what—you don't apologize, and then I won't have to apologize. Let's just say that all is forgiven and never speak of it again."

"But I want to speak of it."

That seemed to surprise him. "You do?"

"Yes. I'm sorry that I've behaved the way I have. It's no excuse, but I'm still trying to find out who I am, so it's difficult for me to know exactly how to behave at times." It felt good to say this out loud. "Also, I've never really had anyone in my life I could trust, no one beyond my mother and Silas. You are right to expect it from me, and I want to be worthy of yours, but...neither of us seems to be very good at offering it."

He nodded. "You're right. I suppose we both have some work to do. For my part, I am sorry. I'm afraid I haven't been myself lately."

When it was obvious that was all he was going to say on the subject, she asked, "Is it the Aether?"

"Something feels odd." He shrugged—or maybe it was a shudder. "Never mind that. I want you to be careful tonight. If it doesn't feel right, get out of there immediately."

She nodded. "I will." But she had no intention of leaving without Jasper.

As if reading her mind, Griffin arched a brow. "We don't know if you'll be able to count on Jasper for help."

Finley met his gaze. "You don't really think he's a murderer, do you?"

He scratched his head with a sigh. "No, I don't, but I've been wrong before. That doesn't mean I'm going to leave him with Dalton, though." At that moment, he looked so tired. She wanted to take all of his worries away, but she had no idea how to do that.

She reached over and touched his hand. "We'll get him."

A slow smile curved his lips, and she suddenly wanted to

lean in and kiss him—just press her lips to his until everything else went away.

His fingers closed around hers. "I know."

They sat there for a moment, holding hands until the tension between them grew. One would think this bit of atonement would have made things easier, but this awareness was so thick she could almost taste it.

Something had changed between them. She wasn't certain what it meant, but she was fairly certain that, whatever it was, it was good. And if she survived dinner with Dalton, she just might get to enjoy it.

Chapter 6

After discussing it further with the others—she was try-ing to prove she could be a team player—Finley decided she would let Dalton see that her bruises had healed, rather than trying to re-create them with cosmetics. Her ability to heal quickly could only be seen as an advantage, especially to someone who might want to use her for violence.

She dressed in one of her sleeveless Oriental-style gowns in violet satin, embroidered with tiny red-and-gold flow-ers. It was flashy, but nothing a girl who lived a life of crime couldn't afford. Over it, she hooked a flexible black satin cor-set that matched her square-toed boots. She put her hair up with chopsticks, darkened her eyelashes and painted a light rose color on her cheeks and lips—nothing too garish. She wanted to look like someone with aspirations of finer things, not a trollop.

Finally she dabbed a little sandalwood perfume behind her ears and on her wrists and strapped a blade around her thigh—just above the slit in her skirt. She hoped she wouldn't need it, but even she wasn't stupid enough to go into a lion's den without some sort of protection other than her own fists and feet. And her head. She had an incredibly hard skull.

It was a cool evening so she took a shawl with her, though she doubted she'd need it. She tended to run a little warmer than most people. When she left her room she locked the door and slipped the key into a small pocket inside her corset—no chance of Dalton or anyone else finding it there. A key from the Waldorf-Astoria would cause suspicion. The last thing she wanted was to alert the criminal to her association with Griffin—and therefore Jasper.

Jasper. Would he be glad to see her, or had he already told Dalton who she really was? Would she be walking straight into a trap? No, she wouldn't think that of him. Jasper was her friend, and she would do everything she could for him.

She called for the lift and took it all the way down to the main foyer, which was lit in such a manner as to flatter all the ladies—and their glittering jewels. She hadn't fully realized when they first arrived just how fancy the hotel was. Having been a lady's maid in two fine houses had made it easy for her to move into Griffin's house without much fuss. It wasn't until now, walking across this polished floor with its pristine carpets, that she understood how fortunate she was. She could have just as easily ended up in a place like Whitechapel in London or Five Points if Griffin hadn't found her.

Thankfully, Dalton chose to live just north and west of the desolation—on Broadway. She knew exactly where, because she'd looked for the street on the map of the city she had found earlier that day.

Griffin had given her ample fare for a cab there and back. Before they left London, the two of them had come to an agreement. Finley wasn't about to live in his house and let him pay for everything—she knew what society called women who did that. She was comfortable, however, being his employee and accepting a wage for the work she did with him. He paid very well—more than she'd ever earned at another job, more than her stepfather, Silas, probably made in his shop.

A passing bellman in a spotless, creaseless uniform stopped to inquire whether or not she needed a carriage brought around, and for a moment, she felt very posh indeed. "Actually, I'm in need of a cab," she told him. "Might you acquire one for me?" She even sounded posh.

The young man replied that he could and headed off to do just that. That left her standing alone, off to one side of the lobby, where she could watch other guests leave for their evening's entertainment.

A fine figure of a gentleman caught her eye as she studied her surroundings. His back was to her, allowing her to admire the breadth of his shoulders beneath his fine black coat, his impressive height and the way the light brought out red and gold in his hair. Then as though feeling the weight of her gaze upon him, he turned and looked right at her.

Breath deserted her lungs. *Griffin.*

She had thought him handsome the first time she laid eyes on him, and before that, she'd heard Phoebe, a girl she used to work for, talk about him and how all the young ladies admired him. Perhaps it was the lighting or the danger of the situation she was about to walk into, but she didn't think he had ever looked as breathtaking as he did at that very moment in his black-and-white evening attire, his thick hair brushed back from his handsome features. Amusement danced in his gray-blue eyes.

Her mouth hung open like an old door off its hinge.

This was the Duke of Greythorne, and it was no wonder young ladies whispered about him. Though Finley would admit that she often found Griffin more attractive when he was slightly scruffy, there was something about the way he was so perfectly dressed—something about how he stood and held his head. He radiated power and authority; confidence but not arrogance.

She realized then what he and Jack had in common. They liked themselves. They knew their own strengths and their weaknesses and had made peace with them both. She envied that. Respected it.

She still didn't know what her strengths—the nonphysical ones—were, but she was pretty certain her weaknesses outnumbered them. Someday, though... Someday, she hoped to feel comfortable in her own skin. She already felt better about herself than she had two months ago. Again, she owed some of that to the gorgeous specimen standing across the foyer from her.

So when Griffin smiled at her, she glanced away—embarrassed, scared that he might have somehow divined her thoughts and emotions. She wanted to be more like him. She wanted to like herself. But first, she had to know herself.

Out of the corner of her eye, she watched him as he left the hotel, and then through the glass, she saw him climb into a fine carriage driven by two gleaming brass automaton horses. Someone had sent a private vehicle for him so he wouldn't have to take a hack. Nice.

Finley stepped out into the evening air just as Griffin's vehicle pulled away. She, of course, didn't have a private carriage waiting on her. It was difficult not to be a little envious of Griffin when she climbed into an interior that smelled of smoke and sweat.

New York, like most modern cities, was humid—the air filled with steam from factories, vehicles and automatons. In the winter, it would make the cold seep into one's bones. In the warmer months, it would make a body so moist you'd think people had bathed with their clothes on. Thankfully, this night was cool, so she didn't have to worry about her kit sticking to her skin.

She gave the driver Dalton's direction and sat back as the carriage rolled into motion. Hers was driven by a real horse, which added to the bouquet of the cab. She stared out the window at the passing city.

New York might be a newer city, perhaps a little more modern, but life was the same here as in London—the wealthy mingled with the poor as little as possible, but often had little choice in the matter. The have-nots would always outnumber the haves, as she had seen the other day in Five Points. It rivaled any London slum.

The lights of a dirigible drifting overhead briefly illuminated 5th Avenue, its engine a low hum over the hustle and bustle of the city. She had heard that the air machines avoided flying over the poorer areas, because they didn't provide a pleasing view for their passengers. Only the very wealthy could afford air travel. The rest of the world still had to rely on rail and boats to get where they wanted to go.

The dirigible continued north toward the landing port in Central Park, and Finley's carriage continued south and a little west, inching farther and farther away from the grandeur of the hotel and the party Griffin would enjoy. Not too far, though. She wasn't headed for the slums tonight.

Dalton was wise to keep his household just on the fringe of Five Points. He didn't impinge on anyone's "business" that way and avoided anyone trying to take a piece of his. The gangs didn't take well to strangers, and if Dalton was from San Francisco the same as Jasper, then he hadn't been in the city long enough to fully establish himself. He obviously fancied himself above the gangs and their ilk, judging from the way he dressed and spoke. Perhaps that was something she could use to her advantage.

His was a moderately sized, slightly shabby redbrick town house with a freshly swept walk and a weathered brass knocker on the door. It looked like the sort of place where a middle-class merchant might have once lived with his wife and children—not a den of thieves. There were even flowers in the tiny gardens tucked on either side of the steps.

"Are you certain this is where you want to go, miss?" the driver asked as she stepped out. "It's not the sort of neighborhood a pretty little thing like you should brave alone."

Finley smiled in appreciation as she dug a few coins out of the pouch concealed beneath the bottom of her corset. If he only knew the damage she could work, he wouldn't be so quick to dismiss her as a "little thing." Though, he was still welcome to think her pretty.

"It's all right," she told him. "I'm meeting friends here."

He looked dubious, but he didn't press the issue as she dropped payment and a generous tip into his palm. "You have a good night, then, miss."

She bade him good-night and approached the front steps, hoping the cabbie wouldn't sit there and wait until she went inside to leave—as though he were her father or guardian.

To her relief, the coach pulled away when the front door of the house opened. It was the behemoth who glared down at her. "You're late."

She glared back. "So?"

He didn't seem to know just what to make of that. Clearly he was not a man accustomed to being talked back to. "Mr. Dalton's waiting for you. Follow me."

When Finley crossed the threshold, it was as though she'd stepped into another world. At that moment, she realized there was no turning back. Jasper would prove to be either a friend or enemy, and she would either survive this or she wouldn't. She didn't doubt for a minute that Dalton would try to kill her if he found out she'd lied to him—it was what any criminal would do. She could only hope she would have backup with her when the time came.

The house was comfortable and clean—much like the home her mother and stepfather owned. She'd grown up surrounded by lemon scent and furniture polish, the slight, sharp tang of vinegar. The smells brought a pang of home-sickness to her chest as she followed the silent giant across the foyer through another doorway. He knocked and opened the door to reveal a small green parlor.

Jasper sat on the sofa. He looked up as soon as she walked in. There was absolutely no recognition on his face, but she thought she caught a glimmer of something in his green eyes. The girl was there, too, watching her like a mouse eyes a hawk—or perhaps the other way around. Finley's own eyes narrowed.

Why were pretty girls always so eager to get all territorial when another girl entered the room? It wasn't as though

Finley was competition or wanted that ugly-arse necklace she was wearing.

Dalton was at the bar, fixing himself a drink. He turned and grinned at her, bright eyes crinkling at the corners. Did he stand at his mirror and practice that smile? Did he know just by how it felt on his face how charming it was? He was almost too perfect to look at—like an angel sent to earth.

Only Dalton was no angel.

"Miss Bennet," he greeted in a low drawl. "Good evening. Care for a drink?"

Finley shook her head. She needed all her wits about her. "No thanks. My apologies for being late."

A quick glance at the clock above the mantel, and Dalton frowned. "You're not late at all."

She couldn't help but throw a triumphant smirk at the giant, who glowered in response.

Her host appeared not to notice the exchange. He gestured with his glass toward the sofa. "You remember my associates, Jasper Renn and Mei Xing?"

Mei Xing? As in a-mazing? Poor girl getting stuck with such an unfortunate name. Or perhaps she thought it was cute. Finley nodded at each of them. "How d'you do?"

Chuckling, Dalton walked around to the love seat and gestured for her to join him. "I love how you English speak."

"Really? I've always been intrigued by what I believe is referred to as the 'Southern drawl.'" She seated herself beside him, forcing herself to act relaxed and affable. This was how it was supposed to go—he had to like her for this to work.

"Most English are." Jasper spoke. "'Least in my experience."

Finley arched a brow. "Really? Have you been to England?" She wanted to ask what he was doing there. If he was a prisoner, then why was he allowed to walk around freely? It didn't look well for proving his innocence.

"I spent some time there" was his response.

Her gaze skipped to Mei. "What about you, Miss Xing? Have you ever been to London?"

"No," the girl replied in a deceptively soft voice—like a cloud wrapped around steel. "But I doubt you have ever been to San Francisco, let alone Peking."

Forcing a smile, Finley crossed her legs. "No, I haven't." She was accustomed to other girls not liking her, so she didn't take it personally this time. Girls didn't need a reason to despise each other.

"As fascinating as this conversation is," Dalton said with a dramatic roll of his eyes, "I'm starving. Let's eat." When he stood, he offered Finley his arm, just like a gentleman would.

She placed her hand on his elbow and allowed him to escort her from the room. She made her grip just a tad tighter than it should be and felt the solid muscle beneath his sleeve. He wasn't some noodle-limbed ponce. He was strong and she would do well to remember it. When he turned those dark-rimmed blue eyes at her and flashed a lopsided smile, she felt like a deer being sized up by a lion. Griffin's words about Dalton being nothing like Jack echoed in her head. He was a real villain.

The dining room was small, with a table set for four and accented with fresh flowers. The walls were painted a soft coral, and a sideboard of rich ebony held heated silver dishes. Their contents smelled delicious. Finley's stomach growled softly.

Dalton held out a chair for her—at his right. He seated himself at the head of the table. He asked her several questions over dinner, which she assumed were to divine her character, though she was surprised by the seemingly genuine interest behind them. She tried to be as honest as possible, because lies were often difficult to remember, but avoided telling him anything too personal or anything that might link her to Griffin—or Jasper.

"I could use a girl like you, Finley," he told her as he cut into a thick beefsteak.

Finley forced her lips into a coy smile. "I know. What did you have in mind?"

There was no mistaking the predatory interest in his eyes. "I'd like for us to work together as *friends*. But first, I need to know you're right for the job. What would you say to a test?"

She chewed and swallowed the bite of potato in her mouth, appearing nonchalant, even though the palms of her hands grew moist. "What sort of test?"

"There's a document I need in a house uptown. I'd like for you to go there with me and help me steal it."

"Are there people in the house?" Her heart began to hammer in her chest. Anxiety or anticipation, she wasn't certain.

"They're having a party," he replied with a grin. "Everyone will be nice and distracted."

She'd never stolen anything before. Hitting people who deserved it was one thing, but stealing... It wasn't as though she could refuse, though, could she? Not if she wanted to gain his trust. She glanced down at her clothes. "I'm not exactly dressed for a party."

"I can fix that. All you have to do is be your lovely, ruthless self if we run into trouble. Are you game or not?"

It was all she could do not to look at Jasper for a sign of how she should respond. Instead, she grinned back, twirling a lock of her hair around her finger. "Always."

The house was huge and ornate, situated near the corner of 58th and 5th, not far from Central Park, in the wealthier section of the city. Lights blazed in the windows, carriages of different colors and sizes were parked out front, and music drifted down to the street, along with the sound of conversation and laughter.

All in all, it seemed everyone was having a bang-up time.

Finley turned from the carriage window to Dalton. "How are we getting in?"

He leaned across her to glance outside. "I reckon we'll saunter right on in through the front door."

She raised a brow. "There's an automaton guarding it." She had taken on metal before, but wouldn't it call attention to them if she ripped the thing apart on the front steps?

"You leave the tin can to me and keep those sharp eyes of yours peeled for any sign of trouble."

A footman from the house opened the carriage door for them. Dalton stepped out and then offered Finley his hand. She had to give him credit for behaving exactly as he ought.

He looked the part of a gentleman, as well, dressed in a stark black suit with white shirt and cravat. He'd found a rich plum silk gown for her that fit remarkably well and had only needed to be let out a bit in the bust. Surprisingly, Dalton had taken care of the alteration himself on the spot.

"My father was a tailor," he explained to her as he had pulled apart a seam. "His clients were San Francisco's elite." That explained his impeccable clothing.

Arm in arm, they climbed the steps to where the automaton stood along with another footman.

"There's a man watching us from across the street," Finley whispered near her companion's ear. "I saw him earlier outside your house." She'd noticed the man because he was dressed like a cowboy, and the only other cowboy she knew was Jasper.

Dalton didn't bother to glance over his shoulder. He only smiled in that caustic manner of his. "That's just Whip Kirby, a lawman who followed me from California. Don't pay him any mind. He has no power here."

Finley nodded, but she would keep a look out for the man later. He might prove useful one day.

Dalton approached the small polished automaton standing at the door. From the inside pocket of his evening jacket, he withdrew a punch card trimmed with paper lace and inserted it into the slot on the machine's front. Then he turned the key to the right of the slot.

A whirling sound came from inside the creature. Cogs and gears came alive as the card was processed. The automaton chugged and clicked for a few seconds, then a bell dinged and a small bulb on top of its "head" lit up.

"Thank you, sir," the footman said, opening the door for them to enter. "Enjoy your evening."

The sharklike smile that was already becoming familiar to Finley slid across Dalton's face. "We intend to."

"How did you do that?" she whispered, once the door had closed behind them.

"I snagged the invitation during a poker game last week. Fella was so drunk he probably thought he lost it."

Finley couldn't help the appreciative smile that took hold of her lips. "I don't suppose you were responsible for his drunkenness?"

"Not at all," he replied so innocently that it was an obvious lie. "The papers I want should be in a study upstairs.

Let's find them before people start to realize no one knows us, shall we?"

She had to hike the skirts of her gown to keep from tripping as they climbed the winding staircase, but she kept up with his quick stride. At the top of the stairs, she tugged on his arm, forcing him to stop.

"They'll notice you don't belong a lot sooner if you don't slow down. You look like a man on a mission rather than a party guest."

Dalton immediately slowed his pace. "You're right." Then he snagged two glasses of champagne from a footman on his way to the ballroom and gave her one.

Because of her experience with wealthy houses, Finley had a fairly good idea where a gentleman's study might be located. There were few enough people outside the ballroom that no one really noticed that they were peeking in rooms, but enough so that they didn't stand out as the only couple.

The second door they opened proved to be the one they were looking for. Dalton shot her a triumphant glance. "Get in."

"You say the sweetest things," she cooed and slipped into the room. He followed and closed the door behind them with a soft click.

There wasn't much light in the room—a lamp on the desk and a sconce on the wall—but it was enough. The room was large, definitely masculine with its oak wainscoting and dark green paper. The desk was huge, and a massive leather chair sat behind it.

"What are we looking for?" Finley asked, voice low.

"Floor plans," he replied, riffling through a stack of papers. "They will be large sheets, either folded or rolled."

She opened the top drawer of the cherrywood desk. "If they're important, wouldn't they be in a safe?"

"They're only important to me." He didn't look up from his search but moved on to the other set of drawers. "To anyone else, they're just pictures of a building."

She wanted to ask what he wanted them for but didn't want to give him reason to be suspicious of her. Instead, she kept pawing through the drawers.

"I like you, Finley," Dalton commented, glancing up. "You don't ask a lot of questions."

So curbing her curiosity had been a good thing. She shrugged. "Part of my charm." Something at the bottom of the drawer caught her eye, and she pulled it out. It was several large, folded sheets of paper with diagrams on each sheet. "Is this it?"

Dalton took them from her and unfolded them. She watched as pleasure softened his face. "They are indeed. Well done."

She was a fool for praise and preened accordingly. Her enjoyment was short-lived, however, when they heard the doorknob turn, and the door started to creep open. They were caught.

The way Finley saw it, they had two choices—stay and pretend to be lovers sneaking off for a bit of privacy as Dalton had joked or make a run for it. Since they had what they came for, their best bet was to try to get out of there with as little fuss as possible.

"Go." She jerked her head toward the opening door. "I'll take care of it."

Dalton stared at her for a split second before whirling toward the door. He pulled it the rest of the way open and brushed past the intruder. "You shouldn't just walk in, son," he said in a haughty tone. "You never know what you might see." Then he disappeared from her sight.

Finley followed after him, but then the intruder turned his head, and his gaze locked with hers. She groaned. He stepped into the room and closed the door behind him. "What the hell are you doing here?"

She forced a smile. "Hullo, Griffin."

He should have stayed in the ballroom—then he never would have known that Finley had snuck into the party with Reno Dalton. Instead, Griffin had fled the crowd to avoid interacting with Miss Lydia Astor-Prynn, a very determined young woman bent on landing herself a duke. The fact that he was only eighteen and had no intention of marrying for many more years seemed to have no effect on her. She'd been a second shadow for most of the evening, and people were starting to whisper.

Other mamas had been throwing their daughters at him, as well. It was like he was a starving dog, and everyone was trying to force-feed him a steak. If he'd stayed there, he would have continued to feel like a piece of meat, but at least he wouldn't be staring at a guilty-looking Finley.

She tucked a strand of black-streaked honey hair, which had fallen loose, behind her ear. "I reckon I'm the last person you expected to see here."

"You've got that right," he replied as he approached her, still frowning. "What are you doing here?"

When she moved around to the front of the desk, he saw that she was wearing an evening gown that fit her almost perfectly and made her skin look as smooth as cream. She looked lovely. Then again, he was beginning to think the girl could wear a sackcloth and he'd still fancy her.

"Committing robbery. It's a test to prove myself to Dalton," she told him. "I didn't know this was the party you were invited to."

Griffin tried not to stare at her bare shoulders—he had seen them before, but with her all dressed up, looking like a debutante, it seemed different. "Robbery? Good Lord, Fin! What if you get caught?"

A lopsided smile curved her lips. "I have been caught—by you."

His scowl returned. "Did Dalton give you the dress?"

She flounced the skirt of the gown. "Yeah. Not bad, eh? He picked it out."

Griffin's eyes closed. Silently, he swore. "What did you steal?" Since Dalton had whipped by him like the house was on fire, he determined that the outlaw must have whatever they had been looking for in his possession.

"Floor plans for the New York Museum of Science and Invention."

He cleared his throat. "What does he want with those?"

"Dunno. As soon as I find out, I'll let you know. I think this will secure me a place within the gang."

She didn't have to sound so bloody pleased about it, though he had to admit he was proud of her. "Have you spoken to Jasper?"

"Not yet, but I will. He hasn't ratted me out, so I'm pretty certain he's not with Dalton of his own choice."

Griffin rubbed the back of his neck. "I don't like this."

Talking her out of this was not an option, not if they were going to help Jasper—or determine if Jasper even needed their help. Her plan was working. Still, Griff wished there was another way. If she was caught, arrested... He didn't know if even he could help her. Worse, there was a slight gleam in her eye that worried him. Was she enjoying this bit of crime and intrigue?

Was her darker side going to prove to be dominant over the light?

"It's getting late," she said, interrupting his thoughts. "I need to get back before Dalton starts to wonder where I am."

He nodded. "How will you leave?"

"Out the front door. I doubt the carriage will still be waiting. I'll have to get a cab."

"A hack?" He didn't mean to sound alarmed. "A hired driver could tell police about the girl he delivered to Reno Dalton's doorstep."

Finley shook her head. "I'll get out a block earlier."

He didn't like not being in control. He didn't like not being able to protect her—never mind that she was more than capable of protecting herself. But instead of ranting about it, he only nodded. "I'll check the corridor."

"Griffin, you can't be seen helping me."

He didn't listen. Instead, he went to the door and opened it just enough to peek out into the corridor. Miss Astor-Prynn was headed in their direction. "Damnation," he muttered. "You'd better hide. We've company coming."

"I have a better idea." Her voice came from directly behind him.

He turned his head. "What's that?"

He barely saw her fist before it connected with his jaw. Pain exploded in his skull, and then everything went black.

Chapter 7

Finley caught Griffin as he fell and lowered him gently to the carpet. "Forgive me," she whispered, but he was out cold.

She leaped to her feet, gathered her skirts and bolted from the room. Her shoulder collided with a pretty but snooty-looking girl who made some snide remark. Finley really didn't care what this bit of fluff thought of her. What concerned her was what Griffin was going to think of her once he woke up.

Actually, at that moment, what concerned her most was getting out of this bloody house before the police were called. Sometimes—most times—she enjoyed a good fight, but she didn't want to call any more attention to herself than she had to. Plus, Griffin would be ridiculed for being knocked out by a girl, so the less people who knew about that the better.

She'd only done it so he wouldn't try to help her and cause trouble for himself. She'd brought a far bit of it down on him in London and had no desire to do the same to him now.

Thankfully, the loud music would mask any noise she made. Still, there were a few guests who stopped to stare as she raced by them, skirts hiked up around her knees.

At the top of the stairs, she leaped into the air, dropped in a flutter of petticoat and silk, and landed in a crouch at the bottom, the jolt reverberating in her shins. Then she sprang up, toward the door. Angry voices rang out behind her. Someone shouted, "Stop her!"

The poor footman tried to oblige, but she pushed him aside. The automaton next to him wasn't programmed for security, so it didn't even move.

Down the steps she ran, into the night. A steam carriage passed by, and she ran for it, hopping easily onto its back and clinging to the bar. She couldn't resist glancing over her shoulder at the small crowd gathered in front of the house, spilling down the steps to the street. A tall man shook his fist at her.

Exhilarated by her escape, Finley blew him a kiss.

She rode the carriage as far as she could down 5th Avenue before hopping off. She bought a meat pie from a vendor on the corner of 42nd and gave the money she would have used for a hack to a beggar-woman who had a child with a tarnished brass prosthetic leg. The woman hugged her, and Finley almost gagged at the smell of her, poor wretch. She made sure the mother bought a pie for herself and the boy before she moved on.

It was a beautiful night, and the walk soothed her heightened senses. She walked the rest of the way to Dalton's house with a spring in her step and a full belly.

She wasn't certain, but for a second, she thought she saw a man on the street ahead of her—one wearing a long coat and a cowboy hat. Whip Kirby again? Whoever he was, he was gone in a blink, and Finley was left wondering if maybe she'd imagined him.

It had been fun sneaking into the party and stealing those papers. Hitting Griffin was a bit of a low point, but at least she'd had the chance to tell him just what Dalton had been after before she did it. She could only hope that his pride could handle the ribbing he might get. Outside of that... Well, she couldn't dwell on it.

If nothing else, Dalton would have to be convinced she was a worthy addition to his gang.

So it was with a smug smile on her face that she strolled into Dalton's parlor, heavy skirts swishing around her legs. Dalton was there, as well as Jasper and Mei. Mei had changed into a simple blouse and skirt, but she still had that strange collar around her throat. Now that she looked at it, it appeared to have cogs and gears in it—as though it were machine instead of jewelry. Maybe it was. For a second, she had the macabre thought that perhaps the collar was the only thing keeping the girl's head attached to her neck.

She'd seen people do some pretty scary things in the name of science, but she was still tempted to poke at the collar, just to see what would happen. She resisted the temptation.

"Miss Finley," Dalton said with an arched brow. "It is good to see you."

She grinned. "Sorry it took me so long. I had to hoof it part of the way."

"You dealt with our visitor?"

"He'll have a sore jaw tomorrow, and bruised pride, but nothing too serious."

"Meanwhile, I escaped with the papers relatively unnoticed." He flashed her an appreciative smile. "I'm much obliged, Miss Finley."

"You're welcome. May I ask what you're going to do with them?"

Dalton was still smiling as he set aside his cup of coffee. "You may, but I'm not inclined to answer just yet."

Her spine stiffened. "I thought I've proved I can be trusted."

Dalton's lips curved in a manner meant to mollify. He could probably charm his way out of dying. "You did a good job, and I'm impressed. I'd like for you to join my gang. Do that, and I might see fit to start trusting you with important information."

She shrugged. She didn't like it, but if she wanted in, she'd have to accept it. "Fine. What's next?"

No one had ever stared at her with quite the same intensity as Dalton. Under those sharp brows of his, icy-blue eyes gazed at her as though trying to look right through her.

"You know, I could always have a photograph taken, then you can stare at that as long as you want," she informed him.

Dalton smiled, then turned his attention away from her and fixed it on Jasper, who was so quiet she'd almost forgotten he was in the room. That wasn't like him. Mei had been silent, as well; the pair of them acted like children who knew to be seen and not heard.

"I want you to accompany my friend Jasper on an errand tomorrow. Make certain he gets the job done and return with him. Be here by eleven o'clock tomorrow morning."

When Finley's gaze locked with Jasper's, she saw all she needed to see. He might have made some bad decisions in his life, same as her, but there was no way he was part of Dalton's scheme by his own free will. Tomorrow, if she did what Dalton asked, she might discover just what the devil was going on.

She shrugged again. "All right. Eleven it is."

Dalton raised his cup. "Bring your belongings. You'll live here from now on out."

It was only for a split second, but she froze—and Dalton saw it. She narrowed her eyes. "What's the rent?"

He took a sip of coffee and set the cup on the table once more. "Relax, darlin'. There's no catch. You're part of my crew now—my family. You live with me."

It would make getting information to Griffin, Emily and

Sam that much more difficult, but she'd have her portable telegraph, and she might be able to sneak out on occasion. Besides, this is what they wanted. This would put her in a position to help Jasper.

Still, it wouldn't do to look too happy about it. "Just so we're clear, I won't abide any improper behavior."

"Improper behavior?" He mimicked her accent in such an awful way she wanted to slap him on behalf of Queen Victoria. "Sweetheart, I won't deny that you're the kind of gal who sparks my tinder, but you're not here for my entertainment. I can get that elsewhere. You just do what I say, and we'll get along fine."

Finley almost sighed. Why was it that all the pretty boys thought so highly of themselves?

She leaned closer, looked him dead in his sparkling eyes and said, "You do know I could snap your neck like a chicken bone."

Across the room, she heard Mei gasp, but she didn't bother to look. No doubt Jasper would shoot daggers at her with his eyes. She might very well just have ruined everything.

Then Dalton reached out and patted her on the shoulder. "That's why you're here."

He was mad as a bloody hatter, but he hadn't tossed her out, so that was something. One thing was for certain—she wasn't going to start snapping at his heels anytime soon.

He lifted his hand. "You've had a busy night. Why don't

you skedaddle? I imagine you have a lot to do before morning."

A dismissal if she ever heard one—and she was thankful for it. "I'll just go change."

He waved a hand at her. "Take the dress with you. Keep it. What am I going to do with the thing?"

What did he think she was going to do with it? It wasn't exactly her style of gown. Still, it would be rude not to take it.

"Thanks." Then because she couldn't think of anything else to say, "I'll see you all in the morning."

She hastened another glance at Jasper, only to find him looking at her with rueful green eyes. She wondered what it was that he looked so apologetic over as she left the room.

Then again, maybe she didn't want to know.

Griffin would have left the Astor-Prynn party immediately after regaining consciousness—which was about two minutes after Finley hit him—had the police not been summoned and he'd not been pressed into talking to them. He had just finished his interview, and his pride smarted from the amused look in the officer's eyes when he'd told him what had happened.

Bloody Finley.

He roused to the sound of a high-pitched voice practically screaming at him. It was Miss Astor-Prynn, and to be fair, she had seemed genuinely concerned for his well-being.

Would have been nice if she could have expressed her concern without sounding like a bloody banshee, though.

The entire side of his face throbbed, especially his jaw. Hit by a girl—that would follow him for the rest of his stay. He was beginning to wish he'd never left England. No one would know that Finley hit with about the same force as a battering ram. No one but him.

He moved his jaw and winced. Did she have to hit him quite so hard? She hadn't needed to knock him out. He pressed his fingers to the back of his head. No pain, no lump. Obviously she'd caught him rather than let him hit the floor. How ruddy wonderful was that? Hit by a girl and then supported by one. She'd once picked him up and carried him after he'd absorbed too much Aether. Next thing, she'd be cutting his food for him or perhaps tying his shoes.

He said his goodbyes to Mr. and Mrs. Astor-Prynn—both of whom had apologized several times already for an incident they believed to be their fault. He assured them he was fine and that he didn't blame them. Then, because he felt badly for them, he agreed to come for dinner one night. Luckily, they hadn't pressed him to set a date.

He kissed Miss Astor-Prynn on the hand and bade her good-night, then went outside and climbed into the carriage they'd loaned him. He could have hailed a cab, but they had insisted. He would have agreed to let Mr. Astor-Prynn piggyback him all the way down 5th Avenue if he'd thought it would get him out of there any faster.

When he returned to the hotel, Griffin found Sam and Emily waiting for him in Sam's room. They were sitting on the bed playing cards. Emily's cat sat on the carpet within arm's reach. Ever since being injured in the fight against The Machinist, Emily kept the metal animal close—her protector. It was more than that, though. With her ability to "talk" to machines, the cat was more than just a thing to her. It was as much a friend as something without a heart could be.

"How was the lecture?" he asked, closing the door behind him.

"Brilliant," Emily replied enthusiastically, looking up from her cards. Her face practically glowed. "Griffin, Tesla is a bloody genius."

"If he's such a genius, why can't he find words that everyone can understand?" Sam growled.

Emily shot him an amused glance. "Someone fell asleep halfway through."

Griffin chuckled, then swore as pain rippled down the left side of his face. Both of them stared at him.

"How was the party?" Emily asked, somewhat hesitantly as she stared at his bruising jaw.

"Boring," he replied as he unbuttoned his coat. "Until Finley showed up, that is."

Emily straightened, cards totally forgotten. "Finley was there? At the party?" A frown tugged at her forehead. "What happened to your face?"

As he tossed his coat over a chair, Griffin sighed. "She

was there with Dalton. Apparently he wanted her with him while he stole a set of building plans. As for my face, Finley happened, that's what."

Sam scowled so hard his eyebrows almost became one solid black line. "She hit you? What the hell for?"

"I assume to keep up appearances, but who knows what goes on in that head of hers."

"Did you start ordering her around?" Emily asked. "Maybe she just wanted to shut you up."

Griffin shot her a droll look. "Maybe."

Sam looked thoughtful. "You know what, Em? You're the only one of us Finley hasn't hit."

The Irish girl stared at him. "I haven't given her reason, now, have I?"

"Can we talk about something other than who Finley has and hasn't punched and why?" Griffin asked—somewhat testily. "Like, what Dalton would want with floor plans to the Museum of Science and Invention?"

"Maybe he wants a tour," Sam suggested. When Griffin glared at him, he went on. "Won't Finley tell us that when she comes back? If she hasn't decided to run away and join Dalton's gang for real, that is."

The pain in Griffin's jaw increased. Perhaps it had something to do with the fact that his teeth were clenched. "That's assuming Dalton trusts her so quickly with that kind of information."

"Do you reckon she's talked to Jasper?" Emily asked, hope

in her wide eyes. "Maybe she's found out what Dalton wants with him."

Sam scowled and began gathering up their cards. "Or maybe she's found out Jasper's a crook, too."

"Maybe," Griffin allowed, ignoring the shocked look Emily shot him. "But I don't think so. If Jasper was a willing party in this, Dalton never would have hired men to bring him here."

"He went willingly enough."

Griffin opened his mouth to debate but hesitated when he saw Emily place her small hand on top of Sam's much larger one. "I know thinking the worst of people makes it hurt less when they disappoint you, lad, but not everything is as it seems."

"She's right," Griffin said. And that was why he'd wait until he'd talked to Finley before getting *too* angry over the fact that she'd hit him.

Shifting uncomfortably, Sam turned his hand so that his fingers wrapped around Emily's. Suddenly, Griffin felt like an intruder.

"Not everyone sees the good in people like you do, Emmy," Sam said.

"She even sees the good in you" came a new voice from the door.

Griffin's heart leaped in response. *Finley.* He glanced at her over his shoulder. She had changed into her own clothes and looked so completely unaffected by the evening that he thought perhaps he had only imagined seeing her at the party. But then he saw the bundle of plum-colored silk beneath her arm.

Emily bounced off the bed and came forward with an excited countenance. "Did you really hit Griffin? How's Jasper? Did you find out what Dalton's up to?"

Finley drew back from the smaller girl's enthusiasm. She shot Sam a look from the corner of her eye. "Did you give her coffee again?" Then to her friend, "Yes, I hit Griffin. I'm sorry, but it was necessary. Dalton hasn't told me much of anything, and Jasper was…quiet."

"Quiet?" Emily's nose wrinkled as her demeanor calmed. "That doesn't sound like him."

"It isn't." Finley turned her attention solely to Griffin. "There's definitely something not right there. I think Dalton's somehow forcing Jasper to work for him."

"What kind of work?" Griffin asked, rubbing his jaw. When he noticed the flush in Finley's cheek, he dropped his hand.

She glanced away with a shrug. "Dunno, but I'm supposed to accompany Jasper somewhere tomorrow, so I'll hopefully have the chance to get some answers from him."

"Or he might get some from you," Sam cautioned. "Dalton might use him to spy on us. You don't know that Jasper didn't tell him who you really are."

"You don't trust anyone, do you?" Finley asked, incredulous.

Sam scratched his jaw. "I trust them." He pointed at Emily and Griffin.

"Did you get a sense that Jasper has betrayed us?" Griffin asked, ignoring the fact that Sam had deliberately left Finley out. The two of them seemed to like picking on one another.

Finley shook her head. "No. He's being used. I'm certain of it. I'm just not sure what the game is. I'm fairly sure Mei's in the middle of it."

"Mei?" Emily's eyes narrowed. "The Chinese girl who was at the fight?"

And Griffin added, "Mei Xing?"

Finley nodded. "Has Jasper ever mentioned her to you?"

"Once." He ran a hand through his hair as he tried to remember the circumstances. "I believe he had a photograph of her in his lodgings in London. I think they had been romantically involved."

"Then it makes sense if Dalton is using her to keep Jasper in line," Finley remarked. She shifted on her feet, her gaze not quite meeting his. "Dalton wants me to move into his house."

It was as though the world stopped—even Emily and Sam went eerily silent. Griffin gave the words a moment to sink in and fought his immediate instinct to forbid her to leave the hotel ever again. If it was Sam in this situation, he wouldn't be the least bit worried. Then again, Sam wasn't really Dalton's type.

"Are you comfortable with that?" he inquired. "Or do we need to come up with another plan?"

Was it his imagination, or did her shoulders actually relax? "I'm fine. Dalton's flirty, but he's more interested in what I can do for him." Her gaze locked with Griffin's. "Honestly."

"But why did you hit Griffin?" Emily demanded, hands on her hips. "Why are the two of you looking at each other like that? What are we going to do about Jasper? We can't let Finley walk into what could be a trap. What?" She turned her head to look at Sam, who had put his big hand on her shoulder.

"You have had too much coffee," he said, taking her by the hand. "Let's go for a bit of a walk. Get rid of some of that energy."

She protested, but it was weak, and Sam managed to drag her from the room without much fuss. The door clicked shut behind them.

Griffin ran his hand through his hair—it must be a mess by now. No doubt it stuck up in all directions, making him look like a hedgehog. "My jaw really hurts, and this plan of yours had better work, because by tomorrow morning, I'm going to be the laughingstock of Manhattan Island."

She winced. "I'm sorry for that, but Dalton has to believe I'm on his side. He took me there to fight anyone who got in our way. He was there when you came in. If I hadn't hit you, he'd be suspicious."

"I know. He would be even more suspicious once he found

out it was the Duke of Greythorne who stumbled upon you. Doesn't make my jaw ache any less."

Finley moved toward him, a sorry expression on her pretty face. She tossed the silk gown on the bed and lifted her hand to his face. He tried not to flinch, but part of him actually expected her to haul off and cosh him again.

She noticed that he pulled away. Her mouth tightened, but she went ahead and placed her palm against his cheek. Her skin was cool; her touch seemed to ease the ache.

"Part of me likes to hit people," she informed him as she looked him dead in the eye. "But not you. I want you to know that. I did what I thought I had to do."

He believed her. "Did you like it?" he asked. "Stealing the plans, I mean?"

This time she withdrew from him. She dropped her hand. The ache in his jaw tripled.

"I did." It came out as a whisper. "I didn't want to, but I did."

Griffin's stomach clenched at her honesty. How was he supposed to feel about her candor? He appreciated that she'd told him the truth, but what did he do with it?

"What did you like about it?"

"The excitement. The danger." Her eyes and cheeks seemed to brighten. "It was like when I was out on the bow of the airship, or like when we went up against The Machinist. I knew there was a chance it could go bad, but it didn't."

"Adrenaline," he told her. "A perfectly normal reaction."

"You think so?"

She looked so hopeful it was hard to breathe. Griffin forced a smile. "Of course. I've felt the same way myself." That was true, but not when committing a crime. Then again, he had never committed a crime, so he didn't know if it was the same or not. It could be that Finley simply liked being...bad.

Her shoulders sagged in relief, and when she put her arms around him, he put his around her, as well.

"Thank you," she murmured as she hugged him. "Thank you for being my friend."

Griffin swallowed hard against the lump in his throat. "I'll always be your friend." He meant it, and that was what made it so difficult. He would do anything for her, but if Finley gave in to the darkness inside her, he would have no choice but to stop her—even if it meant losing her forever.

Chapter 8

Jasper wasn't really surprised to see Finley walk into Dalton's house at five minutes to eleven the next morning. He was, however, surprised to see that she had shabby luggage and dust on her boots. Dirt was easy enough to find around these parts, especially the closer a body got to Five Points, where the grimy automaton street sweepers would be stripped down for their parts, but the Duke of Greythorne was the type of fella to share his wealth with his friends.

So he was left to reason that Griffin—or Finley—was as smart as he assumed and picked up the obviously worn items to protect the ruse that Finley was a girl looking to make a little blunt on the wrong side of the law.

Didn't she look the part, as well, standing there in knee-length gray trousers, heavy-soled boots and a leather corset over a linen shirt.

He was plumb touched at the amount of effort that had already gone into trying to help his sorry hide. Guilty, too. She shouldn't be involved in his mess.

"Can I help you with those, miss?" he asked as he walked toward her. He knew full well she could easily carry both bags, but showing her to her room would give them a chance to talk.

She eyed him warily. Either she was a good actress or she truly didn't trust him any further than she could throw a buffalo. "All right." She handed him the lighter of the two pieces. "I wouldn't want you to hurt yourself," she said sweetly. There was a sparkle in her eye that made it impossible not to grin in response.

He tapped the brim of his hat. "Much obliged. Follow me."

They made it perhaps two or three steps before Dalton arrived. He strutted into the foyer like a banty rooster on a spring morning, all decked out in head-to-toe gunmetal-gray.

"I admire punctuality in a woman," Dalton remarked as he joined them, his pale eyes glinting at Finley. And didn't she look at Dalton as though he was the prettiest thing she ever saw. She wasn't really infatuated with him, was she?

"My papa—" she said it the English way, *pah-pah* "—used to believe that tardiness was a sin. It only takes a few blows from a strap to knock that out of a person."

Dalton inclined his head. "A very efficient man, your father."

"I'll tell him you said so."

It was all Jasper could do not to stare at her in open-mouthed amazement. He knew for a fact that this was a lie—Finley's father had died before she was born—but his mind wanted to accept it as truth from the simple, sincere way she'd delivered it.

"I was just going to show Miss Finley to her room," he told Dalton, hoping the other fellow would leave them alone once more.

"I can do that." Dalton held out his hand to take the luggage from Jasper. "You go tell Little Hank to bring the carriage around. He'll take the two of you to your destination. Shall we, Finley?"

Jasper looked at her, but Finley didn't so much as blink in his direction. She merely smiled at Dalton as though they were the only people in the room. "Lead on, good sir."

He watched them walk away, torn between wanting to protect her from Dalton—or perhaps protect Dalton from her—and wanting to walk out the door and run as far away as he possibly could, like a coward. Instead, he went to the kitchen, where he knew he would find Hank.

"It's time," he told the giant. "Dalton wants you to get the carriage."

Little Hank, who was sitting at the table eating what appeared to be an entire apple pie in the company of a tired-looking kitchen maid, stared at him for a moment before nodding his head. "Fine."

Jasper didn't bother to wait for him but went outside to sit on the steps. He'd gathered other bits of the machine faster than he'd wanted, and there was only one more piece to collect after this one was recovered. He couldn't stall much longer. Dalton had him running other "errands" for him, and each left a sour taste in his mouth. He hadn't had to do anything serious, but standing there while Little Hank beat up a man because he hadn't yet delivered some forged documents was bad enough.

He'd been made to pick out a rifle, as well—a good one that felt right in his hands and had sights so accurate he could have shot a fly from two hundred yards.

Whatever Dalton had planned, he was making certain Jasper played a part in it, so if there was trouble or things went south, he would share the blame—and the hangman's noose.

He hadn't figured out how to get Mei and himself out of this situation without letting Dalton win. There was no way to get the collar off her—the fear in her eyes when she spoke of it was enough for him. He could only imagine how it felt when the thing began to tighten, but short of putting a bullet between Dalton's eyes, what else could Jasper possibly do?

Dalton had wanted the machine badly enough in the first place that he had killed a man when he originally stole it. Whatever it did, Dalton would use it for his own purposes— and those were never good.

He wished he had his guns. He'd feel better with them strapped around his hips. Cleaning them helped to clear and settle his mind. Without them he felt naked—vulnerable. Which was exactly how Dalton wanted him to feel. He wasn't allowed to have the rifle, either. Dalton knew him too well.

Since being exposed to the Organites Griffin's grandfather had found, Jasper doubted anyone could beat him in a gunfight. He was faster than a blink. Dalton was smart to keep him unarmed, because he'd take the outlaw out in a second.

But that chance wasn't worth risking Mei's life. What if Little Hank or another of Dalton's henchmen also knew how to work the collar? If Jasper did anything to Dalton, Mei would be the one to pay for it.

His only choice was to do exactly what Dalton demanded and wait for the right opportunity. It was his own dang fault for getting involved with the gang in the first place. His mother had warned him not to be swayed by the promise of big money for little work, but he'd needed the money, and he would be the first to admit that the dangerous life was also fun and exciting at times. It hadn't taken long, though, to realize how stupid he'd been.

A fella couldn't outrun his past, no matter how fast he was.

The door opened behind him, and he leaped to his feet. He should have known better than to leave his back open like that.

Dalton smiled, as though he knew the direction of Jasper's thoughts. "Jasper, there you are. Don't keep my Finley out too long." He smiled in a way that reminded Jasper of a shark.

Dalton went back into the house, leaving Jasper and Finley alone for a few moments before the carriage arrived.

"What did he tell you to do?" Jasper asked, pretending to watch for the vehicle in case they were being observed.

Finley's eyes narrowed as she glanced up at the sky. "To make sure you found some mechanical item. And to put a 'serious hurt' into you if you try anything dodgy."

He kicked a tiny pebble off the step. "Not surprising."

"What's this thing do?" she asked. "The thing you're supposed to retrieve?"

"Damned if I know, but whatever it is, it's bad or Dalton wouldn't want it. I brought it here to Manhattan and dismantled it, thinking that would keep Mei safe back in San Francisco, but I was wrong. There's only one more piece to get after we collect this one."

"He wanted it bad enough to send men to London after you."

"Their payment is part of the debt he figures I owe him." He took off his hat and ran his hand through his hair. "I should have left the damn thing where it was. He wouldn't have cared less what happened to me."

"He's gone through a lot of trouble for it. Anything that important can't be good. We have to find out what he's up to and stop it before anyone gets hurt."

Jasper rubbed the back of his neck. "If we can."

"He's threatened Mei, hasn't he?" She shot him a sideways glance. "That's how he's making you do this."

There was just enough hope in her voice that Jasper's throat tightened. That was friendship—she and Griffin had no idea if he could be trusted, but they acted as though he was.

He set his hat on his head. "Yeah. That collar she wears, it…it tightens if she tries to leave or does anything to upset Dalton." He met her gaze. "He'll kill her, Miss Finley. He'll do it in a blink. He's done it before."

She didn't say anything, just nodded, but he could tell from her grim expression that she believed him, and like him, she had no idea just how they were going to get out of this situation without anyone getting hurt. Going to the authorities was not an option, not when Mei's life was in Dalton's hands.

The sound of hooves on cobblestones drew their attention, and Jasper watched as a somewhat scuffed and dusty carriage pulled up to the curb, Little Hank at the reins.

"Hasn't Dalton ever heard of steam engines?" Finley asked, eyeing the archaic mode of transport.

"He fancies himself a proper cowboy," Jasper told her as they walked down the steps. "Horses all the way. Only thing a steam engine's good for is robbin'. Plus, Little Hank's afraid of steam, aren't you, big fella?"

The behemoth glared at him, but Jasper saw him cast a glance at his left hand—which was encased in a leather glove. Hank had scars from a steam burn he got during a robbery. It was cruel to tease him about what had been a horribly painful experience, but Jasper figured he owed him a couple of insults after the beating Hank had given him upon his arrival in New York.

He held the carriage door open for Finley. Before he followed her inside, he looked up at Hank. "Mulberry Street. Bandit's Roost."

If nothing else, he had the pleasure of seeing the big man's face pale. Mulberry Street was part of Five Points and one of the worst areas of the slums. Little Hank would have to be far dumber than he looked to not be worried. Even a man his size couldn't survive an attack by an entire gang.

Jasper grinned. "Don't worry, Hank. I'll protect you." Then he ducked inside the carriage and closed the door.

Finley regarded him with an arched brow. "You simply cannot help that tongue of yours, can you?"

He touched the brim of his hat. "No, ma'am. I cannot."

She smiled and glanced out the window as they started to move. Jasper leaned back against the worn cushions and enjoyed being out of the house. He felt calm—calmer than he had in the long months since leaving Dalton's gang. Maybe it was because the smell of horse reminded him of home. Or maybe it was because he knew that he might very well die in this city and never see San Francisco, his family or even London again.

At least he'd die having seen Mei one last time. At least he wouldn't have any regrets there.

Other than getting her into this mess, that was.

"I hear they're going to raze the Five Points neighborhood," Finley remarked, pulling him from his maudlin but strangely serene thoughts.

Jasper nodded. "Apparently they tried to a couple of years ago, but a new gang headed by a gal named Wildcat McGuire stepped up and put the kibosh to that. Some think she bribed or blackmailed the right people. Others say she's a witch."

Finley's lips curved into a skeptical smile. "What do you think?"

"I think she's effective." That was all he cared to reveal on the subject for now. He glanced out the window to see if Whip Kirby was following them. He'd spotted the lawman outside Dalton's house on a couple of evenings, just watching—waiting for the opportunity to grab Jasper and drag him to the nearest noose, no doubt.

He almost wished Kirby would make his move—at least that would put a dent in Dalton's plans.

He and Finley didn't talk much for the remainder of the trip, mostly because there was no way of knowing if Dalton had installed any kind of devices in the interior of the carriage that might allow Little Hank to overhear their conversation. Jasper didn't much mind the silence. He liked Finley, but neither of them needed to waste time jabbering. What they needed to do was think of a way to stop Dalton. They needed the others. If anyone could figure out how to get the collar off Mei without causing injury, it was Emily.

He felt guilty thinking of the pretty little red-haired girl when he ought to be thinking of Mei. It felt like being un-faithful, but that didn't change the fact that Emily was the smartest and most capable girl he knew.

A few minutes later, he was saved from having to justify his own thoughts to himself by the carriage coming to a stop. He peeked out the window. Bandit's Roost.

He opened the carriage door and stepped out, followed by Finley. They were at the mouth of a narrow lane—not much bigger than an alley—which ran between crammed, sagging buildings, most housing more people than they were ever intended to hold. Lines of clothing ran from second and third floors, from one house to the opposite. Worn trousers, stained and grungy shirts, mended socks and the odd pair of yellowed drawers waved in the breeze, but smoke from cooking fires kept all laundry from ever smelling completely clean.

"Wait here," Jasper instructed to Little Hank, who had a look on his face that dared anyone to try and fight him. That arrogance of his—the belief that he was the baddest of the bad—was going to get him killed one day. The giant was too stupid to realize that Finley could snap his neck like a chicken bone, and even she was no match for the whole neighbor-hood.

Which was another reason he felt guilty. He shouldn't have brought her here, but it wasn't as though he had a choice.

He jerked his head toward the lane. "This way."

Finley followed him silently, but he noticed how her amber

gaze took in their surroundings, not missing anything. If there was anyone he'd want at his back going into a situation like this, it was her.

The sun was almost directly overhead as they made their way down the lane, aware of faces watching from windows and from the shadows. The flapping laundry over their heads alternately blocked out the light or let it blind them, depending on the wind.

Doors opened behind them, and Jasper knew without looking that they were being followed. He didn't turn, and he suspected Finley didn't, either, though she was undoubtedly even more aware of their stalkers than he was.

At the end of the lane stood a house that was in only slightly better repair than the others. Someone had tried to whitewash it, but it had turned a dull gray, and the eyelet curtains in the windows were dull and frayed. It was at the door to this house that he stopped—and knocked.

The battered wood swung open on hinges that screeched like an angry hawk—no sneaking into this house—to reveal a tall, muscular young woman, perhaps his age or a little older. She had long black hair, which she wore in two loose ponytails on either side of her handsome face, a leather vest, snug trousers and scuffed leather boots, which came up over her knees. But it was her eyes that commanded a fella's attention—they were the color of lilacs, and while you were gazing into them, you were likely to get a knee in your privates. They were brightened by her dusky complexion.

"Jasper Renn." Her voice was as smoky as the air in these parts. A slight smile curved her mouth as she leaned her shoulder against the door frame. "What brings you round these parts?"

He tugged the brim of his hat at her in greeting—and respect. "You look good, Wildcat. I'm here for that item I gave you a while back."

Those brilliant eyes narrowed. "You remember what I told you before you left here last time?"

He nodded. "I surely do." Did he ever. Their relationship had been intense and unexpected and over before it really had a chance to get started.

Wildcat turned her attention to Finley. "I know you. You're the one that was here with the Irish witch."

"She would prefer to be called a scientist" came Finley's drawled reply. "I'll give her your regards."

The dark girl turned back to Jasper. "She's almost as much a smart-arse as you. She all you brought?"

"I got a driver, but he'd rather see me dead than do me a favor." Then he grinned. "But if you know my friend, you know she's enough."

The girl nodded, grime-streaked face serious. "All right, then. You know what has to be done." And then she stepped across the threshold, a baseball bat in her hands. Its wood was smooth and stained brown with old blood. A dozen other girls and fellas followed after her—some armed, some not.

"Jasper?" Finley asked warily. "What the devil's going on?"

He turned to her with what he hoped was a suitably apologetic expression. "When I left the piece with Wildcat, she told me if I ever came back she'd 'beat the snot out of me.'" Technically, he hadn't left the part with Cat. It had gotten left behind when she kicked him out. He was simply relieved she still had it.

Finley's eyes widened. "Are you telling me we have to fight? All of them?" She gestured at the gang standing in the street behind Wildcat.

Jasper nodded. "That's exactly what I'm saying."

"At least we don't have to take on the entire gang," Jasper offered with a sheepish smile. "Just Cat's best."

Finley was tempted to leave him to fight on his own. "Oh, that makes it so much less insane. There's only thirteen of them. Piece of bloody cake." She reached into her trouser pockets and pulled out the knuckle-guards Emily had made for her out of brass. They were fingerless gloves with caps of brass molded to fit over her knuckles. If all she had were her fists, she was going to have to make every punch count.

Jasper flushed, but his gaze never wavered. "You don't have to do this."

Of course, that immediately softened her, because she knew that he meant it. He was fully prepared to do this on his own—and probably die doing it. At the very least he'd end up severely injured.

She bent her neck to the side and was rewarded with a

sharp crack. Then did the same to the other side. Jasper grimaced but made no comment. Wise boy. "Let's get this done."

"You sure you want to do this, San Fran?" Wildcat asked, coming down the steps.

"I have to, New York." Jasper pushed his hat down farther on his head—Finley wondered if she would be "London" when all this was over. "Otherwise I wouldn't be here."

The girl shrugged. "That's the worst apology I've ever heard. Break a girl's heart and can't even say you're sorry? What sort of man are you?"

As much as she dreaded meeting the bat held in Wildcat's hands, Finley had to admit it was difficult not to like the girl. She had an easy yet dangerous air to her that felt oddly comforting, perhaps because, Finley suspected, they were very similar.

"He's sorry," Finley piped up. "He's so very, very sorry. Can I have a bat, too?"

Wildcat smiled and tossed hers aside. It hit the dirt with a solid *thwonk,* which Finley felt in her teeth. Getting hit with such a weapon would not tickle.

"How's that?" the girl asked.

Finley shrugged, noticing that Wildcat had wicked-looking metal claws on one hand that were more than a match for her brass knuckles. "Fair enough."

The fight began almost immediately, without any dancing about. Finley took on Wildcat and anyone else she could between blows. Jasper was able to use his speed and agility against the others, who—fortunately for him—were simply "normal" humans. Wildcat, on the other hand, was decidedly more than normal. She was fast, vicious and had those blasted claws—no doubt these factors contributed to her apt nickname.

Blood ran down Finley's cheek from a particularly nasty swipe. It stung and burned, but she ignored it as best she could, consoling herself with the fact that her opponent was also bloody.

Strike. Dodge. Reel. Swipe. Kick. Stagger. It was almost like a bizarre dance they had going on between the two of them, and neither was about to surrender. But they both knew neither of them was going to win anytime soon. And Jasper swayed on his feet. Even though he could still move faster than his opponents, he simply had too many to avoid.

Finley grabbed Wildcat by the throat and shoved her up against the side of the house—a nearby window shuddered. Wildcat's own hand came up and seized Finley's neck. They faced each other with opposite hands poised to strike.

"This been enough of a fight for you?" Wildcat asked, a touch of Irish in her voice, which Finley hadn't noticed before.

Finley didn't lower her hand. "It was your idea."

The other girl smiled, and Finley thought she caught a glimpse of fang. "I made a promise, and I had to keep it. Point of pride, you know. Tell you the truth, I'd rather just give him the thing and send you both on your way."

Since Finley wanted that also, she lowered her striking hand. Wildcat lowered hers, as well, and once that was done, they released one another.

Finley turned to find Jasper on the ground, face bloody but not too badly battered. Half a dozen of Wildcat's followers were also down, and the rest all wore signs of battle as they panted from exertion. At least Jasper had managed to tire them out.

Before Finley could help him up, Wildcat offered him her hand and easily drew him to his feet.

"Come inside, cowboy. Clean yourself up." She cast a glance at Finley. "You, too."

Shrugging, Finley followed Jasper inside.

The interior of the house was as surprising as Wildcat herself. It wasn't much, but it was neat and clean. It was obvious that someone had put effort into making the place feel like a home. The furniture was worn but comfortable, serviceable. Photographs and paintings hung on the walls in chipped frames, and frayed rugs covered the bare-board floors. The air smelled of wood smoke and cinnamon—a strangely pleasant scent.

Jasper seated himself at the table, so Finley did, as well. One of the girls brought them a bowl of water and cloths to clean their faces while Wildcat disappeared from the room. When she returned, Finley had just wiped the last of the blood from Jasper's face.

"Keep on with this kind of behavior, and you won't be so pretty anymore," she warned him with a teasing grin.

One side of his mouth quirked—the other side was cut and stayed still. "I've heard ladies like rugged men."

"Ladies like intelligent men," Wildcat interjected, setting a small dusty crate on the table in front of him. "Something which you are not, San Francisco. Here's what you came for."

Jasper stared at the box. He didn't attempt to open it to check the contents, so it was obvious that either he trusted Wildcat or knew better than to challenge her integrity.

"Thank you," he said.

The girl shook her head. "No thanks necessary. Just make sure whatever that thing is, it never finds its way back into my neighborhood again. Same goes for you. Am I understood?"

"Perfectly."

Finley noticed that he hadn't agreed to her terms, but then again, the chances of the crate coming back here were slim. Dalton struck her as an ambitious bloke—he would set his sights on something bigger and more…well, just more…than this part of the world.

Now that they had the piece, there was no need to hang about—not that they had been invited. They needed to get back to Dalton, give him the thing. Finley wondered how Little Hank had fared while waiting for them. Would it have hurt the lummox to help them out in the fight? So what if Jasper had told him to stay put? Then again, he probably still wouldn't have come to their aid—he didn't like either one of them, and the feeling was mutual.

Jasper took the crate, said his farewells to Wildcat, who gave him a hard smile, and walked out the door. Finley followed close behind, but before she could step outside, Wildcat grabbed her by the arm. Finley immediately tensed, expecting the girl to continue their earlier match. Instead, Wildcat stepped close to whisper in her ear.

"It's her, isn't it? The reason why he wanted the crate? It's got to do with Mei Xing?"

There was that unfortunate name again. Finley nodded, her gaze sliding to meet serious lavender eyes. "You know her?"

"Jas told me about her when we met. He loved her."

Finley's eyes narrowed. "You make that sound like it's a bad thing."

Wildcat's top lip curled ever so slightly into a sneer. "Ever have a feeling that someone's bad news—even though you've never met them?"

Opening her mouth to call the other girl mad, Finley hesitated. Now was not the time to be a smart-arse or glib. Besides, she felt that way about Lydia Astor-Prynn, the girl whom she had learned over breakfast was hoping to snag Griffin. "Yes."

"That's how I feel about Mei, and it wasn't just jealousy. Trouble seems to follow that girl, whether she invites it or not. I know you're a friend to Jas, so I'm asking you as another of his friends, make sure she doesn't hurt him again."

"I would think you'd like to see him get hurt, after what he did." She really had no idea just what Jasper had done to this beautiful girl, but he had to have broken her heart for her to be so eager to kick his arse.

Sadness darkened Wildcat's gaze. "Just because he hurt me doesn't mean I want to see someone else hurt him."

Finley nodded. Now she understood. Wildcat still had feelings for Jasper, and here he was doing all he could to save Mei. No wonder Wildcat wanted to beat the "snot" out of him. Finley was tempted to take a few swings at him on her behalf. *Bad form, cowboy.*

"I'll keep my eye on her," she promised. Other than that, there was nothing else she could do. Mei might be pretty and the reason Jasper was in this mess, but that didn't mean she was evil.

Wildcat released her arm and offered her hand, which Finley accepted. The girl had hands like hers—hands that worked and fought, hands that Lydia Astor-Prynn would probably cringe at. She pushed the thought aside. Now was simply not a good time to compare herself to another girl.

"Take care. And if he gets into trouble, come get me."

Loyalty, Finley suspected, was not something this girl gave easily. "I will," she replied, and then took her leave.

On the way back to the carriage people stood aside, lining the street as they passed. They didn't speak or make any sound. They simply watched—a fact that unnerved Finley. It was awfully creepy to be stared at—like they were a funeral procession. But maybe they knew something Finley and Jasper didn't.

Like perhaps this mess they had gotten into—with strange machines, exotic girls and dangerous criminals—might actually be too much for either of them to escape.

Chapter 9

Griffin considered himself a believer in science and rationality. Everything that happened in the world—no matter how fantastic—he believed could be explained by science. Even ghosts had their place in the scientific realm—the Aether was the one place he believed the spiritual and the mathematical met.

But even he wanted to puncture his own eardrums after an hour of listening to Emily and Nikola Tesla chatter excitedly about each other's theories and gigantic, big brains. They kept talking about theories and things he couldn't quite wrap his own mind around—things that didn't pertain to his areas of interest. In short, he was bored.

When they first arrived at the Gerlach Hotel on 27th Street, where the inventor lived and conducted experiments, Tesla had greeted Griffin enthusiastically—full of questions about Ganite, the ore his grandfather discovered. Griffin was impressed he knew the name of it, since most people tended to refer to it as "Greythorne Ore."

What the older man was particularly interested in was the power cells derived from the ore. He wanted to know what made the ones manufactured by King Industries that much more effective than those made by a California company, which had also discovered a pocket of Ganite.

Griffin merely smiled and said that it had to do with quality and craftsmanship, purposefully neglecting to mention his family's secret process for purifying the ore before it was used to make the King Cells. Who knew what sort of invention Tesla would come up with if he knew how to purify the ore himself. The man seemed a little too interested in weapons— and a tad paranoid—for Griffin's taste.

The discussion eventually turned to alternating versus direct current, a topic that Tesla was very passionate about. He had no problem giving his opinions on Edison's work on the topic, either. At least the awkward Serbian gentleman didn't seem to make a habit of electrocuting animals as Edison did. Afterward, the inventor's attention moved to Emily and her obvious interest in his work.

Tesla was amazed at Emily's pocket telegraph machines and showed a keen interest in her work in the field of what she termed "telautomatics"—the use of radio waves to control mechanical devices, such as automatons or even torpedoes. Tesla believed such a method would be of great use to the military. All Griffin could think of was how much damage a man such as Leonardo Garibaldi—The Machinist—could have wrought with such technology. The man had done enough damage as it was and had almost succeeded in taking over the entire British Empire.

When they began discussing the theoretical uses of "cosmic radiation" and the mathematical computations necessary to derive the resonant frequency of Earth itself, Griffin lost whatever tenuous hold he once had on the conversation.

"That's how I felt the other night," Sam remarked quietly from the chair next to him, a bored expression on his face. "At least you could follow some of it. I don't understand a single bloody word. It'll be more fun when he gets out some of his inventions."

All Griffin could do was smile wearily in response. It wasn't that he wasn't impressed by Mr. Tesla—who in his right mind wouldn't be? It was just that he was worried about Jasper and Finley and what every moment they spent in Dalton's company might do to them. He already had Finley committing crimes against the upper classes. What was next? The two halves of her nature might have begun to come together, but she was still vulnerable to her darker half. What if she liked being part of Dalton's gang?

What if she decided her life was going to be one of crime, rather than with Griffin?

Instead of helping his friends—a matter which appeared to be out of his hands—Griffin was forced to act the aristocrat and visit scientists who could benefit from his patronage. Granted, he had another motive for visiting Tesla: there was a slim chance Dalton might need the help of a genius with his machine—or that Tesla might at least hear of such requests if they were made. It was all Griffin could think to do.

He felt like a helpless idiot. It was not a feeling he bore well.

Griffin rose to his feet and began to snoop about a bit. He listened without paying much attention as Emily and the Serbian discussed the beneficial properties of having Aethertowers placed at regular intervals around the globe to make transmissions without the use of wires and cables easier. It would mean that the pocket telegraph machines would work at much farther distances than they did now. He should really pay attention, but he couldn't quite bring himself to do it.

Sam appeared at his side. "That's nice, leaving me on my own to suffer," he hissed in Griffin's ear.

Griff smiled as his gaze skimmed over a series of mechanical inventions spread out on a bench. Tesla's intelligence was astonishing. Most of these inventions were new, or a reconstruction of items lost in a fire of his 5th Avenue laboratory in '95. How painful it must have been to lose all that research and work. That was why he had Emily lock all of her plans and diagrams in a fireproof cabinet in her laboratory beneath his London mansion. All of her prototypes were kept there, as well. Not only did it keep everything safe from fire, but also from thieves, though they had plenty of security in place for those occasions, too.

As his gaze fell upon a strange device that looked something like a candelabra with connected glass coils instead of candles, Griffin frowned. One of the coils ran into a rudimentary automaton hand that held a pencil in thin brass fingers, its lead poised above sheaves of paper.

Out of the corner of his eye, Griffin saw Sam flex his own hand—the one that had metal inside of bone. Would his friend ever accept the fact that he was part machine?

It wasn't a question he wanted to ponder, so Griffin turned his attention back to the mechanism, which seemed to call out to him. Slowly, he reached out his hand.

His fingers touched cool metal, and then he felt it—the Aether. Heat flowed gently through his hand, tingling in his veins as the energy assaulted him. The glass tubes on the device began to glow—where the fluorescence came from he had no idea. A soft scratching noise, almost like whispering, came from the machine, growing louder. The mechanical hand had begun to move, the pencil lead marking the paper.

It was writing.

Suddenly, Tesla and Emily were there at his other side. "How did you do that?" the tall, slender man asked in his accented English.

Griffin glanced at him but didn't remove his hand. "I touched it. It's an Aetheric transference device, isn't it?"

Dark brows furrowed as Tesla nodded. "It has only worked sporadically until now and never like *this*." He gestured toward the hand that was busily scribbling all over the paper. "This is astounding."

Smiling, Griffin gave a small shrug. "The Aether and I have always had a strange affinity for one another." He removed his hand from the machine, and it stopped immediately. Before he could remove the paper to see what was written there, an odd clunking noise rose from behind him.

They all turned. There, in the far corner of the room, on a pedestal table, sat a small device that had begun to hum and whir, the frequency of both sounds steadily increasing.

"Griffin?" Emily shot him a glance out of the corner of her eye. "Are you doing this?"

He shook his head. "No." But when he allowed himself to "slip" into the Aetheric plane, he could see energy crawling all over the device. It made sense—the Aether was power, just like electrical current, and could be channeled as such. Still, he didn't know where this burst had come from, because the flow was not emanating from himself. So what...?

He whipped his head around as something flashed in his peripheral vision. What was that? A shadow? Whatever it was, it was gone now. Maybe he had imagined it.

"Mr. Tesla, what is that thing?" It was Sam who had the presence of mind to ask. Sam, who had a distrust of all things mechanical.

The inventor looked confounded. "It is part of my Directed Energy Amplification mechanism."

Griffin watched as Emily's face became even paler beneath her freckles. "Which part?" she asked.

Tesla turned to her, his worried expression mirroring hers. "The part that amplifies and emits the energy flow."

A fellow didn't have to be a genius to figure that one out. Griffin ran a hand through his hair. "Basically, a weapon that could obliterate us all, then?"

The older man nodded. Fascination mixed with the concern in his eyes. "Perhaps the entire building. The entire city block, if it overloads, that is. And it sounds like it is about to do just that."

"We'd better shut it down, then, eh?" Griffin forced himself to be calm as he turned to Emily and Tesla. "How do we do that?"

He look absolutely flabbergasted—not the sort of expression Griffin found overly comforting. "It should not even work. It is not connected to its Aether engine. I have no idea why it is working."

Griffin began to see why this was such a strange and terrible thing. Somehow something had given power to an otherwise inoperable machine—one that could kill them all—and its maker had no idea how to turn it off.

Had he done this? Had his toying with the transference device somehow caused a spike in the Aether? He'd never had anything like that happen before—it couldn't have happened now. When he peered beyond the physical world into the Aetheric, he couldn't see any connection between himself and the machine. This was not his doing. But if not his, whose?

Now was not the time to stand around thinking. He had to act. The thing was practically whining now, it was operating at such a high frequency. It wasn't going to hold together for much longer. It could detonate at any moment and reduce the four of them—and possibly the entire building, perhaps the entire block—to ash.

"Can I crush it?" Sam asked.

"Don't you touch it!" Emily exclaimed, cheeks red. "It will kill you, you great oaf."

Sam scowled, but didn't do anything. They all knew Emily only called him "oaf" when she was worried about him. "It's going to kill us, anyway." Then he surprised both his friends by asking, "Can you tell it to stop?"

Cautiously, Emily reached out her fingers toward the vibrating device, obviously trusting her affinity for machines to keep her safe. The moment she made contact her ginger eyebrows snapped together. "I can't understand it. It's like it's screaming, and I can't make out the words. Ow!" She jerked her hand away, her face a mix of astonishment and hurt. "It shocked me!"

"I'll stop it," Griffin informed them—sounding much more confident than he felt. Obviously this was a lesson in being careful what he wished for, because he had wanted to feel useful, and now if he couldn't be useful enough, people would die. He would die.

He looked at Sam, who watched him with a grim expression, and then moved toward the machine. The Aetheric energy that swarmed around it wasn't right. Normally, the Aether was filled with the brightness of organic auras or soft and gray with ghosts, but this energy was dark and sooty. It looked like a smear of something viscose—dirty automaton grease on a clean white glove.

And it seemed to be watching him, but that wasn't possible. Unless...unless it was a ghost, but there was no form to it. Just a feeling of darkness.

He didn't know what touching it, letting it into him, might do, but he had no choice.

It slithered toward him as he held out his hand, black tendrils curling around his fingers. It felt almost slippery, like the tentacles of an octopus. And sharp. His fingers began to bleed where it touched him. What the hell?

"Griffin?" It was Emily who called out. She'd seen the blood, no doubt. To her, it would look as though his hand had suddenly begun to bleed for no reason. He gritted his teeth and extended his hand even farther, until he touched the device, which was now shaking so violently, it was certain to explode at any second.

The moment his fingers touched the hot metal—so hot— the machine began to quiet. Griffin clenched his jaw even tighter against the double onslaught of pain and placed as much of his hand as he could over the shivering heat. Tendrils wrapped farther up his arm, cutting into his exposed forearm. Blood dripped to the carpet as what felt like a dozen razors slashed at his flesh, and his palm burned.

Once most of the dark energy had gathered around him, he drew a deep breath, pushed past the pain and focused all of his will at the curling black. He drew it toward him, into him.

He was not prepared for the assault. He thought it would put up a fight, that it would take a great force of his power to overcome it.

He was wrong.

The swirling black tendrils drew back. For a second, they seemed to come together, arching upward to form a mist-shaped cobra that undulated before him.

The blackness struck before he could think to defend himself.

It was like shards of glass exploding in his chest. Pain screamed through his body, slamming him to his knees, bringing the taste of blood to his mouth. He opened his mouth to scream, but nothing came out. It felt as though his vocal chords had been cut in half.

And then there was nothing. The vice of agony that gripped him let go as suddenly as it had attacked, sending him sprawling face-first onto the floor, gasping for breath. It hurt to breathe. It hurt to think.

He heard someone call his name from a great distance.

He tried but couldn't answer. His eyes rolled back into their sockets as darkness swamped his mind. He was either going to pass out or die—either was preferable to the pain. He coughed, tasted blood in his mouth.

Finley's face swam in his mind. If he could hold on to the thought of her, he just might live. She just might keep death away.

And then she was yanked away, and there was nothing.

Finley was in a bad mood.

The fight in Bandit's Roost had been just the start of her current glower. She didn't like being injured, and she liked it even less when she didn't have any of Emily's beasties to help heal. It didn't matter that she would heal faster than a "normal" person; she wanted to be healed *now*.

The insult added to that injury had occurred once they'd returned to Dalton's abode. Her Personal Telegraph had gotten broken in the fight, so she couldn't contact Emily, and then Dalton had absconded with the mechanical piece Jasper had given him, without a comment to either about their well-being.

She was beginning to think that for all the criminal's charm and good looks, he was a top-class arse.

Then Mei appeared and fussed over Jasper like a mother hen, glaring at Finley, as though it was her fault Jasper had gotten hurt and not the other way around. It was obvious the girl didn't like her, was jealous of her. Well, if Mei would like to take her place the next time there was a fight, she was more than welcome to it. The girl was a proper cow.

Yes, it was so tempting just to reach out and give that collar a tap.

Instead, she went to the kitchen and helped herself to some bread and roast chicken. Fighting always made her hungry, and food seemed to help her natural healing process.

Never mind that she needed something to do so she wouldn't actually backhand Mei. She shouldn't let it get to her when other girls treated her like dog excrement on their shoes, but she had to admit—and only to herself—that it hurt almost as much as it pissed her off.

She ate her food while sitting on the sideboard and washed it down with iced tea. It didn't taste as bad as she'd thought it would. In fact, it was pretty good, despite being just plain *wrong*. Everyone knew tea was meant to be served hot.

Afterward, she was on her way to her room—a black cloud lingering over her head—when she heard a knock at the door. One of Dalton's men answered it. A girl spoke—asking for her. She recognized the voice as Emily's. What was she doing there?

Finley turned toward the door. Dalton's henchman blocked her view, but she heard him clear enough. "Get lost, pikey."

Finley stiffened at the derogatory term. No one called her Emily such an awful name. She walked up behind the man, grabbed him by the arm and slammed him face-first into the wall, twisting in a manner that popped his shoulder out of joint. He screamed and dropped to the ground.

She crouched over him. "I'll put it back in when you apologize," she told him in a low voice.

He swore at her, but she merely smiled. "Uh-uh. That sort of attitude just makes me want to hurt you more."

"Finley."

Her head jerked up, and she saw the fear in Emily's eyes. This was real fear—not disgust at Finley's behavior but real terror. Something had happened. Something had happened to Griffin.

It was as though someone took a rag and wiped away all her anger—all her emotions. She was numb as she snapped the bounder's shoulder into place. She stepped over his prone body and joined her friend.

"Is he dead?" she asked, her voice surprisingly strong.

Emily shook her head as her wide eyes filled with tears. "I don't know. He was alive when I left to get you."

She swallowed against the lump in her throat. Griffin could not be dead. He had survived a knife wound when they fought The Machinist and rallied. He would simply have to survive this, as well.

"Take me to him." She didn't care if leaving meant Jasper would be on his own. She didn't care if her absence destroyed whatever fragile trust Dalton held for her. Dalton could go to hell.

The door slammed behind her as she walked out into the

bright afternoon sunlight. She barely felt the heat. At the bottom of the steps sat Emily's big metal cat. There were bars sticking out of the side of its head. Emily straddled its back and gripped the bars.

"Get on," she said.

Finley didn't ask any questions—she knew better. And to be honest, she really didn't care. She sat on the cat's back and wrapped her arms around her friend's waist. A moment later they were tearing through the streets, northbound toward the Waldorf-Astoria. The cat ran so fast the wind stung Finley's eyes, or that's what she told herself, because she was *not* crying.

At the hotel, she took the stairs rather than the lift because she could take them two at a time and a lot faster than most people. She reached Griffin's room a full two minutes before Emily did. She opened the door to find him on the bed. Sam sat in a chair beside him.

Finley barely glanced at Sam, who stood up as soon as she came in. Her gaze was for Griffin alone as she approached the bed.

His face was cut in several places, and there was dried blood at the corners of his mouth. His hands, resting on the blankets, had been bandaged, and there was a large square of bloodstained linen over his bare chest.

"What happened?" she rasped, her throat so tight it hurt to breathe.

To her surprise, Sam put one of his big hands on her shoulder and gently squeezed. "We don't know. There was a machine at Tesla's that malfunctioned. Something to do with the Aether. Griff shut it down, and this is the result."

Finley looked up and noticed the slim older man with dark hair and moustache sitting in a chair in the corner. He had to be Mr. Tesla—no one else could possibly look so guilty.

She wanted to blame him for this. Wanted to pound his fine-boned face until it split beneath her fists, but she didn't. She hadn't been there, where she should have been, to help Griffin. She'd been off scrapping in a dirty lane with Jasper to help a girl who didn't even like her.

She hadn't been where she belonged. Look what happened to him when she wasn't there. Something always happened to him when she wasn't around.

"The device shouldn't have worked," Tesla informed her. His accent was strange to her ears. "I do not know how this happened."

The genuine regret in his accented voice diminished much of the turmoil inside Finley's chest. He wasn't to blame any more than she was or Emily and Sam. Griffin was like a white knight, rushing in to save the day with little thought for his own safety—the gorgeous idiot.

"I treated his wounds." This came from Emily, who now stood with Sam. He had his arm around her shoulders. For the first time, Finley noticed the blood on her sleeves and vest. Griffin's blood. "The Organites will do their job. All we can do is wait."

Wait and see if the Organites worked fast enough, she meant. If they would heal him before he died.

"Would the three of you give me a moment with him?" Finley asked, glancing around the room.

No one said a word; they simply filed out the door and closed it behind them.

Finley didn't bother to sit on the chair Sam had used. She sat on the edge of the bed instead, careful not to disturb Griffin for fear of hurting him.

She couldn't even take his hand, so she wrapped her fingers around his naked biceps—where his arm wasn't cut. His flesh was cool beneath hers and hard with muscle.

"Why is it I only get to see you with your shirt off when you're hurt?" she asked in a desperate attempt at humor. A sob caught in her throat. "Don't you dare die. You have to live so I can curse you up and down for scaring me like this."

He didn't respond. She reached up and smoothed his hair back from his face. A tiny cut on his forehead was already healing thanks to the Organites and their magic. To think just a short while ago she was angry because she had to suffer through her natural healing, and now here was Griffin, fighting just to survive.

"Don't leave me," she whispered, blinking furiously against the tears that dripped down her face to plop onto his skin. And then, because she didn't know if she'd ever get another opportunity, she leaned forward and pressed her lips to his.

She kissed his forehead, as well, before finally raising her hands to her eyes to wipe away the wetness there.

"Finley?" His voice was weak, but there was no mistaking it.

"Griffin?" Joy skipped in her chest. "You're awake."

His forehead wrinkled, and his eyelashes fluttered. "Are you crying? My face is wet."

"Of course not," she lied. "Sam was here before me. It must have been him." Gently, she used her thumb to brush the drops from his cheeks.

One corner of his mouth lifted slightly. "Liar." Then his eyes opened a fraction. When the stormy blue of his gaze locked with her own, it was as though her heart fell over.

"You are crying," he whispered. "You didn't think I'd actually die and leave you without anyone to boss you around?"

A huff of laughter escaped her like a hiccup, her throat was so tight. "That wouldn't do, would it?"

His smile faded. "I think I need to sleep for a bit."

"You do that," she replied, but he was already gone. Frantically, she placed her fingers to his neck, searching for a pulse. She didn't breathe until she found it—weak but steady. He was still alive.

Finley dropped her head, squeezed her eyes shut and began to silently do what some might call praying. She called it begging.

★ ★ ★

It was dark when Griffin opened his eyes. It had to be late at night, because there was hardly a sound from the streets outside. He didn't know how he'd gotten back to the hotel, but he assumed that Sam and Emily had brought him after he passed out.

His head ached, and it felt like needles piercing his chest when he drew a deep breath, but other than that, he felt whole and healthy. Not bad, considering he'd been certain Death had finally come to collect him a few hours earlier.

He shifted between the sheets, tugging them up over his chest. It wasn't until his efforts met with resistance that he realized there was someone else on the bed with him. He only had to draw breath—not so painful this time—to know that it was Finley. She smelled like freshly baked cookies.

He turned toward her as his eyes adjusted to the moonlight. She lay on top of the quilt, her boots still on. There was a bloodstain on her white shirt. Hers? Or someone else's? And her hair had slipped from its usual perch on the back of her head and now lay over her shoulder.

When they first arrived in New York, he had made a comment about where else she could sleep. She should have slapped him for being such an arse, but she hadn't. And now here she was, asleep beside him.

He reached out to touch her, but his hand was bandaged. He remembered burning it on the machine and how the black tendrils had cut into his skin. What was that thing? What was it doing in the Aether? These questions ran unanswered through his mind as he slowly peeled the gauze away. His hand was tender, but already, it was well on its way to healed. By morning, he would be back to normal. If not for the Organites, which his grandfather had discovered years ago along with the Ganite, he'd most likely be dead.

He touched the tips of his fingers to Finley's face. Her cheek was soft and warm. Her thick eyelashes fluttered and opened, and when her gaze settled on him, she smiled.

"You're still alive," she whispered. The relief and joy in her voice made his battered chest tight. She had been afraid for him.

"So it seems," he replied. "How long have you been here?"

Finley glanced away. Her sudden shyness seemed strange and out of character. "Since this afternoon."

"You stayed here the whole time?" He was touched but surprised. "What about Dalton and Jasper?"

"They'll wait. Neither one of them is going anywhere."

"But Jasper—"

"Isn't as high on my priority list as you are" came her sharp reply. "You let me worry about the Americans, all right?"

Griffin blinked. "You're angry."

Her gaze locked with his. In the moonlight, her eyes were eerily bright—almost like a cat's. "You're bloody right I'm angry. You could have been killed today. You read my head about how I go running off and all that rubbish, but you always have to be the big hero."

She was *really* angry. "I had to do something. If the machine had blown up, it would have killed all of us—and a lot of other people, too."

"I know Sam offered to smash it."

"Emily wouldn't let him," he argued.

"You wouldn't have let him do it, either, even though he would have been the best choice. You just had to be the one to save the day. What is wrong with you?"

Now he was getting angry. "Forgive me for wanting to prevent people from dying."

"That's not it, and you know it. Of course you wouldn't want people to die—none of us would—but why do you always have to risk your life for other people? You daft git."

"You're a fine one to talk, Miss 'I'll risk getting beaten to death to infiltrate a gang.'"

She glared at him. "You said it was a good plan."

Griffin glared back. "Sometimes good plans are also stupid plans."

"You're stupid."

"Not as stupid as you."

Silence fell between them as they stared each other down. Griffin wasn't certain which of them broke first, and it didn't matter. It was only a matter of seconds before they were both laughing at their childishness. Every chuckle was like a kick to the chest, but he couldn't seem to stop. Finally they both quieted.

Finley wiped at her eyes. "We're a bloody fine pair, aren't we?"

"We are." And he meant it—more than he would ever admit. "I'm sorry I scared you."

She opened her mouth and hesitated. For a moment, he thought she might deny it. "You should be. I'm sorry for being such a cow about it."

He grinned. "You should be."

A brief smiled curved her lips but faded when she took his hand—the unbandaged one—in her own. "Promise me you'll be careful from now on. We can't lose you."

Griffin noticed that she said *we* rather than *I*. There was something in her expression that made him ask, "What aren't you telling me?"

She shook her head, but he pressed forward. "Finley, tell me."

"Emily made me promise not to tell you until she was certain you were better."

"I am better, and Emily's not here. Tell me."

Finley glanced down at his chest, which Griffin then remembered was naked. Embarrassed, he pulled the blankets up. She raised her gaze, and though it was too dark to tell, he was certain she was blushing.

"Emily showed me the paper from the ghost machine."

The ghost machine? "The Aetheric transference device? You mean the writing actually made sense? I assumed it was nothing more than scribbles."

She laughed—but it was humorless. "No, it wrote coherently, if not cryptically."

"So tell me. What did it write?"

Her gaze locked with his, and she gripped his fingers tightly with her own. "It said, 'I'm coming for you, Griffin King.'"

Chapter 10

Finley didn't want to leave Griffin the following morning, especially not after Emily showed her what the ghost machine had written. There could be no doubt that it was a threat against Griffin. Except he was the only one of them who knew anything about the Aether, and all he could tell them was that the energy flowing around Tesla's device had been dark and that it had somehow managed to injure him. He had no idea what it meant, or how such a thing had come about. One thing was for certain—nothing like this had ever happened to him before.

How was she supposed to fight something she couldn't see or even touch?

More to the point, how was she to help him when she had to return to play Dalton's lackey?

She was in a fine and terrible mood when she walked into

the foyer of Dalton's house wearing the same garments she had been in when she left. The heels of her boots clicked on the polished floor as she stomped toward the stairs. She needed a bath and a change of clothes and something to hit.

"Where the sweet hell have you been?" Dalton's voice echoed in the open hall.

Finley's fingers clenched into tight fists, her nails dug into her palms. The pain kept her in control, because Dalton's face looked like a perfect target. "None of your business," she replied.

"It is too my business," he replied with a scowl as he strode toward her, looking sinisterly handsome in his dark gray suit. "You work for me."

"Not that I've seen one cent," she retorted—as though money mattered. "And I might work for you, but you don't own me."

His eyes narrowed. "Your loyalty is to me."

Finley scoffed. She wasn't certain if she was looking for a fight or to get herself kicked to the curb. "I'm just hired muscle to you, so don't preach to me about trust and loyalty, Dalton."

He shook his head, dark hair waving about his face, and folded his arms across his chest. "Ain't you full of gumption this morning? Someday you're going to talk back to someone who doesn't find it half as charming as I do, Miss Finley. Then you're going to be in trouble."

He was right, and she despised him for it. She could take

care of herself and most threats that came her way, but some-day her temper was going to get her into a situation she couldn't simply smash her way out of.

"I don't have many friends," she admitted, "but one of the few I do needed my help, and I went. I'm sorry I didn't tell you, but it was an emergency, and to be honest, you were the last thing on my mind."

It wasn't difficult to meet his gaze because what she told him was the truth. He watched her for a moment. Blokes had looked at her in similar ways before. In fact, Lord Felix had worn a similar look right before she kicked him in the fore-head. She knew she should be afraid of him—was stupid not to be—but she just couldn't bring herself to feel any fear. He just annoyed her. Finally he nodded. "I admire a person with a sense of loyalty. I have no objection to you having outside interests, but when you're with me, I want to be your top priority."

Griffin was her top priority. "Fair enough," she lied. "I'd like to go clean up, if that's all right with you."

"Sure. You'll want to get that gown I gave you ready to wear. Tomorrow night, we're going to the theater. Appar-ently you and Jasper have work to do there."

The final piece of the machine was in a theater? Tricky, but at least she wouldn't have to fight anyone for it—or rather, she assumed she wouldn't. "That won't take me all day. Is there anything else that needs to be done?"

He waved a hand in the air. "Nothing you need to be concerned with. The boys will take care of it."

Finley didn't argue. The free time would give her the chance to poke about a bit—see if she could find out just what Dalton was up to. What she really needed to do was get word to Griffin that they were going after the final piece, and where. That only gave them a little over twenty-four hours to figure out what the machine was and what Dalton planned to do with it.

She just hoped it wasn't too late.

Finley took her leave of Dalton and jogged upstairs to the room she had been given. It was nice—nothing like the one she had at Griffin's, though. Once the door was closed behind her, she withdrew her pocket telegraph from a secret pouch sewn inside her corset. Quickly, she sent a message to Griffin, saying that they were going to the theater the next night and that she would provide more details when she had them. She didn't want him pushing himself to be there, but he had to make plans.

She wasn't going to try to fix this on her own, no matter how much she wanted to. Leaving Griffin out would only make things worse, of that she was certain.

As water filled the tub in the bathroom she shared with Mei, Finley gathered up her soaps and creams and the silk kimono Griffin had bought her when she first came to his house. She hugged the garment to her chest, as though it was her only link to him.

She had been so relieved last night when she opened her eyes and found Griffin watching her. She'd never been so happy in her entire life.

Since she'd met him, she'd bounced back and forth between wanting to be with him and wanting to run away. She told herself they couldn't be together while secretly hoping that they could. Yesterday she'd almost lost him, and now she couldn't think of anything that mattered more than being with him. Worry about what people would think or say was stupid under those circumstances.

Now she just had to figure out what to do about it. When they got back to London, they'd figure it out.

And that was all the thought she'd give it for today—her head was too tired. She turned the taps on the tub, undressed and slipped into the hot water with a sigh.

She must have dozed off, because by the time she came to her senses, the water had cooled and she resembled a prune from shoulders to toes. She jumped up, sloshing water over the sides, pulled the plug and set about drying off.

When she returned to her room with her bundle of dirty clothes, she found Mei sitting on her bed. The girl looked like a porcelain doll in her high-necked violet gown, her thick hair piled on top of her head. For a prisoner, she was sure kept in fancy clothes.

Good thing she'd taken her telegraph machine into the bathroom with her and now had it in the pocket of her kimono. "What are you doing?" she asked.

Mei glanced up from the book in her hands. Finley recognized it as her copy of *Pride and Prejudice*—the book she was reading for the sixth time. "Waiting for you," the girl replied. Her English was excellent, touched by just the faintest Chinese accent. "I thought maybe you had drowned in there."

Finley arched a brow at her tone. Wishful thinking, perhaps? "Your concern humbles me." She said it with just enough sarcasm to let Mei know that if she wanted to get bitchy, she was more than happy to reciprocate.

Lips tightening, Mei rose from the bed and gracefully approached—as though her feet didn't touch the floor. She was so dainty and graceful, but Finley knew better than to lower her guard. This tiny little girl was just as much a threat to her as Dalton was, though Finley wasn't certain why.

"I don't know why you are here," Mei said slowly. "I don't know why he likes you, but I want you to know that I was here first."

Feeling the urge to kick the bee's nest, Finley smirked. "Is this the part where you tell me to stay away from your man because you're afraid I'll take Jasper away from you?"

Incredibly full lips curved into a smug smile. "Jasper adores me."

"Really?" Finley tossed the bundle of clothes into a hamper in the corner. "Because it seems to me that if he loved you that much, he would have taken you to England with him instead of leaving you behind."

The slap came so fast, Finley barely saw it. She felt it, though—all the way through her skull. Fire blossomed in her cheek before the sharp sting had even begun to fade. She drew back her fist but caught herself just in time. As much as she wanted to retaliate, it wouldn't look good for a girl her size—with her strength—to hit a little thing like Mei. Also, Jasper wouldn't like it.

She touched her cheek. "Just so you know, if you ever do that again, I'm going to make you swallow your own teeth."

Mei smiled mockingly. "You will do no such thing. You don't want to upset either Dalton or Jasper."

Finley poked her in the neck—right where the clockwork collar curved around her throat. "If Dalton thought you were that valuable, he wouldn't have given you that lovely bit of frippery."

The other girl shoved her hand away with a gasp. Her own hands went to her throat, clawing at the high neck of her dress. Finley watched in confusion. What the devil... The collar. She had set off the collar, and now Mei was slowly being strangled by it.

She grabbed the smaller girl by the shoulders, holding her upright as her knees sagged. "How do I stop it?" she demanded, fighting the urge to shake her. "How do I turn the bloody thing off?"

Suddenly, Mei stood upright and shrugged off Finley's grip with a tinkling laugh. Finley froze. Mei had only been pretending to suffocate. "You are not as tough as you boast, Miss Bennet."

Finley felt both cold and hot at the same time. She hadn't wanted to be responsible for Mei's death, but now...

She seized the smaller girl by the twist of hair on the back of her head and pulled.

"Ow!" Mei cried. Her hands clutched at Finley's, nails digging in. "Let me go! What are you doing?"

Finley didn't ignore the pain—she let it fuel her anger—as she dragged her captive toward the window. "I'm going to toss you out the bloody window and see if your collar tightens then. The fall might break your legs. You'd have a hard time getting back inside with your legs broken, wouldn't you? Don't worry, I'll save you—eventually."

Mei struggled all the harder. Blood ran down Finley's hand to trickle down her arm and drip to the floor, but she did not let go. She opened the window with her free hand and tossed Mei across the sill so she was half in, half out.

The girl started screaming. Passersby looked up to see what all the commotion was about. A woman cried out, and a young man laughed, making a joke about how girls fought.

When Finley was done with Mei, that little cretin was next.

"I'm sorry!" Mei cried. "Let me in. Please!"

While publicly humiliating the girl went a long way to soothing Finley's anger, the apology was far more effective.

She yanked Mei back over the sill and slammed the window shut. Only then did she finally release her hold on Mei's hair.

The Chinese girl glared at her as she rubbed her scalp. Her face was red with rage, but there wasn't a tear to be seen, except for the usual watering that came with having one's hair pulled.

"You'll pay for that," she promised, her voice low and even.

Finley smiled at her. "Do your worst, sweetheart."

Mei shot her another filthy look before sweeping from the room like an arrogant queen. Finley watched her go with a vaguely amused smile, though she knew better than to entirely dismiss the threat. She and Mei were officially enemies now, and the worst thing she could do was underestimate the girl.

Never underestimate a girl, she reminded herself as she washed the blood from her arm in the basin.

What did Jasper see in the awful little thing? It couldn't be her personality.

Whatever it was, she didn't much care. She just made a mental note not to leave her back open anytime Mei was around. The girl was liable to stick a knife in it.

Jasper was sitting in the parlor, whittling an elephant out of a small block of wood, when Mei came in. Dalton might have "given" him his freedom, but Jasper didn't trust it, and he didn't like leaving Mei alone with the scoundrel any more than he had to.

When he saw the expression on Mei's pretty face, his first thought was that Dalton had dared to touch or harm her in some way. He'd put a bullet right between the criminal's eyes if that was the case.

If he ever got his hands on a gun.

"What's the matter?" he asked, rising to his feet as she closed the door.

"That Finley girl," she replied tightly. Her face was flushed, and her eyes looked as though she had been crying.

"She's back?" Relief swept over Jasper. He'd been so worried when he heard that Finley had just up and taken off after a "little redhead pikey" had shown up. Dalton's man hadn't much liked being roughed up by a girl and had made a comment as to what he was going to do to Finley if he ever saw her again. Dalton fired him on the spot.

Reno Dalton was a lot of things, but he was a might protective of what he thought of as "his," and Finley was a valuable possession, as far as he was concerned.

But for Finley to just up and leave—for Emily to come for her—something bad had to have happened. Something to either Sam or Griffin.

"Yes, she's back." Dark eyes snapped with anger. "You don't have to sound so pleased about it."

Her tone made his brows rise. "I'm not pleased," he lied. "I'm surprised. I figured she skipped out."

"I hoped she had."

"Why don't you like her?" He was genuinely confused.

He had liked Finley the moment he met her, and that was when she had been almost two separate people.

"I don't trust her," Mei said, lips settling into that little pout he found so cute. "She came out of nowhere, and Dalton took her in without question, even though she's English and the duke of whatever was asking questions about you."

Her astuteness made a frisson of discomfort run down his spine. "Dalton did ask questions. I told him she wasn't in league with the duke. She's not his class."

"Neither are you," she reminded him sharply. "He associated with you."

He wasn't sure why, but her words stung a bit. "Because English society treated me like some kind of strange being. You know they sometimes display people like animals in a zoo." It was true, but it was nothing that wasn't done in America, as well. Griffin, however, had never treated him like that. "Miss Finley doesn't strike me as the type to allow herself to be treated as such."

Dark eyes lifted to meet his. He had never seen her like this before. It was as though she was bitter. His Mei had never been bitter. "You like her." It was an accusation, not a question.

"She's all right. I got her into a brawl in Five Points, and she never complained." That was true. "Dalton likes her, too, so I'm not sure what that says about her character."

"Hmm."

"Are you jealous?" He couldn't stop the grin that spread incredulously across his lips.

Mei shrugged. "*She'd* never be a victim with a collar around her neck."

Jasper placed his hands on her shoulders and gave a gentle squeeze. "You're not a victim."

She sniffed. "I feel like one. First Dalton and his collar, and then that girl threatened to throw me out the window."

"What?" Jasper frowned. "*Finley* threatened you?"

Her dark eyelashes glistened with tears. "She grabbed me by the hair and held me out the window. She said the fall would break my legs, and then I'd probably die when the collar choked me."

He didn't know Finley well, but it sounded like something she might do. He didn't think she'd ever really kill anyone, but why would she say such a thing to Mei?

What had Mei said to her? a little voice in his head asked. He pushed the suspicion away. He'd talk to Finley about it later.

"Probably for the best if you just stay away from her," he suggested. "Soon this will be over, and Dalton will let both of us go."

Her gaze swept up to meet his. "Are you sure of that?"

"He's a scoundrel and a thief, but I've never known him to be a liar."

Silence grew between them, but when she stepped close,

he took her into his arms and rested his cheek on her soft hair as she placed hers against his chest.

"Jasper, you care about me, don't you?"

He closed his eyes. "You know I do." Once, she had been his sun and his moon. She wouldn't be in this mess if it weren't for him.

"Then promise me you won't do anything foolish like try to double-cross Dalton. Just get him the rest of his stupid machine and let him do whatever he's going to do."

"I will." It was a promise he didn't think he'd be able to keep—not the part about letting Dalton go off and have his fun. "Tomorrow night, I go for the last piece."

"At the theater. He's making us all go, you know."

He nodded. "I know." Probably so they could all witness what Dalton would see as his triumph and Jasper's defeat. He wouldn't be surprised if Dalton put a bullet between his eyes afterward. That stuff he'd said to Mei about Dalton not being a liar wasn't exactly true, which he supposed made him just as much a liar lately, since untruths had been coming out of his mouth with ease.

Mei's arms tightened around his waist. "I can't wait until he releases me from this collar, and we can be together again. We can go back to San Francisco."

"We could," he remarked—another lie. He could never return to San Francisco while he was wanted for murder there.

"We could go anywhere," he added. This was something they could discuss later. First they had to survive the next couple of days. If they were still alive the morning after Dalton got his machine put together, there just might be hope for the two of them.

And that was as far into the future as he would let himself look.

It was late afternoon before Griffin finally felt well enough to leave his bed. The Organites were doing their work—not as fast as he would like, but it was better than dead. By tomorrow evening, he should be as good as new. Just in time to go to whatever theater Reno Dalton would be at.

He had gotten Finley's telegraph message earlier, while lying abed, sipping the Organite tea Emily made him. She was convinced it would help his insides heal faster. For a moment he had hesitated, wondering if it was the Organites and their effect on human evolution that had made him encounter that thing in the Aether. But it seemed too much of a stretch and didn't make enough sense for the theory to stick.

More than likely it was the machine itself that had caused the dark energy. It might have conjured a malevolent spirit. That would explain the mysterious threat the other machine had "written." He would advise Mr. Tesla to destroy the blasted thing.

Gingerly, he eased off the bed. For a moment he considered calling Sam for help, but he was not an invalid. He might not be as physically strong as Sam or Finley, but he was not weak.

Still, he could have used the help at that moment.

His arms and chest were bandaged, so he bathed as well as he could and managed to wash his hair.

He was in front of the wardrobe with a towel around his waist when the door to his room opened. Startled and practically naked, Griffin hid himself behind the open armoire.

It was only Sam.

"Don't you ever knock?" he demanded, feeling like a girl for having hid his state of undress.

Sam scowled at him, but that was nothing new. Sam scowled at everyone. "I knocked a while ago. You didn't answer. I was worried."

"I was in the shower."

"So I can see." Sam's dark gaze raked disapprovingly over him. "You need to eat more."

Griffin glanced down. "I don't look *that* bad." All right, so maybe a couple of his ribs were beginning to show and his abdominal muscles were sharply defined, but he had always been lean.

"You haven't taken proper care of yourself since that night at the warehouse."

He had almost died that night, too. This was a habit he did not want to continue.

"You're right. Do me a favor and call down to the kitchen, will you? Ask them to bring something up. Order something for yourself if you like."

A rare smile curved his friend's lips. "As if I wouldn't do that, anyway."

Sam called down using the telephone on the desk. After that, he assisted Griffin in getting dressed, despite Griffin's protests that he was quite capable.

"Finley mentioned something interesting last night," the larger boy began, while Griffin buttoned his shirt. "She said that she'd spotted a man outside the Astor-Prynn residence the other night who Dalton identified as Whip Kirby. She thought he might have been watching Dalton's place, as well."

Griffin frowned. "He must be waiting to catch them in the act."

"The act of what?" Sam asked. "We still have no idea what Dalton's up to."

"Except that it has to do with a strange machine and the Museum of Science and Invention."

Sam's expression was wry. "That still doesn't tell us much."

"Maybe we should check the schedule of events for the museum. Maybe that will give us an idea of what Dalton's up to."

"I'll ask downstairs if they have a listing of events."

Griffin ran a hand through his hair. "It's worth a look."

Then conversation turned to Finley—a topic Griffin was surprised by. Sam hadn't liked Finley when she first showed up; Sam didn't like most people in general. But it seemed as though the two of them were slowly, very slowly, becoming tolerant of one another, if not friends.

"She refused to leave your side all bloody night," Sam remarked with something that sounded like respect.

"She's a good friend," Griffin replied.

His old friend stared at him in amused disgust. "Griff, I'm your friend, and even I wasn't about to sit here and watch you heal."

Griffin looked away, annoyed by the sudden heat in his cheeks. "Yes, well, she was a much prettier sight to wake up to than your ugly head."

"I'll have you know I've been told my eyes are like a night sky" came the mock-indignant reply.

From there, the conversation spiraled into a bout of good-natured insults. Griffin was much more comfortable with that than discussing Finley and how she'd stayed with him. He wasn't entirely certain how he felt about that himself, and most of that was because he didn't know how she felt.

Perhaps it would be better not to think of it at all.

When the food arrived, it seemed to Griffin that Sam had ordered everything on the menu. Regardless, the two of them managed to eat it all. In fact, they had just polished off two slices of thick, flaky-crust apple pie when the phone rang. It was the majordomo from the reception desk downstairs. He was terribly sorry to bother His Grace, but there was a Whip Kirby waiting upon him in the lobby. Would he care to come down, or should the gentleman be sent away? Griffin replied that he would be there directly, thanked the man and hung up.

"Whip Kirby wants to see me," he informed Sam. "He's downstairs now."

"What the devil does he want?" Sam demanded, scowl back in place.

"I don't know, but perhaps he has information about Jasper or Dalton. I'm going to meet with him."

"You sure you're up to that?"

Griffin nodded as he rose from the chair. "I feel much more myself, now that I've bathed and eaten. I'm certain I can give Mr. Kirby a few moments of my time."

"Do you want me to come with you?"

"No thank you. I need you here in case Finley comes by or sends another message. Is Emily still at Tesla's?"

Sam's brows clenched. "Yes. Finds him bloody fascinating, she does."

Griffin offered a supportive smile. "It would be the same if you met the author of some of those dime novels you like so much. She respects his mind, Sam. And he's impressed by hers—that's all. He's old enough to be her father."

Thankfully, Sam did not remind him of how many society marriages joined an older man with a much younger lady. "You're right. I just hoped with Renn out of the picture that we might spend some time together."

"You could always pick her up and cart her off," Griffin suggested with a grin. "If that doesn't get her attention, nothing will."

Sam seemed to consider this a viable plan. He helped Griffin into his coat and was left pondering aloud the possibility of perhaps having an entire pie sent up.

Griffin took the lift down to the foyer, his dislike of small spaces raising its head just enough to make his heart beat faster. If it weren't for the lad operating the bloody thing, he'd probably break out in a sweat. His fear was always calmed by having another person with him.

He adjusted his coat sleeves as he stepped out into the blessedly large entry area and spotted Kirby standing not far away. He started toward the older man.

"Your Grace! How delightful to see you again!"

Griffin stifled a groan as he recognized who had stopped him. He turned to the petite blonde with a forced smile. "Miss Astor-Prynn. Good afternoon. I trust this afternoon finds you well?"

She rolled her bright blue eyes. "You would not believe the day I've had, Your Grace. First my maid—" she jerked her head toward the timid-looking little thing standing a few feet behind her "—*ruined* my favorite hair ribbons, and then Cook served the most dreadful luncheon, and my dressmaker had to cancel my appointment, because she was bitten by a spider and is under the weather. I swear, it is impossible to find good help these days."

Sweet Hades. Could she honestly be this shallow? Yes, he could see it in her face; she could. "My sympathies. I hate to be rude, but I must ask you to excuse me. I am on my way to meet someone."

She stopped him with a hand on his arm. The pressure didn't hurt, but made his wounds itch uncomfortably. She wore a large-brimmed hat decorated with ostrich plumes, and when she leaned in closer to him, the feathers almost brushed his face. He had to blow on them to keep them away.

"I do hope you're feeling better after that unfortunate... altercation the other night. Why, you don't even have a bruise!"

Of course he didn't—the Organites made certain of that. "Yes, well, like I said to the police, I'm fairly certain the girl used chloroform or something similar. She couldn't have knocked me out otherwise." Thank God the authorities had agreed with him. That was easier to understand than the fact that Finley was extraordinary—not that he could have told them that, anyway.

"I am very glad to see that you survived the ordeal unscathed. My shoulder still aches where the awful creature ran into me."

"I'm sorry to hear that. Perhaps you should see a doctor." Perhaps she could do that right now and leave him alone. He was in no mood to flirt and be charming; he wasn't very skilled at it even on a good day.

The girl waved a dismissive hand. She was a pretty little thing, but something about her got under his skin and annoyed him—like a tick. "It's nothing serious, and it won't stop me from attending the theater tomorrow night. Will you be there, Your Grace?"

"Which theater is that?"

She laughed, as if she thought he was trying to be funny. "Why, the Olympia, of course! It's the only one with a production worth seeing at the moment."

Could that be the theater where Finley and Dalton would be? It seemed a little too coincidental not to be. "Is that so? I may have to attend, then. I've heard the theater in New York is tremendous."

She shrugged. "Though nothing like the London stage, I'm sure. After all, you have Lillie Langtry."

"I believe she's moved to this side of the pond," he replied with the one bit of information he knew about the aging actress. Kirby still stood by the wall, watching them. He redoubled his efforts to extricate himself. "Miss Astor-Prynn, will you excuse me? I'm supposed to meet someone, and he's waiting for me."

The blonde smiled prettily. "Of course. I hope to see you tomorrow evening." Then she offered her hand, and he was forced to take it in his own and kiss the air above her knuckles. It would have been rude of him not to.

He said goodbye and turned toward his next visitor with a sigh of relief. He felt as though he had just been pulled out of the path of a runaway carriage.

Whip Kirby watched as he approached. Once they were within a few feet of each other, the lawman tipped his hat. "Your Grace, thank you for seeing me without a prior appointment."

"Of course. Shall we find somewhere a little more private to talk?"

They found a small seating area not far away, which wasn't currently in use. Griffin made himself as comfortable as he could, but his torso was still a little tender. Having one's chest perforated would do that.

"I'll get right to the point," Kirby said, leaning forward so that his forearms rested on his knees. "Have you had any contact with Jasper Renn?"

Griffin arched a brow. "Who?"

"Come now, Your Grace, don't play games. I saw you at the Tombs, and I know Renn was seen in your company in London. Your presence in New York is no more a coincidence than mine. Plus, you've been asking around 'bout Dalton just as much as I have."

"If you know this, then you also know that I'm not about to tell you anything that might endanger my friend, or myself."

The lawman tipped his chair back. "You assume I'm interested in harming the boy."

"Aren't you?"

"I'm interested in justice." Kirby's eyes were flat—entirely empty of emotion. "I won't let some well-meaning English dandy stand in my way. I'll ask again—have you made contact with Renn?"

Griffin could lie, but there was something in the old man's

tone that confused him—a hint of desperation. Could it be that they were on the same side?

"I haven't been in direct contact, no."

The older man smiled, causing lines to fan out around his eyes. "So that English girl running with Dalton's gang is yours. I wondered about her. You know about Dalton, too, right?"

If Finley belonged to anyone it was herself. He was tempted to tell the marshal that. Instead, he nodded. "I do."

"Then you know what kind of trouble your friend is in."

"Is that all you wanted to talk to me about, Mr. Kirby?" Griffin was still sore and more than a little cranky, so he was done with this conversation.

The lawman met his gaze with one that was the color of a wolf's and just as unnerving. "During your association with Renn, he never once talked about San Francisco or why he left?"

"We might have talked a little about his family but not much else." Come to think of it, Griffin hadn't offered up much personal information about himself, but they had managed to become friends, anyway.

"You're sure? He never once mentioned Venton or Reno Dalton? Not even a girl? I find it hard to believe that young men your age wouldn't talk about girls."

Griffin arched a brow. "Not one in particular, no." What did this man think, that he had nothing better to do than sit around chitchatting about girls all day? "I didn't learn about Dalton until I arrived in Manhattan."

"Damnation," Kirby mumbled, rubbing the stubble along his jaw with the palm of his hand. "I suppose he wouldn't talk about Venton's murder, not if that's what he was runnin' away from."

Just what sort of information was he after? And was that concern he heard in the man's tone? Griffin went ahead with the obvious. "Jasper is not a murderer, Mr. Kirby." He didn't care what kind of evidence the lawman had. He refused to believe the young man he knew would kill someone in cold blood.

Kirby regarded him for a moment. "Your faith in your friends is admirable, Your Grace. But regardless of that, I want to talk to Renn myself."

He wouldn't be much of a lawman if he simply took Griffin's word for it, and Griffin respected that. But if Kirby wanted information, then he was going to have to share some. "Tell me, Mr. Kirby, what is it that leads you to believe that Jasper murdered this person?"

Kirby hesitated, as though considering his words. Perhaps he decided to trust Griffin, just as Griffin was prepared to trust him. Sometimes a man had to listen to his gut. "Your Grace, I don't think Renn murdered Mr. Venton."

"You don't?"

"No," Kirby asserted with a shake of his head. His eyes were serious, his expression unguarded. "I believe Venton was killed by a girl named Mei Xing."

Chapter 11

Finley didn't get much of a chance to poke around in Dalton's business. She managed to sneak into his bedroom but found nothing of any interest—not even a safe—except a book filled with stories and pictures that made her face hot and the rest of her feel twitchy. After looking at it, she had a pretty deep suspicion that this was exactly the sort of book her stepfather, Silas, kept in the locked cupboard at the back of his shop.

Once she was done with his room, she moved on to the parlor but didn't expect to find anything. Anything important—that wasn't hidden in his bedroom—would be in his study, and that's where Dalton was at the moment.

Jasper and the others weren't back yet, so there was nothing for her to do and no one for her to talk to—unless she went to Dalton. She was pretty certain he had Mei with him, and she'd rather swallow live leeches than spend any more time than she had to with that girl.

There was something of a training room set up in what normally would have been a drawing room, on what some of the people around here referred to as the first floor. This was confusing because she was used to calling it the ground floor, which was followed by the first, second and so on. There was a sparring square and a sandbag for punching, along with other equipment to improve physical health and strength. Dalton shared the modern belief that exertion was good not only for the human body but the mind, as well. It was the perfect place for her to go to burn off some of this nervous energy dancing through her veins.

She was already dressed in loose knee-length trousers with lace trim on the hems and a comfortable shirt with a supple leather corset over the top, so she didn't need to change. She jogged downstairs, her thick-soled boots quiet, and headed straight for the training room.

She began with some stretches to limber up her muscles, then moved on to climbing the rope suspended from the ceiling. When she reached the top, she turned and went back down the rope headfirst, coiling the rope around one of her legs to keep steady. She reached the bottom and was just about to turn around and go back up again when she heard footsteps. She looked up to see Jasper walking toward her. He didn't have his Stetson on, and the ends of his hair stuck out a bit from where the hat had set.

"Ain't you just like a monkey," he remarked with a grin.

Finley smiled back. "I'll take that as a compliment."

"You do that. Want me to hold that for you?"

She had moved on to the sandbag, and the extra weight would make it more difficult for her to move. "Thanks."

Jasper put himself flush against the leather bag and anchored himself by wrapping his arms partially around it, using his elbows as added security.

A quick glance over her shoulder confirmed that they were alone in the room. "Where did you go?" she asked, keeping her voice low just in case.

"Forger," he replied. "Dalton paid him for three copies of an invitation to the Museum of Science and Invention."

Finley swung at the bag with her left fist and connected with a solid *thwap*. "What's going on there?"

"Don't know. Little Hank grabbed them from me before I could read the whole thing. But I did see something about it being a gala event. There can't be too many of those going on, can there?"

"Your reckon is as good as mine," she allowed, taking another swing. "During the Season, the upper class can get dozens of invitations to similar affairs. However, they're normally at different places, so no, I don't think there could be too many galas going on at that museum. I'll send a message to Griffin later."

Jasper grunted when she hit the bag so hard it actually

moved him back a couple of inches. "You need to tell him we're going to the Olympia tomorrow night, too."

"How did you manage to hide a piece of the device in a theater?"

"They were still building it at the time. I got a job on the construction crew." He leaned into the bag, and this time it didn't move as much when she hit it. She could send a full-grown man flying with a good punch, but there was no point doing that to the bag—it would only break, and then she'd have hundreds of pounds of sand to clean up.

"Clever." Another punch. "I'll let Griffin know. He should be recovered enough by then. Bloody fool's likely to go even if he isn't."

"You never did tell me what happened."

She'd forgotten that. They hadn't been alone since she'd returned that morning. Lord, had it only been yesterday that Griffin almost died? "He was attacked at Mr. Tesla's home."

Jasper looked startled, but he maintained his hold on the sandbag. "Did Tesla attack him?"

"No," she replied with a chuckle, despite the seriousness of the situation. "Apparently Griffin saw a shadowlike creature in the Aether, and it was attached to this machine that came 'alive' on its own. That's what attacked him. Sam's convinced it was a ghost—a mean one."

"What does Griffin think?"

She threw a left uppercut. "He can't think of any other

explanation, though he's never seen anything like it before. It hurt him bad, Jas." She lowered her fists.

Jasper eased his hold on the sandbag and leaned his cheek against the side of it as he looked at her. "You all right?"

Finley shrugged. "Yeah. It was scary seeing him like that."

"He does come across as somewhat invulnerable, don't he?" Jasper smiled. "The two of you are like a twister colliding with a mountain."

There was no need to ask which one of the two she was, Finley thought with a smile.

"I bet His Grace doesn't like you being around Dalton very much."

She leaned against the bag, as well. "You mean because Dalton's so pretty? Maybe. He'd never admit it, though."

Jasper arched a brow. "I meant because you seem to have a liking for fellas of dubious character. You like being on the wrong side of the law."

A frown pinched between her eyebrows. "I do not like fellows of 'dubious character.' And I'm not certain I like being accused of enjoying a life of crime."

He tilted his head. "Tell me you don't enjoy it."

Now, that really would be a lie. "It's exciting, of course. But so far, being a friend of Griffin's has been far from dull."

Jasper watched her with an expression that was either amusement or pity. "You like the adventure and the danger of it, just like I did when I first joined up. It's fun to do things and not get caught—so long as no one gets hurt. But people do get hurt, Miss Finley. Especially when Dalton's around."

"Is that the voice of experience I hear?" she asked with forced levity.

He nodded. "It is. I've seen him kill a man just to make a point. I'd hate to ever know that you had become like that."

"Me, too," she agreed.

A moment of silence followed. She watched as Jasper frowned, as though contemplating something important in his head. "Miss Finley, there's something I need to ask you."

He usually only called her Miss Finley when trying to be charming, so to hear it in this grave tone was just wrong. "You talked to Mei," she guessed. It was the only explanation for the way he couldn't quite look at her.

"Did you threaten to throw her out the window?"

Only biting the inside of her mouth kept her from laughing. It sounded so absurd, especially in that slow, melodic accent of his. "Yes. I did."

Now he looked at her, his green eyes full of hurt and anger. "Why would you do that to someone smaller and weaker than you?"

Instantly defensive, Finley braced her hands on her hips. "She might be small, but there's nothing weak about her. She's like a little wild animal that might look cute and sweet but will try to eat your face if you get too close."

Jasper scowled. "She is not."

"I didn't even hurt her," she added. "All I did was pull

her hair a bit and lean her over the windowsill. I wasn't really going to drop her." That was only a tiny lie. She would have dropped the little cow if she'd felt she had good enough reason.

"You scared her," he chastised. "What did she do to deserve that?"

"She came into my room being a proper bitch. When I returned the sentiment, she hit me, and she then made me think that collar of hers was trying to choke her. What do you say to that? You know I could have hurt her if I wanted, and I didn't. I'm not Dalton." That was a big part of this, wasn't it? That he was worried about her getting in so deep with Dalton she wouldn't be able to find her way out?

"I know." He looked like a child whose favorite toy was lost. "Why don't you like her?"

Finley snorted. "I think a better question might be why do you like her so much?"

"You haven't seen how sweet she can be. It's hard not to be on edge when your life's in danger."

"For a prisoner, she has it pretty good here. Dalton treats her like a doll."

An angry flush rose in Jasper's cheeks. "He could kill her whenever he wanted, and he doesn't even have to touch her."

"Look, I'm not defending Dalton, all right?" Finley's own temper was on the rise. "I just don't like Mei."

"She's had a hard life. When I found her, a man named Venton had been trying to force her into prostitution. She and her family hadn't been in the States long, and they were scared. Mei was so brave. I took her to Donaldina Cameron—she rescues and educates Chinese girls."

That banked Finley's anger a little bit. She had been attacked by the son of her previous employer, so she had a little sympathy for the girl. At least Finley had been strong enough to knock the bounder unconscious.

"She never complained about her life. And when Miss Donaldina took in new girls, Mei always helped them. Sometimes she went on dangerous rescue missions by herself."

All right, now she was starting to feel bad for hanging Mei out the window. "She's had a tough time of it. I'll give her that."

Jasper shook his head. "You don't understand, because you weren't there. Mei tried so hard to change things, and she couldn't. One night, Dalton told Venton where to find her. I didn't get there in time."

For one horrifying moment, Finley thought Mei had been raped, but the expression on Jasper's face didn't look quite that horrified. It was more like…regret. Then the pieces all fell into place.

"Jasper, is Venton the man you're accused of murdering?"

He glanced at her—then away—and nodded. "He is."

"You didn't kill him, though, did you?"

He shook his head. "No."

Mei had. Mei had killed the man who tried to force her

into prostitution. No doubt he would have raped her first—men like that tended to be monsters through and through.

Blast it all, but this revelation did a lot to make her feel for Mei. Hell, she almost *liked* her. Any girl with the stones to defend herself to that degree deserved a little respect. She was just about to say so when she heard the door to the room open.

"There you are." Dalton's voice rang through the room with false cheer. "I was looking for the two of you. Jasper, a word, please?"

Jasper didn't glance at her before he walked away. Finley marveled at his acting ability. Gone was the concerned boy of just a few moments ago, replaced with an edgy young man who could shoot you without so much as a blink.

What was worse was that she knew she often had that same expression on her face, because part of her would do anything to survive. To win.

Blimey. No wonder Jasper was worried about her. Truth be told, she was a little worried herself.

She went back to hitting at the bag but not with much gusto. Her hearing could be very acute when she concentrated, and right now, she wanted to know what Jasper and Dalton were talking about.

"Is everything set for tomorrow night?" Dalton asked.

"Yep," Jasper replied. "Finley and I will retrieve the piece during the performance so there's less chance of being seen."

"Good." She didn't have to see Dalton's face to know that

he was pleased. "Once I have the machine assembled and have completed my plan, you and Mei will be free to go."

"You better not be lying, Dalton."

"My friend, I can promise you on my mother's grave that once this is over, you will never see me again."

Finley frowned. Maybe she was paranoid, but that sounded more like a threat than a promise. Surely Jasper had to suspect that, as well.

"What are you doing in here, anyway?" Dalton asked him. "What were the two of you talking about?"

Finley lifted her head and turned. "Oy, cowboy."

Both Jasper and Dalton looked at her just as Mei entered the room. Wonderful. The more the merrier. Whoever said that should be made to swallow their own teeth.

"I thought we were going to spar? I'm restless and need to hit something. Your pretty face ought to do."

Jasper gave her a dubious look—the sort he should give a person he didn't know well who was asking him to fight. "All right." Then to Dalton, "Unless you have some kind of objection?"

Dalton smiled that feline smile of his. "Of course not. In fact, I think I'll watch."

Of course he would. Finley didn't care. At least Jasper didn't have to answer him, and she didn't have to try and make nice with Mei, for whom she now had conflicting feelings.

She was even more glad she'd worn the loose trousers as

she climbed into the square. They made it easier to kick and move. Jasper was fast—blur fast—and she needed every advantage she could, if he decided to use that speed.

She needn't have worried. As soon as Jasper joined her, and they took a few swings at one another, it became obvious he wasn't going to use his abilities against her—not because she was a girl, though. She knew that for certain. It was because he didn't want Dalton to see what he could do—how fast he had become.

They had just begun to find their rhythm—Finley's muscles grew warm and languid beneath her skin—when the formerly demure Mei began encouraging Jasper. Not just encouraging but instructing him. Instructing him how to put the most hurt into Finley.

"Why aren't you breaking free?" Mei yelled when Finley got him in a particular hold. "You know how to escape."

Finley grinned at her. "Maybe he likes it." Then she released Jasper and danced away, never taking her eyes off the other girl. "You seem to know a lot about fighting. Would you like to take Jasper's place?" She might have some sympathy for the girl, but it was obvious the feeling wasn't mutual.

"Yes," the girl replied with a flash of anticipation in her dark eyes.

Jasper hesitated. "I don't think that's a good idea."

But it was Dalton who took Mei by the arm and stopped her progress. "Sorry, ladies, but I cannot allow Mei to risk sporting bruises at the theater tomorrow." He gave the Chinese girl an intense glance, but she didn't look away. "Finley will heal. Won't you, Finley?"

She had deliberately allowed him to see how fast she healed, so there was no point in denying it. "That's right." She couldn't resist adding, "I could always hit her from the neck down."

For a second, Finley thought Mei was going to jerk free of Dalton's grip and leap over the rope. Instead Mei looked from Jasper to Dalton and shook her head.

Oddly enough, Finley was strangely disappointed. At least if Mei came at her, she would have to really fight. Mei would want to hurt her, while Jasper was more concerned with making certain his enhanced speed didn't become apparent to Dalton. Where was Sam when she needed him? She wanted an opponent who would make her work for her victory.

It really didn't say much for her character—at least she didn't think it did—that violence sometimes soothed her in a way nothing else could. Only Griffin had ever managed it—something to do with her "aura" and the Aetheric plane. She didn't quite understand it and she didn't need to. For all his bossiness and infuriating tendency to be right, Griffin had become her anchor; the only person she trusted enough to let down her guard around.

They sparred for perhaps another twenty minutes before calling an end to the sweaty production. Her earlier restlessness was gone, and she wanted to send Griffin the information Jasper had shared with her.

She shook Jasper's hand and thanked him for the exercise, then watched as he left the room with Mei as Dalton commanded. Dalton, she noticed, didn't bother to look at either one of them—he was staring at Finley.

This was it, she realized. This was when he would make whatever advances he was going to make. She'd known this was coming, ever since she found out that he liked "rough" girls.

It took real effort to keep her spine loose as he approached her—much like she thought a hungry cat stalked a mouse—only she didn't think Dalton meant her any harm. He had a different set of rules for women than he did for men.

He stood so close to her that every breath threatened to push her chest against his. "You could have pounded him to a pulp. Why didn't you?"

She arched a brow. Was he serious? "Because we're on the same side. And because it would be difficult for him to do whatever it is we have to do tomorrow if I busted him up. I don't always have to win."

Dalton smiled that indolent smile of his. "That's the difference between you and me."

How many girls had fallen victim to him? She wouldn't be one. Finley knew dark and charming, and Dalton was no charismatic Jack Dandy. Jack had his honor, but Dalton... Dalton was just dangerous. Maybe if her darker self was stronger she would be tempted to run away with him, but all she could think of was that, as soon as this was over, she could return to Griffin and Emily—even Sam. Sure, she didn't mind if it took a little bit longer, because she did enjoy the intrigue and the danger, but that was it.

Pretty soon she might make herself believe it.

He offered her his handkerchief, and she took it. She hated when sweat trickled into her eyes. Dabbing at her forehead, she glanced at him. "Would you have preferred if I had beaten him? Just because I can hurt someone, doesn't mean I should. Sometimes, the threat of violence is more of a weapon than fists or blades." She wasn't sure where that had come from, but it sounded good.

Dalton reached out and touched a lock of her hair that had fallen from the sticks at the back of her head. "You are an extraordinary woman, Finley Bennet."

She knew he was only trying to butter her up, but it was nice being referred to as a woman. "Yes," she replied without an ounce of pride. "I am." It was a plain and simple fact—she was extraordinary. But then again, so was Wildcat McGuire. So was Emily.

So was Mei.

"I'm not much of a fighter, I'll admit it," he confessed, still stroking that lock of hair. "I don't like getting my hands dirty, so to speak. Does that make me less of a man in your estimation?"

She thought of Griffin, who was physically capable of defending himself, she was certain, but whose powers lay in something more than the tangible realm. "No," she answered honestly. "Power doesn't always have to equate to physical strength. Look at Mei. She's a tiny little thing, yet she holds so much power over Jasper. A fact that you are well aware of, I'm sure."

His chin came up. Crystalline eyes regarded her with unveiled interest as he curled her hair around his finger. "Do you know that he took the blame for a murder for her?"

"No," she lied. "I knew they had history, but nothing like that."

Dalton nodded, giving her hair a slight tug before releasing the ringlet he had made. "He did. He would do anything to keep her safe. Jasper's always thought of himself as a hero."

"You don't like him much, do you?"

He seemed surprised by her question. "Jasper? I used to love him like a brother until he betrayed me." His hand cupped her elbow. "I don't really want to talk about him, or Mei, for that matter."

"I don't think you want to talk at all," she remarked drily as his gaze traveled over the length of her.

Dalton chuckled, and for a moment, his features were transformed into something truly beautiful. It was almost painful to look at him. Angels had to weep at the sight of his face. "No," he agreed quietly. "I don't want to talk."

She was prepared for the kiss, braced for it even. It was lovely, as far as kisses went. Her heart gave a little jolt at the contact, but that was it. There was no feeling of being struck by lightning. No desperate urge to grab hold of him and never let go. And there were absolutely no butterflies in her stomach.

Griffin only had to look at her in a certain way, and her stomach quivered.

It was a terrible time to realize you were falling in love with someone—when you were kissing another bloke.

But she had to put her own acting ability to the test right now, because she wanted Dalton to trust her. Wanted him to believe she was completely on his side. She held on to the lapels of his jacket and made herself kiss him back with all the enthusiasm she would give a kiss from…well, Griffin.

That seemed to do the trick, because he held her tighter and kissed her harder. Then just when she thought she might have to forcibly remove his mouth from hers, he lifted his head. He smiled at her, as though he expected her to melt at his feet at any moment.

Finley smiled back. Oh, she had missed her calling. She should have been an actress. "Do all you Southern boys know how to kiss like that?"

He might have chuckled; she wasn't sure. Something caught her attention out of the corner of her eye, and she turned her head just in time to see Mei leave the room. She must have returned after leaving Jasper wherever he had gone.

How long had she stood there? Long enough to see Dalton cozy up to her. She'd stood there and watched them kiss without making a sound. Spied on them—purposefully. There was only one reason a girl did that sort of thing.

Was Mei in love with Dalton?

Chapter 12

After Kirby announced his suspicions regarding the shooting of the late Mr. Venton, Griffin suggested they continue the conversation someplace a bit more private, so they returned to his room. He called for Sam, and the three of them sat down with coffee sent up from the hotel kitchen.

Two hours later, the lawman had told them all that he knew—or all he was willing to reveal—about the murder and to what extent he believed Jasper to have been involved.

Basically Venton was a sack of shite that deserved to be killed, and Jasper took the blame for it, even though Mei Xing had no doubt only done it in self-defense. Kirby wasn't interested in arresting Jasper, so much as he was determined to clear his name. When Griffin asked why, the marshal told him that was one piece of information he didn't feel like sharing just yet. He'd only told them this much because he feared Jasper—and Finley—might be getting in over their heads with Dalton.

"Maybe you'd be kind enough to let them know that?" Kirby asked. "I reckon you'll talk to your girl before I can get anywhere near either of them. Dalton's bad news, and he'll take them down with him if he can."

Griffin looked him dead in the eye. "What are you after Dalton for?"

The marshal finished his coffee. "He got my wife's brother in a heap of trouble. And he's responsible for the death of a good friend. There's a list of crimes as long as my arm that no one's ever been able to pin on him. If I can catch him in the act here, I can petition to have him transported back to San Francisco to stand trial."

"If we help you catch him, will you turn a blind eye to Jasper's and Finley's involvement?"

"As far as I'm concerned, they're working to bring Dalton down, same as me."

Griffin nodded. "I suspect Dalton will be at the Olympia Theatre tomorrow night. I'll let you know when I know for certain. From now on, you'll know what we know."

"Likewise. You'll be sure to let Renn know that I have no intention of punishing that poor girl any more than she's already been punished? I just want to clear his name."

"I will." And he'd ask Jasper why this man would go through so much trouble for him, as well.

"Well, then, I best take my leave." The older man picked

up his battered Stetson from the table and set it on his head. "Thank you for the coffee."

Griffin rose stiffly to his feet and walked him to the door. Kirby gave him his direction. His hotel had a telegraph machine and telephones, but Griffin wanted to avoid any means that might be overheard by curious ears or seen by prying eyes. It was agreed that he would send a messenger or come himself, if at all possible.

Once the door shut, leaving him and Sam alone once more, only then did Griffin sag against the wall.

"You've overdone it," Sam chastised, helping him to the bed. "Stubborn fool."

"Look who's talking," Griffin shot back. "I think I need some more of Em's vile Organite tea, Samuel." As soon as the words left his mouth, Sam was at the phone, asking someone from the kitchen to bring up hot water.

"What would I do without all of you to take care of me?" Griffin asked—perhaps a little harsher than he ought. Right now he felt like the weak link in the chain that was their group. Yes, he could fight, but not like Finley or Sam, and he couldn't heal like them. Emily was so much smarter than he was, and Jasper so fast he was almost untouchable. Sure, he could summon the Aether as energy, but one good cosh to the head would stop that. He was entirely too vulnerable, and he hated it.

Sam glanced at him. "Feeling sorry for yourself, are you?

I suppose you're allowed. I mean, look at how bloody awful your life is."

"Sarcasm doesn't become you," Griffin retorted as he eased out of his coat and boots. The simple action caused a fine layer of sweat to bead on his brow. He was as weak as a child.

"And wallowing doesn't look good on you. You feel feeble. I understand that. But if you want that to change, then change it. For pity's sake, just stop whining about it."

Griffin arched a brow. "Is that experience speaking?"

Sam scowled. "You know it is, you great arse. You think *you're* helpless—Emily and I couldn't even see what attacked you. How do you think that felt?" As he spoke, he casually took Griff by the arms and moved him up the bed so that he reclined on a mountain of pillows. Sometimes it wasn't bad to have friends that were much stronger than he was.

"A little helpless, I suppose," Griffin allowed, suddenly sheepish.

"That's right." A knock sounded at the door. "There's the water for your tea. You stay in bed, understand?"

Griffin nodded, fighting a grin. Sam was such a mother hen. He was also very nosy at times. Griffin was surprised his friend had not asked him if anything had happened between himself and Finley the other night. He and Emily must be beside themselves with curiosity. The two of them were convinced he was in love with Finley and she with him.

He didn't know if he was—and he'd never dare guess at her feelings. He had to admit to himself that it had been nice

to wake up and see her face. To know she'd dropped everything else to be—literally—by his side.

Take that, Dandy, he thought smugly.

Sam brewed him a cup of Emily's tea and a cup of Earl
Grey for himself. Then he took a pack of cards from the desk
and held them up. "Want to play something?"

"May as well," Griffin replied. It wasn't as though he was
in the proper condition to do anything else at the moment.
Once Emily returned from Tesla's, then they could fill her
in on Kirby's visit and discuss where to go from here.

"So," Sam began as he dealt the cards. Griffin took a sip
of the awful tea. "What happened between you and Finley
last night?"

By late that evening, Griffin felt more like himself. He
had drunk several cups of Emily's tea and had gotten Finley's
telegraph that the Olympia Theatre was indeed their destination for the following night and that Dalton had forged invitations to a gala at the Museum of Science and Invention.
There hadn't been anything in the pamphlet Sam found about
the museum, but that hadn't listed much information in the
way of events.

He'd wager Mrs. Astor-Prynn would know—and gladly
tell him, especially if she thought she could throw her daugh-
ter at him in the process.

He sent a note on to Kirby relaying that information and
was now taking a leisurely stroll around the city. Recuper-

ating had been necessary, but now that he had healed, he felt restless.

Sam and Emily had wanted to come with him, but he needed a little time to himself. So he'd listened to his friends' concerns and brought along a walking stick Emily had made for him. It doubled as a club, had a sword hidden inside it and emitted a gas that would put any attackers to sleep when sprayed directly in the face. What Emily didn't know was that he had been practicing with something new. It wasn't a secret that he could use Aetheric energy to destroy—he had done it when he brought that warehouse down on The Machinist. What he had been toying with, however, was controlling the amount of energy he put into an item, so that the thing itself became an Aetheric weapon, charged with the power he'd siphoned.

Sam was right. He needed to stop whining. The incident at Tesla's was the second time in a matter of weeks that he had been injured to the point where his life was in question. That didn't sit well with him, not at all. So rather than brood on how weak he was, it was time to make himself as strong as possible.

To make his little band of "strays"—as his aunt Cordelia sometimes called them—as strong as possible.

So perhaps he should be completely honest and admit that this wasn't just a leisurely stroll. He had intentionally walked in the direction of Reno Dalton's house. He knew where to go because Emily had mentioned the address. He wasn't quite certain why he walked this way—perhaps he wanted to tempt fate and maybe run into the criminal. Perhaps he simply wanted to take a measure of the man.

Or maybe he hoped to catch a glimpse of Finley. He missed her. Sometimes she drove him mad, but she was as much a part of his world as Sam or Emily. From the moment they'd met, he'd felt as though she completed the puzzle that was his life. She just seemed to fit.

When he reached Dalton's unassuming address—a simple brick house with clean windows and freshly swept steps—he kept to the shadows so that he could spy on the occupants, unnoticed. He was surprised that Kirby wasn't already there. The man seemed to have made a habit of watching Dalton and his companions.

The curtains were open in one of the front ground-floor windows. Lamps kept the room well lit, so he could clearly see the two people inside.

Finley and Dalton. They were playing a bizarre and dangerous game, where Dalton threw a dagger at her and she caught it by the handle before throwing it back. Did neither of them have any concept of mortality or respect for their own safety and lives?

He thought of her sitting out on the bow of the airship on the way to New York. The idea of falling hadn't even occurred to her; she thought she was invulnerable, like many young people their age, but a fall from several thousand feet would kill Sam. It would definitely kill her, as well.

His heart stopped as she caught the dagger a mere fraction of an inch from her left eye. It would have killed her if she hadn't grabbed it. The thought rolled around in his stomach, making him feel sick. What did she do? She laughed. The idiot.

This was not one of those moments when he wanted to kiss her. What he wanted to do was storm into that house, punch Dalton in the nose, throw Finley over his shoulder and take her back to the hotel, where she belonged.

He did neither of these things. Firstly, she had to stay there if they were going to help Jasper and make sure Dalton paid for his crimes. Secondly...she obviously liked it there. She trusted Dalton to throw a deadly weapon at her. He trusted her to throw it back. Neither of them had any concern of betrayal or injury.

Dalton was dangerous and likely more than a little mad. That would appeal to Finley's dark side. Lately, it seemed that darker part of her was to become the dominant half of her personality. That part of her would not be content with his world. There was excitement, but usually someone ended up getting hurt, and there wasn't much of a reward for it.

Would she return to him when this was over? Or would she choose Dalton instead?

As the thought crossed his mind, he saw Finley's head turn, and she looked out the window. He hadn't realized, but he had walked out of the darkness into the pool of light from a nearby streetlamp. She could see him. Those sharp eyes of hers could probably make him out plain as day.

The smile slipped from her face as they stared at one another. She set the dagger on the table and crossed the floor to the window. Griffin watched as she placed her palm against the glass, as though to wave at him. Was that guilt he saw on her face, or did she miss him, too?

She glanced over her shoulder and said something. Then she turned back to him. Her fingers curled against the glass before she lifted her hand and took a step back.

Then she yanked the curtains closed.

Griffin shoved his hands in his pockets, turned on his heel and started walking back in the direction of his hotel. She'd done it to keep Dalton from seeing him, obviously. Not because she wanted to shut him out. He told himself that it meant nothing, that he should trust Finley. That he *did* trust Finley.

Only, he realized now that he didn't trust her—not as much as he ought. Not as much as he would expect her to trust him. And that was the worst of it all.

The Olympia Theatre was in Longacre Square, situated between 44th and 45th Streets. The *New York Times* heralded it as "one of the most imposing facades" on Broadway, or so Dalton claimed. To Jasper, the building was ostentatious and sprawling, never mind all that "French Renaissance" nonsense Dalton spouted about its design. Architecture had nothing to do with why Jasper had chosen this particular building as the hiding place for the final piece of the device.

He had hidden it there because he knew it would be hard to recover—even harder than the piece from Wildcat. After all, he knew Wildcat well enough to know that she would have stopped beating on him once she figured he had enough. But tonight, there was no such guarantee that they would get off quite so easily.

"If anything happens tonight, I want you to run," Jasper whispered to Finley as they walked through the large doors into the theater's opulent vestibule.

She shot him what could only be termed as a dirty look. "I won't leave you."

"I need you to protect Mei. Please, promise me."

Her stare was hard, and her mouth tight. "No. You're the one wanted for murder, not me. *You* run. I can't be trusted to protect her. I'd turn her over faster than you can blink, if it would save you."

Jasper knew that it would be impossible—even for him—to carry a torch for three girls, but he fell a little bit in love with Finley right then. No one—and he meant *no one*—had ever been so loyal to him.

"I hope Griffin realizes how lucky he is to have you," he murmured fervently.

A strange look came over her face. She looked sad. "I'm not sure he thinks himself all that lucky."

Jasper opened his mouth to ask why and was cut off. "What

are you two whispering about?" Dalton demanded. "You're
like a couple of old women."

Gritting his teeth, Jasper turned his head to reply, but it
was Finley who jumped in. "Renn just wanted to make sure
my inferior female brain understood what needs to be done
tonight." Her tone was dry as the desert.

"Don't underestimate her, Jas." Dalton chuckled. "She's
as smart as she is pretty."

Jasper and Finley shared a wry glance. "I'll do my best
to remember that," Jasper replied, biting back a grin. He
shouldn't feel any humor in the situation, but he couldn't
seem to help it.

"We'll go to our box," Dalton informed them. "Once the
performance starts, I want the two of you to go collect our
treasure."

Jasper just loved how he said "our" as though he was a
willing participant—or even a partner. Dalton didn't share
well with others, and this was not going to be an exception
to that rule. Once he did this, he was going to be just one
more loose end that Dalton needed to tie up, unless he could
come up with a plan. For all his reassurance to Mei that Dalton would let them go, he didn't really believe it. Dalton was
a man of his word, but he was also the kind of man who took
disloyalty very personally. Jasper would pay for betraying him,
and so would Mei.

Too bad *he* wasn't as smart as he was pretty.

They climbed two flights of crimson-carpeted stairs to the

floor where their box was located. Dalton had won the deluxe seating from its owner—some swell with a season subscription—in a game of cards a few nights earlier. He'd even made the man believe that offering it up was his idea, rather than a suggestion Dalton had planted. It was all handled in a charming and gentlemanly way, which won Dalton the gentleman's regard, and that of his cronies, as well.

Of course Dalton would have to draw attention to himself by having a box for the evening. For a man who claimed not to want to be fancy, he sure made a fine stab at it. He smiled and waved at another man nearby. Jasper recognized him as one of the men from the poker game. The man tipped his hat in greeting.

Dalton sat in the front of the box, placing Mei and Finley on either side of him. Jasper and Little Hank sat toward the back, in the shadows, and the two other ragtag members of Dalton's gang waited outside by the carriage. Jasper didn't remember their names. They hadn't been part of Dalton's racket when he had been up to his eyeballs in it.

Jasper tugged on the cravat around his throat. Dalton had insisted they all dress like gentlemen, and the starch in his collar made Jasper's neck itch. It felt like he couldn't move freely—or breathe comfortably, for that matter. How in a rattler's tail did Griffin stand the blasted things?

As fate would have it, that was the moment Dalton turned to regard him over his shoulder, blue eyes hard and bright as ice. "I see your friend has arrived, Jasper. What a coincidence."

Jasper frowned and followed Dalton's gaze as he turned to face the theater once more. There, across the open expanse above the public seating in a box exactly like this one, sat Griffin, Sam and Emily.

A thick lump formed in Jasper's throat. They weren't there to enjoy the show, of that he was certain. Miss Emily looked like an angel in a copper-colored gown, which warmed her pale skin. Would anyone recognize her as the girl who came looking for Finley? He noted the way she and Sam—the surly oaf—regarded one another and felt a stab of envy. And a little jealousy, for which he immediately felt shame when Mei was so close.

He wished someone would look at him the way Emily looked at Sam. Mei had looked at him like that once. Maybe she would again, if they could manage to get out of this alive. Maybe she'd leave America with him; they could have a good life in England.

But back to the matter at hand. He didn't know how to respond to Dalton's comment. Did the criminal suspect Griffin was there because of him? Did he think Jasper had somehow managed to contact the duke?

Once again, Finley stepped in and took the attention from him. "*That's* the Duke of Greythorne?"

"It is," he replied.

"I thought he'd be older," she remarked, boldly staring across the theater. "He's a little bit of lovely, innit he?"

"He is," Mei agreed enthusiastically.

Jasper's head whipped toward her, and he wasn't the only one who stared—Finley and Dalton did, as well. The Asian girl shrugged her delicate shoulders. "She asked."

Jasper had many options when it came to envying Griffin, but appearance hadn't ever been one of them—until now. But that wasn't his utmost concern at the moment. No, what needled him was the fact that Dalton seemed to feel exactly the same way. Could it be that he had developed feelings for Mei?

No, that was impossible. Mei was just another possession to him. Though, if Dalton had gone soft on her, then it would make him much more reluctant to kill her. More reluctant to let go of her, as well.

Meanwhile, Finley looked as though she'd like to strangle the other girl. "Maybe you'd introduce me to His Grace," she suggested to Jasper.

Dalton reached over and put his hand on her leg, which was covered by the same gown she'd worn to break into the house party. "Not tonight," he informed her. "We have work to do. You can work your wiles on the fancy man another time."

Finley pretended to shrug it off, but Jasper saw the stiff set of her shoulders. If Dalton didn't take his hand from her leg, he was likely to lose it.

Jasper looked to Griffin, wanting to see how he viewed this little display. Obviously he couldn't see where Dalton had his hand, but he could tell that it was near or on Finley. The young duke's jaw was tight, but he nodded in polite greeting at their pointed stares.

Dalton inclined his head, as well, then turned to Jasper once more. "Perhaps you *should* introduce Finley, Jas. He appears to be quite fascinated with her."

Finley laughed and shifted in her chair so Dalton's hand fell away. "Right, he might recognize me as the one who knocked him senseless at that house party."

"You are a difficult girl to forget, Miss Finley," Dalton agreed. "You would be an excellent way to divert the duke's attention. He could be our first test."

"Test of what?" Jasper demanded, resisting the urge to shoot a worried glance at Finley.

Dalton merely smiled. Not for the first time, Jasper was tempted to beat the smile right off the blackguard's face. He could no longer resist glancing at Finley, who looked as though she entertained similar thoughts.

The lights went down, and a roar rose from the crowd in the pit below. A man in a suit came out to introduce the performance, and then the curtains parted, and the entertainment began. The audience quieted.

"Time for the two of you to get to work," Dalton commanded in a low whisper. "Be quick about it."

Jasper rose to his feet along with Finley. The two of them said nothing, just filed out of the box into the empty corridor.

"When this is over," Finley whispered as they walked, "we're going to take turns holding him down while the other beats his pretty face."

Jasper chuckled at her bloodthirsty tone. "Sounds fun." He liked the fact that she just assumed they would defeat Dalton, as though he wasn't a danger to either of them. He didn't know if she was foolish or confident, but whatever it was, she bolstered his own faith in their abilities.

"C'mon," he said, guiding her toward the end of the corridor. "We have to get downstairs."

"Tell me you didn't hide it in one of the dressing rooms," she murmured.

"No," he replied. "It's not in a dressing room."

Beside him she breathed a sigh of relief. "Good."

Jasper winced. "It's in the lobby."

Finley halted in the middle of the carpet, turning on him with astonishment. "Are you out of your ruddy mind? What were you thinking?"

"I was thinking of ways to make it impossible for Dalton to assemble the damn thing. How was I to know he'd stoop to extortion?"

She scowled at him. "He's a ruthless criminal—what else would he do?"

She had a valid point, and it made him feel stupid that he hadn't thought that far ahead. "Dalton's never had much of an attention span. I figured he'd give up looking. Obviously I underestimated how important the damn thing was to him."

Fists on her hips, Finley sighed. "I beg your pardon, Jasper. Of course you took what seemed like the best course of action at the time. Let's just go and see if we can recover it and hope no one else has found it in the meanwhile."

"I doubt anyone has," he explained as they continued toward the staircase. "It's not in plain sight."

Another sigh. "Of course not," she muttered. "That would be too easy for us."

Jasper grinned. "Come on, ducks." He affected an accent much like the slight cockney she used in Dalton's presence. "Where's your sense of adventure?"

She shot a narrow glance at him, but it was softened by her smile.

It would have been too much to ask that the lobby be empty when they entered it. Why did folks bother going to the theater if they were just going to loiter about the entrance and never watch any of it? It didn't make any sense, but then wondering at what went on in another person's mind gave him a headache.

Unfortunately, this smattering of people would make their job more difficult than if the space was packed. A large crowd would do much to conceal them, but as it was, there would only be more witnesses to their actions.

"The far corner." Jasper gestured with his chin. Finley followed his gaze. "There's a loose panel in the wall. Or at least, I'd loosened it at the time. I'm hoping no one noticed and fixed it."

Finley's lips twisted sardonically. "It would be just our luck if they had."

Fortunately, luck had seen fit to smile on them just a little. Someone had placed a large potted plant in that very location. It would provide a little cover—not much, but a little.

When they reached the spot, Finley gestured for him to step behind the plant. She withdrew a fan from the bag she had brought along and began to leisurely waft it. "You remove the panel," she instructed. "I'll keep watch."

Jasper smiled as she positioned herself near the plant. Her body provided extra cover. She kept her gaze raised to where his face would be if he stood, so if anyone were to glance over, they'd think she was just an overheated girl talking to her escort, who was behind the plant. The fan also worked to partially obscure her features, making it harder to identify her.

No wonder Griffin fancied her so much—she truly was a remarkably useful girl. Perhaps this wouldn't prove such an impossible task after all.

Jasper crouched in the corner and began pressing his fingers to the panel in the wall before him. It didn't budge.

"What's the problem?" Finley inquired, still fanning.

"It won't open," he replied.

"Are you certain this is the right spot?"

He shot her a wry glance, but she didn't see it. "Yes, I'm sure. I put it here."

"Quite a while ago."

"It's here," he said firmly. "I just need to work at it. The paint's acted as a glue of sorts."

"Well, get to it." She glanced over the top of her fan. "If we stay here too long we will attract attention."

Jasper clenched his jaw. "I know. Now would you kindly stop talking like you're my ma and keep watch?"

She didn't respond, so he took that as a yes and went back to work. He needed to exert force on the panel to break the seal, but if he exerted too much, the sound would attract unwanted interest.

Finally he felt the wood begin to give. A corner loosened, and he pushed on either side, slowly widening the opening until he could slip his fingers inside. Using his forearm for leverage, he gradually pushed the panel aside, enough to ease his hand into the darkness beyond. Now all he had to do was pray a rat hadn't carried the part off or—worse—that a rat wouldn't be waiting to take a nibble on his fingers. He shuddered at the thought.

Slowly, he felt around for the pouch he'd wrapped the piece in. The panel dug into his wrist as he searched, and he reached deeper, gritting his teeth as the wood bit into his skin. Then his fingers touched dusty cloth, and he smiled. He strained his arm, now ignoring the pain, as he managed to grab hold of the pouch and tug it toward the opening.

"I think I have it," he told Finley.

"Good," she replied. "There's a man walking this way who seems a little too nosy for my liking."

Jasper pulled his arm and his bounty from the wall. The panel fell back into place, leaving only the slightest gap. No one would even notice it unless they were as near the floor as he was. He shook the dust from the pouch and rose to his feet.

"Here," he said, holding a piece of dusty paper out to her. "Put it in your bag, quick." He didn't have to say it twice as Finley snatched the paper and shoved it through the drawstring opening of her bag.

Jasper stuffed the piece of the device into his inside jacket pocket. Then stepped out from the corner just as the man he assumed Finley had spotted approached them. Jasper took one look at the fella and wasn't certain if he should shout for joy or curse.

"Remember when we talked about which one of us should run if there was trouble?" he murmured.

She gave him a slightly panicked look. "Yes."

"The fella coming toward us is Whip Kirby."

Finley's eyes widened, and she gave him a shove. "Run."

Jasper did.

The rugged lawman tried to brush past Finley to go after Jasper, but she stopped him by grabbing his arm. He looked at her hand, then her face in surprise. Obviously he wasn't accustomed to being detained by a girl.

He glared at her and tried to pull his arm free of her grip. He failed.

"Damn it, girl," he snarled at her. "I'm trying to help him."

"So I hear," she replied, stepping closer so as not to call attention to them. When she'd sent him the name of the theater, Griffin had mentioned that he thought Whip Kirby might be more of a friend to Jasper than an enemy. It appeared as though the lawman was more interested in arresting Dalton. "But I don't know you, so you'll have to forgive me if I don't just let you have him."

Kirby shot her a frustrated look. "Saucy little thing, aren't you?"

"A 'saucy little thing' that can break your arm like it was a peppermint stick, Mr. Kirby. So would you mind listening for a moment so I don't have to resort to violence? I've been told I'm very good at it."

He regarded her as though she was some kind of wild animal, which was all right with Finley, because she was getting rather used to being looked at that way. "What do you want?"

"You know I'm a friend of the Duke of Greythorne, right?"

He nodded, his expression hard. "Though, now that I've made your acquaintance, I'm afraid I don't understand how."

That stung a little bit, but she had threatened to break his arm. "I wonder the same thing myself at times, but you don't have to understand, sir. What you need to do is stay here with me long enough for Jasper to get back to Dalton, because if you don't, Dalton won't get his machine, and he won't do whatever it is that's going to get him arrested. You do want him to be arrested, right?"

It was obvious from the look on his face that the older man didn't like what she had to say. However, it was also obvious that he realized she spoke the truth. He swore—very colorfully. Finley's eyebrows rose in appreciation.

"Was your mother a fishwife by any chance?" she inquired. "Because you certainly sound like one."

He flashed her a disgusted glance. "You realize that there's a very good chance Renn will be arrested along with Dalton? You, too?"

Actually, Finley hadn't realized that. She assumed she'd be back with Griffin and the others by then—Jasper, too. But there was a very good chance she and Jasper would be forced to participate in whatever Dalton had planned, if it was going to happen in New York.

She had gotten in plenty of trouble in the past, but she'd never been arrested. She wasn't keen on it now.

"There's a very good chance the duke won't be able to help you, either. This ain't England. As much as some folks seem to like his title and fancy ways, most folks in this country hate the English, and you'll be the one who suffers for it."

Finley swallowed—hard. It could be that he was just trying to scare her—and it was working—or he could mean every word. Suddenly, these past few days running with Reno Dalton didn't seem half so exciting as they had earlier this evening.

But she had to get out of there quickly. If she and Jasper didn't return, Dalton would send someone out looking for them, and if she was seen talking to Kirby there would be even more trouble—for Jasper.

She glanced around the foyer for any sign of the criminal and saw none. What she did see, however, made her heart freeze in her chest.

Lydia Astor-Prynn—the girl she had run into after she'd knocked out Griffin—stood on the stairs talking to several men in black suits. With her was an older woman, who looked so much like her she had to be her mother. They were all staring at Finley. Lydia pointed at her, and when the men moved away to start toward Finley, the blonde girl shot her a smug glance.

Finley swore. This time, Whip Kirby was the one who was surprised. "What was that about a fishwife?"

She ignored the remark. "Mr. Kirby, I have to get out of here. Now."

His amusement turned to a frown as he looked at her. No doubt she looked a fright. She could fight these men—probably—but could she do it before the police arrived? What if they had guns?

Kirby glanced over his shoulder and saw the men approach. Finley barely had time to react when he wrenched his arm free of her grip and whipped her around so that her back was to him. He had handcuffs on her before she could even think to fight.

"I'm going to get you out of here," he murmured close to her ear. Then loudly, "You're coming with me, you dirty thief." He flashed his badge at the men and introduced himself as a federal marshal. They immediately backed off, and Kirby marched her across the foyer to the exit.

Finley's cheeks burned in embarrassment, and her knees trembled. She was scared, and she was angry at herself for it. Griffin trusted this man, and she should, as well, but it was hard to trust someone when they had you in irons.

She glanced up to see Sam at the top of the stairs. Her eyes burned at the sight of his scowling face. Of all the people to witness her being treated like a common criminal, she was glad it was him and not Emily or Griffin.

Finley reached into her bag and groped blindly until she found the piece of paper Jasper had given her. It was a big risk she was about to take, but she quickly—as quickly as the restraints would allow—folded it into a small square and dropped it on the floor behind her. Sam's dark gaze followed the paper as she nudged it toward the wall, where it was less likely to be seen by someone passing by. Then his gaze lifted to hers.

He gave her a tiny nod—silently promising that everything would be all right.

As she was shoved out into the warm night, she wished she could believe him.

★ ★ ★

When he'd slipped into the seat beside Dalton, his old friend had looked at him with an expression of annoyance. The lighting in the box—in all the audience—was dim so that the stage was the center of attention, but Jasper could see good enough. He could also tell that Griffin and the others were watching from their side of the theater.

"Why are you sitting there?" Dalton asked softly.

Jasper glanced at him. "Whip Kirby just took Finley." He knew this because he had hidden around a corner and watched the entire scenario play out. Finley had told him to run, but he couldn't bring himself to completely abandon her—not until he had to.

Dalton's face paled at the man's name. The reaction intrigued Jasper. So Dalton was afraid of something—someone. "This is unfortunate," he murmured. "Did you get the piece?"

Was that all the consideration Finley got? Jasper wanted to punch Dalton in the face. Instead, he patted his jacket. "Right here."

"Good." Dalton shot a glance over his shoulder at Little Hank. "Let's go. It seems we'll have another way to test our device. The Duke of Greythorne can wait. We have a much more important agenda now." He took Mei by the arm and hauled her to her feet as he stood.

Jasper rose behind him. He cast one last glance across the theater before he departed and saw Griffin watching them.

He shook his head, hoping his friend saw how sorry he was. Maybe someday, Griffin would forgive him, but as he turned to leave the box he figured it was highly unlikely—especially now that Finley was in Whip Kirby's custody.

Dalton waited for him outside. Mei was with Little Hank now, and the two of them were already a considerable distance down the corridor, poor little Mei rushing to keep up with the giant's long strides.

The criminal glanced at him as they began to walk. "Don't mope, Jas. It doesn't become you."

"Bugger off," Jasper growled, borrowing an appropriate phrase he'd picked up in London.

"Now, don't be like that." Dalton nudged him with his elbow. "Cheer up. We have work to do."

"You mean putting together your precious machine?"

Dalton grinned. "Of course, and you know what we're going to use it for?"

"What?" Jasper asked warily.

He smiled, lips curving sharply. "A jailbreak. We're going to bust Miss Finley out."

Where was Finley?

Griffin's heart seemed to be struck in his throat as he watched Jasper return alone to Dalton's box in the theater. Jasper looked worried—Dalton, too. That couldn't be good.

He gripped the arms of his chair as he waited for Sam to

return. He'd sent his friend to spy on Finley and Jasper, and he should have returned by now.

Unless something had happened to Sam, as well.

He turned to Emily. "If he's not back soon, I'm going looking for him."

Emily nodded, ropes of hair swinging around her face. "I'm coming with you." She nodded across the way. "Where do you suppose they got off to?"

"No idea."

Silence fell between them for a couple of heartbeats— which he felt in the back of his mouth.

A small hand settled on top of his. "She's all right, lad. You know she's tougher than most men."

He nodded. Physically, Finley was one of the strongest people he knew next to Sam. She was strong in other ways, as well, but they were in a country that wasn't their own, up against an enemy they really knew nothing about.

A charming, handsome enemy who made crime seem exciting and fun, something he feared she wasn't strong enough to resist. Finley liked danger. He could offer her danger readily enough. Perhaps not a steady stream of it, but the work they did wasn't without risk. But Finley was drawn to the darker side of it—her friendship with Jack Dandy was proof of that, as was how deeply she'd thrown herself into this mess with Dalton.

He had known when he saw her fight all those people to get close to Dalton that this might tip her toward her more base nature. He knew, because there had been a moment where unadulterated joy had shone on her face. He'd been jealous because she never looked like that with him.

His thoughts were thankfully interrupted by Sam. He couldn't waste any more time worrying over Finley's morals, because which way she went was nothing he could control.

"What happened?" he demanded when his friend sat down on the other side of him.

"Finley's been taken by Kirby. He led her off in irons."

Emily gasped, drawing a cross look from a lady in the box next to theirs. Emily frowned at her before turning back to Sam. "Why would he do that?"

Sam leaned closer so as not to earn them more dirty looks. "That Astor-Prynn bird set some gentlemen on Finley. I wager Kirby took her with him to keep her safe. Either that, or he fed us a line of shite and he's going to use her to get to us."

"I believe he was sincere when he spoke to us," Griffin argued. "Taking Finley serves no purpose except to keep her from trouble."

Sam offered him a folded bit of paper—yellowed and stained. "She dropped this."

It unfolded to reveal a schematic of a machine. Griffin wasn't stupid, but he couldn't generally tell what a machine was just by looking at it. This needed Emily's attention. She took it and tipped it toward what little ambient light there was. "It looks like some sort of oscillator, but what kind, I'm not certain." She raised her head with a pinch between her brows. "It looks like Tesla's work."

"Tesla?" Griffin echoed. "Is that possible?"

"I don't know, but it looks like his signature smudged at the bottom. If we show him this drawing, perhaps he can identify it."

"And tell us how Dalton managed to come by it in the first place." Had Jasper brought it to New York from San Francisco? Or had Dalton stolen it right out from under Tesla in his home?

"Does this mean we can go back to the hotel now?" Sam asked.

"Yes." Griffin rose to his feet. "Let's go." He needed to start planning. He needed to get in touch with Kirby and maybe try to get some sleep.

As they approached the foyer, Mrs. Astor-Prynn and Lydia stopped him. "Your Grace. You will be happy to know the girl who accosted you at our party has been arrested," the older woman told him smugly.

At that moment Griffin was tempted to summon enough Aether to send the woman flying across to the other side of the theater. Perhaps farther. Somehow he managed to incline his head toward her. "Indeed." That was all he could say. He didn't care if it was rude. He turned and walked away from them, leaving the two ladies staring after him in shock.

He didn't care if he'd behaved badly. He didn't care what they thought of him or if they told their friends. He just wanted Jasper safe and Finley back. And he wanted to punch someone. Hard.

Perhaps he and Finley weren't that different after all.

Chapter 13

Jasper was woken up at five o'clock the next morning by a gunshot. He bolted out of bed, grabbed a pair of trousers from the floor and made for the door. He'd kick it down if he had to. Oddly enough, it was unlocked for the first time since his arrival. This would be the perfect time to make a run for it, and yet he ran downstairs instead, wearing only his trousers, toward the sound of the shot.

He stopped in the doorway of Dalton's study/library. Dalton stood over the desk at the back, which had been converted into a worktable. On it were the pieces Jasper had collected, fully amalgamated into one machine. On the floor beside the desk, there was a dead man, blood soaking into the carpet around him from what appeared to be a gunshot wound in his chest. He was facedown, so Jasper couldn't tell for certain, but it seemed to be the most likely answer.

Jasper's mouth went dry, and his chest squeezed tightly. He'd seen dead bodies before, and it was always sad and shocking. But to see someone who had been murdered, and their killer standing right beside them… It made him think of that day when Mei had shot Venton. He could see her so clearly in his head, a fine splattering of blood on her face and clothes. Years from now, he would remember this moment just as clearly.

The only difference was that Mei had done it in self-defense and Dalton was just a monster.

Drawing a deep breath, he summoned his courage, straightened his spine and strode into the room with a bored look on his face. "What happened? Did he insult your waist-coat?"

Dalton looked up and smiled. "Did you kick the door to your room down to get here?"

"It was unlocked." He made himself move closer and tried another tactic. "You all right?"

His companion wiped his hands on a black handkerchief. Blood didn't show on black. "Thanks for the concern, but the good engineer didn't attack me. He simply made the mistake of giving in to his curiosity. He wanted to see what the machine did once he put it together for me."

"And you couldn't let him live once he saw that." Jasper's tongue was thick in his dry mouth.

Dalton tossed the handkerchief aside. "Exactly. Word might get around, then everyone would want my new toy."

Jasper turned his head. If he hadn't given Finley the schematic, this man would still be alive. Dalton wouldn't have needed an expert to put the pieces together, and this man would be with his family right now. Instead, he'd no doubt be fished out of the harbor later today or tomorrow.

The sound of heavy footsteps signaled the arrival of Little Hank. Jasper wasn't surprised to see the giant. What did surprise him was that Mei hadn't come down. Surely she had heard the shot? Then again, she might figure it was safer to stay in her room. At least she didn't have to see the corpse on the floor.

"Where was she taken?" Dalton asked, glancing up from admiring his machine.

Hank wiped his nose with the back of his hand and sniffed. Jasper grimaced. "Kirby took her back to his place. Some bounty hunter's setup. Couldn't tell which cell."

"We'll have to figure that out." Dalton rubbed a hand over his jaw. There was gunpowder on his fingers. "How many guards?"

"Just Kirby, far as I could tell. Could be more."

"It doesn't matter." He stroked the assembled machine on the table before him. "This sweet little contraption will make everything all right."

"Are you sure of that?" Jasper asked, moving closer. He made an effort to avoid touching the body on the floor.

Dalton's light eyes twinkled as he shot him a sharp glance. "Dead certain."

★ ★ ★

Nikola Tesla was not known for being particularly gregarious, but when Emily, Sam and Griffin showed up at his lodgings early in the morning with the schematic Finley had dropped for Sam, he became almost animated.

The inventor paced the rug with the paper in hand, as though committing every bit of it to memory. Then he seemed to remember his company and begged their pardon. "Please, sit. May I offer you tea?"

Personally, at that moment Griffin would have preferred something stronger, but he accepted their host's hospitality and seated himself on the slightly worn sofa. He felt as anxious as Tesla appeared. Once they knew what the machine did, they would be better prepared to stop Dalton.

"Please, forgive me," Tesla went on. "It has been many months since I last saw this invention. It was stolen during a trip to San Francisco. You believe it is here in New York?"

Griffin nodded, ignoring that the inventor had a habit of compulsively adjusting the items around the tiny stove where he set his kettle to boil. "We do. Please, can you tell us what it does?"

"Of course. It is a Matter Transmutation device."

"It moves matter?" Emily inquired.

Tesla shook his head, looking momentarily frustrated with her. "Not in the way you think. It does not move matter from one location to another but allows matter to be moved."

Sam glanced at Griffin. "Isn't that the same thing?"

He was given an exasperated look by Emily. "He means that it makes it possible for matter to be displaced. Is that correct, sir?"

"Yes," Tesla replied with a nod. "If you directed the device at a wall, it would displace the particles of that wall so that they would no longer be tangible."

Griffin shook his head, uncertain he heard him correctly. "You mean that I could use this thing to walk through walls?"

The inventor nodded. "Precisely. As well as human flesh, if the machine is properly tuned. It was designed for warfare."

"Good Lord," Emily breathed as she and Griff exchanged horrified glances.

The machine would allow Dalton to walk into any vault he wanted. Locks would no longer be a problem.

Tesla obviously didn't share their concern. "But you say the device has been dismantled?"

Griffin nodded. "Yes. Into several sections."

"There are no instructions for the device. Unless this person knows how to put it together correctly, he will not be able to make use of it." Tesla took the boiling kettle from the stove. "Your Grace, I should very much like my machine back."

It was all Griffin could do not to laugh. "I will do my best to retrieve it for you, sir." He didn't bother to ask the man why he had invented such a contraption in the first place. There wasn't any point. Men with brilliant minds like Tesla did things because they could, because that was the way their genius worked. They were driven by their visions and compulsions to create.

Unfortunately, Griffin didn't share the older man's conviction that no one would be intelligent enough to put the machine together correctly. He wasn't about to underestimate Dalton.

Mr. Tesla offered him a cup of tea, and he took it, even though it would not be the same as the tea he was accustomed to. Tea abroad never tasted as good as what he had at home, even if it was the exact same tea.

Sam accepted a cup, as well, his big fingers circling the rim rather than attempting to hold the delicate handle. He had his gaze fixed firmly on Emily, as though gauging his own reaction on hers. Emily looked worried—more so than Griffin. Of course, she was a lot like Tesla in the way her mind worked. To her thinking, it wouldn't be that difficult to put that machine together and quickly figure out what it did.

Tesla joined them a moment or two later, seating himself on the opposite end of the sofa from Griffin. They sat in silence as they drank. When he turned his head, Griffin noticed that Tesla was watching him with a curious expression on his narrow face.

"Is there something you wish to say, Mr. Tesla?" he asked. Like, what the hell they were supposed to do now? There was only one thing to do—go to Kirby and get Finley back. She was the only one who could tell them if Dalton knew how to use the machine.

"Yes." The strange but brilliant man leaned forward, as though by taking a closer look he might discern what made Griffin work—as though he was the inner guts of a clockwork stripped bare. "Your abilities, they allow you to interact with the Aether, correct?"

Griffin nodded. "That is correct, yes."

"I have seen you use Aetheric energy to power my machines and to render them inactive, as though you emit some sort of mechanical-disruption field. Tell me, when you do these things, are you actually channeling the Aether through your body?"

"If you are asking if I'm a conduit for Aetheric energy, I suppose the answer is yes. I think of myself as something of a stone placed in a hearth—I will absorb the Aether just as that stone absorbs heat."

Tesla crossed his legs. "And like that stone, will you also explode if you absorb too much?"

Unbidden, thoughts of blowing all the water out of the pool in London and the destruction of The Machinist's lair flashed in Griffin's mind. "I assume so."

"So when you release the Aether, I assume it has to go somewhere. What happens then?"

If it were anyone else asking these questions, Griffin would tell them it was personal. He was normally suspicious of curious people, often assuming that they would inevitably want something from him if they knew too much about his abilities. Once, when he was a child, an old friend of his grandfather's had wanted to use him to contact his dead wife. Griffin had done so out of kindness, but then the old man kept coming back, slipping further and further away from his life, until communications with a ghost was all he had. When his father told the old man that Griffin would no longer work as a medium for him, the old man had gone mad and had to be escorted from the estate. He died shortly thereafter—by his own hand.

Griffin took a sip of tea and pushed the past to where it belonged. "I find water to be the best receptacle, though it has the unfortunate tendency to render everything rather damp."

"What if you were to direct it into a structure?"

He cleared his throat, uncertain if he should reveal more. "I would most likely raze it to the ground."

Tesla's eyes were bright, his face lit with excitement. "Aetheric oscillation," he said in a slightly reverent tone, moustache twitching. "You inspired me, Your Grace. I have recently begun work on a machine that I believe will absorb Aetheric energy much like you and then expel that same energy."

"To what end?" Griffin asked. "I could see it being used to replace the treacherous practices now in place for blasting out railway lines or in building demolition, perhaps."

"Or in war," Tesla added. "Imagine if an army marched on New York, one could Aetherically destroy the Brooklyn

Bridge to prevent penetration of Manhattan Island, but without the risk to life or other property that comes with explosives."

War? Griffin didn't like that idea at all.

"Entire cities might be toppled," Tesla went on. "But that's not the manner in which I would use such a creation, no. Imagine being able to peel back the earth's crust like one peels an orange. Only wonder at what discoveries await there!"

For the first time since meeting the man, Griffin wondered if Tesla wasn't a little mad. Certainly he was brilliant, and with brilliance there was often a certain detachment from the rest of the world, but wondering at building something that could destroy the earth, just because you wanted to see if you could build it, well, that was just asking for trouble.

And for that matter alone, Griffin did not tell the man that the Aether was an organic energy, and while small amounts could be harnessed by machines, even manipulated—such as with Tesla's device that could have brought down the building and worse—the amount needed to topple an entire city or split the earth's crust could only be absorbed, and therefore unleashed, by organic material.

Basically, that to the best of his knowledge, he was the only being or thing on the planet capable of such destruction—and even then, taking in that much Aether would undoubtedly kill him.

No, he didn't say any of that. Instead, he raised his teacup in salute. "I wish you the best of luck with that, sir." Meanwhile, he knew in the back of his mind that if Tesla ever did succeed in creating such a machine, he would personally hunt it down and destroy it.

"Now," he said, after taking a drink of tea, "I assume that we need to get close to this machine of yours to stop it."

"No, not necessarily." Tesla smoothed the fingers of his left hand over his moustache. "The device was designed to be operated up close or at a distance. Your criminal will not need to have it on his person to use it."

Griffin clenched his jaw. Nothing had been easy during this trip. Not a bloody thing. And why was Tesla smiling at him? Did the man not realize they were shagged?

"What's so amusing, sir?" He ignored the sharp look Emily shot him for speaking so hotly to the inventor.

Tesla chuckled. "Because it should be obvious to you, Your Grace. *You* do not need to touch the device to stop it. You are one with the Aether. All you must do is locate its signal on the Aetheric plane and use your incredible talent to render it inert."

Had he said what Griffin thought he said? Griffin couldn't help but chuckle. In fact, they all did.

Finally something he could control.

Since Whip Kirby wasn't affiliated with the New York City police, he didn't take Finley to the Tombs, but rather to the set of rooms he'd rented from a bounty-hunter associate, complete with holding cells in the cellar and on the ground floor. The ground floor ones obviously being for the less dangerous captures.

At the moment, Finley wasn't locked up on either floor. She sat at the table with Whip, enjoying a cup of coffee and a hot breakfast of griddle cakes and sausage. She had spent the night on a cot in the small spare bedroom, and she'd been grateful for it, sleeping far later than she should have. Once she realized Kirby meant her no harm, it had been easy to relax. They had stayed up fairly late, talking. She had tried to contact Griffin, but her P.T. was still a bit dodgy, and she didn't know if the message made it to him.

"You don't think I'll run away?" she had asked when he showed her to the guest room.

He shrugged his broad shoulders. For an old man, he wasn't bad looking. He had to be at least thirty. "Don't matter much to me if you stay or leave. But it might be more convincing if you let Dalton come looking for you."

She made a scoffing noise. "He won't come for me."

"I think you underestimate yourself. Dalton considers you his. He sent men to London to fetch Jasper. He'll come for you."

Finley didn't have the energy to argue with him. "Do you really want to clear Jasper's name?"

He nodded. "I do."

"Why?" she asked as she sat down on the bed.

Kirby leaned against the door frame and folded his arms

over his chest. "Because I married his sister six months ago and I promised her I'd find the real murderer."

Her jaw dropped. "Does Jasper know you're family?"

The toe of one of his scuffed boots rubbed against the threshold. "Nope. He doesn't know he's going to be an uncle soon, either. My wife hopes he'll be able to come visit us after the baby's born."

Finley's throat was surprisingly tight. "I see." If she had doubted him before, she didn't anymore.

He gave her something to wear to bed and then retired to his own room. Finley wondered if he spent the night listening to see if she'd leave.

And now here she was, sitting at his table, eating the food he cooked. The man made a delicious breakfast.

A knock on the door made them both freeze. Finley had her cup halfway to her mouth as her gaze locked with Whip's.

"Last cell on the right," the older man commanded, not waiting to see if she obeyed before drawing his gun and pushing back his chair.

Finley raced to the other side of the building where the cells were. She had to go through a heavy door, which would be locked if there were prisoners in residence. There were only four cells on the ground floor; all were empty and clean, awaiting another occupant.

She ducked into the last cell on the right of the corridor and closed the bars behind her. Then she sat down on the cot—which was nowhere near as comfortable as the one she had slept on—and waited, heart in her throat. Was it Dalton? She was worried for Mr. Kirby. Or was it Griffin? Would he be ashamed of her? Or was it the police, coming to take her to a real jail?

What did it say about her that she almost wished it was the police?

By the time Griff and the others managed to get away from Tesla, it was late morning. Kirby welcomed them into his lodgings/jail with a warm but expectant smile—as if he'd been waiting for them.

Griffin didn't waste any time. "Where is she?"

Kirby smiled at them and arched a brow when Sam had to duck his head to come through the door. Sam wore his customary scowl—only a little darker at the moment.

"She's not in shackles, if that's what you're thinking." He jerked his head toward a heavy door. "She's down there. I had her take to a cell until we knew who our company was."

Emily gestured back the way they'd come. "You need a scope on that door—something so you can peer through and see who's come calling."

The lawman nodded thoughtfully. "I'll pass that suggestion on to my friend who owns this place." Then to Griffin, who was grinding his teeth in impatience, "C'mon, I'll take you to Miss Finley."

It was about bloody time. Griffin only nodded in response and followed the older man through the heavy door. Emily and Sam came, as well. They walked down a hall flanked by empty cells, but they'd only gone as far as the second when he spotted her.

She was wearing the gown she had worn the night before, and it was badly wrinkled. Her long honey-blond hair hung in a tangled mess around her shoulders, the black stripe a dark contrast. Her eyes were huge as her gaze locked with his. She looked almost as though she expected him to be angry with her.

He was—or rather he had been. He'd made himself furious, thinking about all the things that might have happened. It was either be angry or terrified, so he'd chosen the former. However, now he didn't seem capable of feeling anything other than relief at the sight of her—and a sharp happiness, which felt like a pinch in his chest.

"Finley!" Emily squealed and bounded over to the bars. She reached through when Finley approached and grabbed the other girl's hands.

Finley blinked rapidly—trying not to cry, Griffin realized. "Em. It's so good to see you. You too, Sam."

Sam grinned, softening his features. "You look good behind bars."

She laughed at that, but her smile faded when she turned to Griffin. "You lot shouldn't be here. Dalton might be watching."

"Hang Dalton," Griffin replied. He couldn't quite meet

her gaze. "I… We had to make certain you were all right. What's this all about, Kirby?"

The lawman shrugged. "Figured if it seemed like I had arrested her, they wouldn't call for the cops. I might not be the best of hosts, but this is a damn sight better than the Tombs."

The thought of Finley being in that place was enough to turn Griffin's stomach. It would be easy to blame himself for this, but he wasn't going to go there. Finley had known what she was doing, and he wouldn't have been able to keep her from it. If he was going to blame anyone, he'd blame Dalton.

"You're right," he agreed, nodding. "Thank you for looking after her."

Kirby pulled a ring of keys from his belt. "Why don't I let her out, and the five of us have some coffee and eats while we compare information? I'm hoping you've figured out what Dalton's up to."

"A little," Griffin allowed. He watched as Kirby unlocked the cell door so Finley could come out. He was barely aware of his feet moving until he stood right in front of her.

No turning back now, he thought, and he hugged her. In front of three witnesses—two of whom were bound to tease him mercilessly for this—he pulled her close and rested his cheek against her hair. He could have stayed like that forever, but he let her go after a second or two. Her hands slid over his shoulders and down his arms. She didn't seem to want to let go of him, either.

They returned to the main area of the apartments and sat

down at the table. Kirby took away the cold remains of Finley's meal with the promise to make more. "Sorry, folks, but breakfast's all I know how to cook."

"I never turn down bacon," Sam allowed.

Emily rolled her eyes at him. "You never turn down anything edible."

Griffin glanced at Finley with a grin. She smiled back. Sam and Emily's banter was always good for defusing an awkward moment. He didn't like it when things were awkward between Finley and himself, but they couldn't seem to help themselves.

As Kirby cooked, he revealed his surprising family connection to the Renns. No wonder he wanted to clear Jasper's name. His sister—and the rest of the family—must be beside themselves with worry. If the marshal had revealed this earlier, it would have kept them from doubting him.

In turn, Griffin related what they had discovered from Tesla in regards to the mysterious machine.

"Isn't that a bit of a coincidence?" Finley asked, speaking for the first time since leaving the cell. She glanced at Griffin, then Emily. "That it just happened to be built by a man you know?"

Emily's pink lips curved slightly. "I prefer to think of it as my sweet Irish luck, my friend. It might seem odd, but Tesla and Edison are the two minds behind the most amazing inventions in this country. Dalton must have heard of the machine and what it was supposed to do—why else steal it? At least now we know what it does."

"Mmm," Griffin agreed as he took a drink of Kirby's excellent coffee. "But still no closer to knowing what he intends to do with it."

"Isn't it obvious?" Kirby asked. "There's not a vault or train—anything—that he can't simply walk right into whenever he pleases."

"Dalton thinks of himself as special," Griffin replied. "He doesn't strike me as the type to simply rob a place because he can. There's no challenge in that. He wants attention, but he also wants respect. No, he'll go after high-profile victims—the kinds of robberies that anyone else would be foolish to attempt."

Finley nodded. "Griff's right. Dalton's vain. He'll want to cause a fuss, right off the mark."

"And what better place to do that than in New York City?" Whip flipped the eggs frying on the stove and turned to Griffin. "You've been something of a celebrity since your arrival. Do you know of any highfalutin shindigs coming up?"

"Dalton stole plans to the Museum of Science and Invention, but from what I've heard, there's nothing that would be of value to a man like him on display there."

Whip's eyes lit up. "Isn't that where they're displaying that rare diamond that's come to town? It's an odd color or something. That Astor-Prynn gent's in charge."

Griffin froze. He had received an invitation to the event,

but he hadn't opened it, because attending would mean spending more time with Lydia. If he had opened it, he would have seen the location. Even though he'd been told about the viewing, he'd never been told where it was.

It was enough to make him want to smack himself in the forehead for being so ruddy stupid.

"Dalton must be planning to steal the diamond," Finley said. "It's flashy, plus he'll have a very upscale audience. It's the kind of thing that would make him famous."

"It would at that," Whip agreed. "And if he's got a machine that allows him to walk through walls, he can get in right easy."

"Not just that," Emily added before Griffin could. "He could reach right into any display or locked box he wanted."

Anticipation stirred in Griffin's belly, just as it always did when he was close to capturing a criminal. But it wasn't just for that. Once Dalton was gone, Finley would come back.

He really wanted her back.

Kirby began setting plates of bacon and eggs and fried potatoes in front of them, and they ate while they discussed Dalton and his plans. Finley told them about the barbaric collar the outlaw made Mei wear and how he used Jasper's feelings for the girl to manipulate him.

Sam shook his shaggy dark head. "There's always a girl."

Emily nudged him hard with her elbow, but the big lad hardly seemed to notice. In truth, he used the fact that her arm was busy to steal a forkful of golden-brown potatoes from her plate.

His joke led Griffin to reveal to Finley what Kirby had told them about the murder Jasper had been accused of committing. What surprised him was that she knew all about it—Jasper had told her.

"Mei and I can't stand each other," she admitted, "but I don't blame her for plugging that fellow full of holes. I'd have done the same myself." A shadow seemed to pass over her face, and Griffin wondered if she was thinking about what she had done to the son of her last employer when the young man attacked her.

"Me, too," Emily agreed.

Sam's scowl returned. "You'd have to do it before I ripped his arms off."

Griffin winced. It was one thing to hear someone make such an overly exaggerated comment and another to know they could actually do it.

A knock on the door put an end to the conversation, and they all snapped to attention.

Quickly, Kirby gathered up their plates and piled them in the sink. "In the back, all of you."

"You think it's Dalton?" Griffin asked, holding the heavy door open for the others.

The marshal met his gaze with his flinty stare. "I'm expecting him."

Griffin only nodded and followed his friends down the

hall. It would be better to have the element of surprise against Dalton. He wouldn't expect Griffin to have come for Finley.

The girls stepped into the cell Finley had been in earlier, while Sam stood just in the entrance of it and Griffin out in the hall. He didn't want to risk the door closing and shutting them all in. They'd be easy targets then.

His gaze slipped to the wall of the cell behind Finley. What the—? He shook his head.

"What?" Sam demanded, glancing over his shoulder.

"The wall. I thought it moved." As soon as he spoke, the strange phenomenon happened again, only this time he was certain of it. The wall rippled.

"Bugger," Griff muttered.

Dalton had arrived.

As if by magic, a figure literally stepped right through that back wall. It was a huge man Griffin recognized as one of Dalton's men. Right behind him came another, then Jasper, then Dalton.

In the other part of the building, there was a commotion, and before Griffin could yell for Kirby, the door burst open and Whip came running in. Past him, Griffin could see a man lying on the floor. Obviously Dalton had sent a distraction for the marshal while he used Tesla's device on the building's outer wall.

Kirby pulled out his gun and aimed it at Dalton, but the criminal had already pulled a pistol of his own and had it leveled not at Kirby, but at Emily. "Put it away, Kirby, or the little redhead gets a haircut."

Griffin stiffened. He thought he heard Sam growl. This feeling-helpless shite was getting to be a bit much. He could try to summon enough Aether to disarm Dalton, but he'd never tried focusing it down to a single bolt of energy. There was too much of a chance he'd seriously hurt his friends.

"Jasper, take Miss Finley outside, will you?" Dalton asked. Griffin's gaze jumped to the fellow standing at Dalton's side. Jasper's face was pale, and when his friend's gaze locked with his, Griffin saw anger and helplessness there. He knew the feeling.

"No one's going anywhere," Whip informed Dalton in a cold tone and pulled back the hammer on his pistol. "Least of all you, Dalton."

Dalton responded by doing the same to his. "Don't think I won't kill her. Should I prove it by putting one in her leg first?"

Finley stepped forward, and from the look on her face, Griffin knew she would gladly snap Dalton's arm in half. He shook his head ever so slightly, telling her not to give herself away. Dalton might just as easily shoot her—or use that damn machine—and he would never forgive himself if anything happened to her.

The second Dalton squeezed the trigger, Sam stepped in front of Emily, taking the bullet meant for her in the leg. He didn't even stumble.

But he ripped the cot from the bolts that held it to the floor and threw it.

Startled—horrified—Dalton fired again and began pushing his people toward the back wall. "Go!" he shouted.

The second bullet hit Sam, as well. This time, in the shoulder. Still, the large lad did not falter. He kept moving toward Dalton, despite Emily shouting at him not to. One of Dalton's men pushed the cot back at him from where it had fallen, trying to trip him with it. Sam grabbed the bed once more and used it to throw the man against the wall.

Dalton raised his gun again. The muzzle was pointing straight at Griffin. For a split second, Griffin felt his mortality slip, and the Aether pulled at him. If only he had something he could charge and throw. If only he was as physically tough as Sam.

Just as he braced himself, committed himself to at least attempt to bend the Aether into a single bolt of energy, Finley grabbed Dalton's arm, lowering it. "We've got to go," she told him. *"Now."*

Dalton nodded. He backed toward the wall as Jasper shoved Finley through it, as though it was nothing more than fog. Only half of Dalton remained when he raised his weapon one more time and fired. Whip Kirby fell to the floor.

He'd been shot in the chest.

Chapter 14

Emily never traveled without her bag of "goodies," as she called them—basic tools that allowed her to work on almost any type of problem, mechanical or organic. She also carried Organites, the primordial ooze from which all life was said to have sprung.

It was fortunate for Whip Kirby that the bullet went all the way through, just below his right collarbone. Sam placed the man on the mattress that had fallen off the cot and ripped open his shirt and leather vest, as though they were tissue paper.

After cleaning the wound, Emily was able to stick the nozzle of her special Organite syringe directly into the bloody hole and inject the unconscious lawman. Sam and Griffin helped her with bandaging and then took care of cleanup while Emily sat with Whip.

"So I guess we can say that Tesla's machine works," Sam commented as he washed the blood from his hands at the sink.

Griffin joined him and chuckled drily at the irony in his tone. "We can at that." He glanced at his friend's bloody pant leg. "Do you need medical attention?"

"I'm fine. Dalton pointed a gun at Em." All trace of humor was gone from his voice, replaced by a hardness that froze Griffin's insides. Dalton was lucky Sam hadn't gotten to him, because Sam would have killed him.

"We'll get him," Griffin promised, even though he had no bloody idea just how to make that happen.

Sam offered him the towel. "If not for Finley, he would have shot you, too."

Griffin kept his gaze on his hands as he dried them. "I know."

"Hope she doesn't break Dalton's neck before I get a chance to."

A reluctant grin took hold of his mouth. "That would be unfortunate. For Dalton."

They shared a grin—the sort that couldn't be helped after such a stressful event. Griffin would never admit it, but he was still a little jittery. He didn't know if it was adrenaline or the Aether, but it ran through his veins like an army of sprinting spiders.

Did Dalton know they were onto him? Did he suspect that Finley was one of them, rather than someone Griffin tried to press for information? If so, Finley could be in danger. She could take care of herself, but Dalton wouldn't hesitate to kill her.

Which meant that they would have to act soon. There had to be a way to extricate Finley and Jasper from Dalton's control. They knew what the machine did, and they had a fair idea of where he was going to strike, so Finley didn't need to be there anymore.

"What do we do about Whip?" Emily asked when she joined the two of them.

"How is he?" Griffin asked.

"Still unconscious, of course. But the beasties have already begun to work their magic. He'll be stiff and sore for a day or two, but at least there's little risk of infection, and his flesh has started to repair itself."

Sam ran a large hand over her hair. It was an oddly gentle and intimate action, which embarrassed Griffin to witness. But it spoke volumes that Sam didn't care if Griffin noticed or not. Usually the bigger lad was terribly self-conscious and private.

"You have such a big, fat brain," he told her. It was obvious from his tone and his smile that Sam meant it as a compliment.

She rolled her large blue eyes at him. "Fool," she muttered, but the only heat to her words was in her flushed cheeks.

Sam grinned. Such an amazing transformation happened when he smiled—it changed his face so much, made him look the teenager he was. Usually he stomped about looking ten years older, for all his brooding.

"What I meant," she said, leaning into Sam's touch, "was what are we going to do with Whip? Even though he's recovering, it doesn't seem right to just leave him here, but it's going to look odd, us lugging a shot-up cowboy back to the hotel."

Griffin nodded. "There's no knowing if Dalton's gang will return to finish him."

"I'll stay with him," Sam offered. "I can handle whatever Dalton throws our way. Wouldn't mind a crack at the knuckle-dragger he's got working for him."

Emily's face pinched. "I don't like the idea of you being here alone."

He smiled, obviously both amused and touched by her concern. "I'll be fine. Plus, I won't be alone."

"An unconscious man doesn't count as company or protection," she informed him.

"Em, I can look after myself—and an unconscious man." As if to prove his point, Sam's statement was followed by a *plink*. The three of them looked down to see a bloody bullet on the floor by Sam's feet.

"Must be the one that was in my leg," he remarked, as though bullets fell out of him every day.

A horrified gasp tore from Emily's mouth as she reached for him. "Oh, Lord! Sam, I'm so sorry. In the flurry to help

Mr. Kirby, I forgot that you were shot. How could I have been so stupid? Let me take a look at you."

Sam chuckled. "Nothing to look at." As if on cue, another bullet popped out from somewhere around his shoulder. Sam caught it before it hit the floor. And held it up between his thumb and forefinger. "See? That's the last one."

It was so absurd, Griffin couldn't help but burst out laughing. Sam looked so comical, standing there, holding up the bullet that had just popped out of him with all the discomfort of a drop of water falling from a tap.

"Don't laugh!" Emily chastised, swatting him on the arm. "It's not funny."

"But it is!" Griffin insisted, eyes watering. Sam began to laugh, as well, and soon the two of them were holding each other up, laughing like lunatics.

Emily shook her head at them and, at some point in their foolish fit, walked away from them in disgust. Griffin and Sam kept going. They hadn't laughed much at all since Sam was killed by an automaton seven months ago. Emily saved him by replacing his heart with a mechanical one, but the attack had changed Sam—made him more serious.

When their laughter faded, they stood shoulder to shoulder, slumped against the counter.

"So you'll stay with Whip long enough for him to wake and ascertain if he's well enough to be left alone."

Sam nodded. "If he's not, I'll bring him back to the hotel

with me. I may, anyway. It wouldn't hurt to have his input into whatever plan you're scheming up."

Of course everyone would assume he had a plan, Griffin thought with a sigh. He supposed he'd better start thinking of one. "Right. Always helpful to have another brain involved." He clapped his friend on the back. "Any trouble, you send for us, understood?"

Sam's dark gaze met his—intently. "I'll send for you."

"Oh, no." Griffin shook his head. "Don't put that on me. I'll be the one who has to tell Emily you want her to stay behind—and you know how she'll react."

Broad shoulders shrugged. "So don't tell her."

"You don't want to do that, Sam. I know you want to protect her, but she'll not take it well, and you know it."

"You don't know what it's like to worry," Sam moaned, running a hand over his jaw. "I'm terrified she'll get hurt."

Didn't know what it was like to worry? Griffin punched him in the arm—hard. It was like punching a wall. "You great arse. I worry about all of you all the time. I've barely eaten or slept since Finley infiltrated Dalton's gang."

Sam made a face. "Finley can look after herself. She could rip Dalton's head off."

Griffin fixed him with a pointed gaze. "She's still human, Sam. Still mortal. And now Dalton knows we know her by sight."

"Bugger."

"Exactly," Griffin agreed, fighting down the fear that

churned in his stomach. "I have to get her away from him. Fast."

Sam shook his head. "Always the hero. Now take Emmy back to the hotel where I know she'll be safe."

"Right," Griffin said, clearing his throat. A bloody hero? "Hopefully Dalton doesn't know where we're staying. Yet."

He waited for Emily to check Kirby's condition one last time, and then the two of them exited the building, and Griffin hailed a cab on the street.

Once back at the hotel, they made themselves comfortable in Griffin's room, both of their portable telegraphs out and within easy reach should anyone try to contact them.

"What do we do now?" Emily asked, slumping onto the bed. "Go after Finley and Jasper?"

Griffin took a pack of cards from the desk. "We do what you and I do best, Emmy. We think. We think, and we wait." They could hardly go charging after Dalton when he had a machine that he could easily use to kill them. As much as he might want to, it just wasn't smart.

She made a face—it was as close to a pout as he'd ever seen on her. "I hate waiting."

Griffin sighed and sat down opposite her. "Me, too, love. Me, too."

Finley didn't get a chance to talk to Jasper immediately when they arrived back at Dalton's. First, Dalton wanted to talk to her. She tried to beg off to go have a bath, but he told her it would just take a second and then she could go get cleaned up.

"What was the Duke of Greythorne doing at Kirby's?" He asked with fake pleasantness.

Finley shrugged. "Kirby told him he had me. Mr. Fancy-Pants asked me about Jasper—and what you had planned. Didn't believe me when I told him I didn't know."

He stared at her with those unnerving eyes. "Which is exactly why I never tell anyone my plans. Good girl. Go ahead and go get your bath. I want everyone to convene in the library in an hour. It's time I told you our next move."

With a promise to be there, Finley went to her room, gathered fresh clothing and went to draw a bath. She didn't linger in the hot, soapy water. Dalton seemed to believe her story, but he believed it a tad too readily for her liking.

Once she was clean and had dried off, she quickly dressed in shin-length pantaloons, high boots and an Oriental blouse of bright blue, embroidered silk. Over that, she laced a black corset. Then she twisted her damp hair up on top of her head and secured it with one of her favorite chopsticks. Now she was ready for whatever Dalton threw at her.

Quietly, she opened the door and peered out into the corridor. No one was there. She slipped out and tiptoed along the carpet to the room she knew was Jasper's. She had remembered to bring her portable telegraph with her in case they needed to contact Griffin.

She tapped softly upon the door. It flew open while her

knuckles were still on it. Jasper stood on the other side of the threshold, a disappointed look on his face.

"Hoping for someone shorter and Chinese?" she inquired, tone deliberately dry as she stepped inside.

Jasper closed the door. "Maybe. How are you? Kirby treat you okay?"

She nodded and rubbed a hand over the back of her neck. There was no easy way to do this, and she wasn't even certain it was her place to reveal it. "Jasper, Whip Kirby is married to your sister, Ellen. That's why he's here. He's trying to clear you of the murder charge."

His normally tanned cheeks paled. "No."

"It's true. You're going to be an uncle soon. Kirby promised your sister he'd help you so you'd be able to meet your niece or nephew someday."

Jasper shook his head, an expression of disbelief on his face. "I'm going to be an uncle?" His gaze snapped up. "Are you certain he wasn't lying?"

"He let me sleep in the guest room. It's only by chance I was actually in the cell when you showed up."

"About that—what did you tell Dalton about Griffin?"

"That he had come there hoping I'd give him information about you."

"Do you think he bought it?"

"Maybe. It's doubtful, though. We need to get out of here before he decides he can't trust either of us. He'd kill us both without blinking."

"You go. I'm going to stay with Mei. If we make it through this, I'm going to ask her to go back to England—or go somewhere else—with me."

What she thought of that must have been written on her face.

"You don't think she'll come."

"Jasper, my friend, I think many things, only half of which are correct—if I'm lucky. I don't presume to know what Mei will do. You'll have to ask her and let her make her own decision."

"No wonder he likes you," he mused. "You must keep him on his toes."

"Who? Dalton?" She waved a hand in the air. "Dalton likes any girl he thinks might slap him."

"Not Dalton. Griff. I bet he's never met a gal like you before."

"I should hope not," she replied glibly, but heat filled her cheeks. "Nature couldn't possibly make two mistakes like me."

"You're not a mistake. Don't you ever think of yourself that way. You're exactly as you ought to be."

She glanced down at her toes as she shook her head, embarrassed by his flattery. "Sometimes I think awful things."

"Yeah, but you always do the right one, Miss Finley. And even if you mess up, you fix it. That makes you a good person, in my mind."

A bright smile spread across her face. He was officially her new favorite person. "Thank you, Jasper. That's lovely of you to say."

"It's true. And I think you're right to want to get out of here as soon as possible. Dalton already shot the man he hired to put that infernal machine together."

Finley's brows arched. "Dead?"

Jasper nodded. "Very much so."

So Dalton really was as terrible as everyone thought. How had she ever thought of herself as a match for him? She could never kill anyone unless she had to. She sincerely doubted Dalton had killed the man in self-defense. She had seen how easily he threatened Emily—something she would make him pay for—and how he hadn't hesitated to shoot Sam. He would have shot Griffin, too.

All right, so maybe she *could* kill someone fairly easily. Right now, it was tempting to march downstairs and beat Dalton until the devil himself came to claim him.

Speaking of Dalton… Her gaze flickered to the clock on the mantel. "We need to go downstairs. He's going to tell us his plans for the machine. Once I know what he intends to do, I'll make my escape." She put her hand on his shoulder. "Promise me you'll run if things go sour."

He nodded. "I will." But she knew he wouldn't go without Mei.

She went downstairs first so they wouldn't arouse suspicion by arriving together. Dalton, Little Hank and the other men, whose names she couldn't remember, were already in the library. Mei and Jasper arrived a few seconds later, arm in arm.

The smaller girl spotted Finley and glared at her. It was very difficult to sympathize with her when she made Finley want to slap her stupid.

Dalton called for everyone's attention. Finley tried to keep her attention centered on him, but Jasper looked so downtrodden, it was difficult to look away.

"Obviously today was a great success," Dalton said with exaggerated bravado, a drink in his hand. "The device has been recovered and proven to be a great success, thanks to our old friend Jasper Renn."

Finley frowned. There was a strange light in Dalton's eyes when he looked at Jasper—a sardonic twist to his mouth. Where was he going with this? That wasn't praise in his tone.

Suddenly, there was a pistol in Dalton's other hand. "And now that he's outlived his usefulness, it's time for our old friend to pay for screwing with me in the first place!" Dalton's voice had grown louder with every word until he shouted the last.

No one but Finley seemed the least bit surprised by this turn of events, not even Jasper. That meant that Jasper must have expected this would happen—and that Dalton had planned it with his cronies all along.

"But first," Dalton continued in a much calmer but still-flamboyant tone, "there's something I want Jas to see. Mei, come here."

Finley held her breath. Was it wrong to hope that maybe Dalton would do them all a favor and shoot Mei, too? She frowned as every instinct she had screamed for her to run. The tiny little girl moved to stand before Dalton, who handed her his drink, which she then placed on a nearby table. His hand free, he reached down and cupped the back of her head, pulling her close to plant a very passionate kiss on her lips.

There were moments in a person's life that they would carry with them until their dying day, and Finley knew the moment Jasper's heart broke would be one of those for her. The color drained from his handsome face, and his eyes— usually full of charm and laughter—flared bright with pain before suddenly going flat and dead.

At that moment, he looked as though Dalton shooting him would be a kindness.

But the two sadistic creatures weren't done with him yet. Mei wore a slightly smug expression as she reached up, around her neck and removed the clockwork collar, which had supposedly held her life in its cogs. She tossed it to the floor at Jasper's feet.

"She isn't yours," Dalton bragged. "She hasn't been yours in a very long time. Not since she killed Venton for me. Thank you, by the way, for being such a hero and trying to take the blame."

"Right," said Finley. She was not going to listen to any more of this, and neither was Jasper. "We're done." Jasper was not going to die today, not if she could help it.

Dalton's attention snapped to her—as did his pistol. "Yes, you are. You had me fooled, you slag. Did you really expect me to believe the duke was only interested in Jasper? Do you really think I'm that stupid?"

"I had hoped," she replied lightly. Then she stopped thinking and simply struck—like a snake—and seized the wrist of the hand holding the pistol.

She snapped it like a twig.

Dalton screamed—not surprisingly, like a girl—and crumpled to his knees. Jasper snatched up the dropped pistol, which was his to begin with, and brandished it as Dalton's gang stared at him and Finley in shock.

Mei was the first to move—and Finley was too late seeing it, but she felt it when the smaller girl landed a stunning roundhouse kick to her temple. It would have knocked a normal human out, but Finley, Mei was about to learn, was not normal. She did, however, stagger a few feet backward under the force of the attack.

Shaking her head, Finley shook off the pain, and when Mei came at her again, she was ready. It took a fist to the throat to make her realize that Mei was indeed the one who had taught Jasper to fight. She was not an opponent to underestimate.

Finley squared off. Out of the corner of her eye, she saw Jasper—or a streak she thought was Jasper—take out two of Dalton's henchmen with lightning-quick ease. It was about time the cowboy showed his stuff. When Mei launched herself at her once again, Finley was prepared and punched the girl in the face before she had a chance to take another swing. Mei recovered quickly and flew up into the air as though she had wings, her leg whipping out to deliver a powerful kick.

But Finley caught her by the ankle and whipped her around hard, releasing her so that she flew back against the wall before sliding down, into a stunned heap.

"Finley!" Jasper shouted.

She ducked and whirled around just in time to see Little Hank level a gun in her direction. Before she could react, she was caught in a rush of wind that sent her soaring backward. There was the crash of glass, a stinging in her back, and then she hit the ground hard, sending stabs of pain from her waist to her shoulders. Jasper sprawled on top of her.

"Sorry," he said, breathless. "I meant to be on the bottom when we fell."

Finley grinned at him. "Worse places to be, my friend. Think those fast feet of yours can get us out of here before they open fire?" Above them, she could see Little Hank rushing toward the window they'd smashed through.

Jasper pointed his pistol at the top of the window and fired, sending a spray of splintered wood into the room and driving the behemoth back. "Let's see," he said as they quickly untangled themselves and jumped to their feet. He turned his back to her. "Climb on."

He didn't have to tell her twice. "The Waldorf-Astoria," Finley cried as she leaped onto his back and wrapped arms and legs around him. Then she hung on for dear life as Jasper took off running—faster than any horse or velocycle she'd ever been on. Tears streamed down her face because of the wind, but she didn't dare lift a hand to wipe them away—didn't know if she could lift her hand.

Jasper didn't stop until they reached the hotel lift. The operator's face turned white when he saw them—probably because both of them had blood on their faces and their hair looked as though they'd been caught in a hurricane.

They went to Griffin's room first. Never had Finley been so glad to see someone as she was to see the Duke of Greythorne. She threw her arms around his neck and hugged him for all she was worth. He hugged her back.

Then he froze. "Finley?"

She pulled back. His face was white, his eyes wide. "What is it?"

He held up his hand—the one that had, just seconds before, rested on her back. It was covered in blood. "Turn around."

Finley did as he commanded, a little ball of worry lying hard in her stomach. His expression scared her. "Blast it, Griffin King, what's the matter?"

"You've glass in your back, love."

"I know. Jasper and I dived through a window, which was unfortunately closed at the time. Can't you pick them out?" She turned and saw his ashen face.

"No," he rasped. "I can't."

Chapter 15

Emily performed the surgery on the desk in Griffin's room.

"Griffin King," she said, hands poised over Finley's bare and bloody back, "if you don't stop pacing and fretting…"

Griffin froze at the threat in her voice. He didn't doubt that she would banish him from the room, and then he wouldn't be there for Finley if she needed him. Not that she was aware enough to know if he was there or not—Emily had given her chloroform to put her to sleep so there was no danger of the shards moving and severing her spine.

It didn't matter that Emily was "fairly" certain that, even if the glass did move and do the worst, she would only have to secure the severed flesh together and Finley would heal. It didn't matter that Finley was amazingly strong. What mattered was that she was hurt and he couldn't help her.

They had all been hurt recently, and some of those hurts

had been life threatening. Who was he to ask his friends to put themselves at such risk? And what for? A country that would probably be terrified of them if they knew what they could do. It didn't seem right or fair, but they did it anyway. And he didn't have to ask why. They did it for him.

All this guilt and responsibility sitting on his shoulders was beginning to feel very heavy.

"What can I do?" he asked. "I need to do something for her."

Emily poured Listerine on Finley's back to clean the wounds and wash away the blood. "Come sit beside her. Hold her hand."

He did. It didn't even occur to him that seeing her naked skin, let alone being so close to it, was highly improper. He had thought about seeing her undressed—what bloke wouldn't?—but this was not how.

He pulled up a chair, sat down by her head and held one of her hands, which dangled over the side of the desk. There was blood on the carpet, and he didn't care. He could afford to replace it if the hotel charged him. What he couldn't replace was Finley.

"Stop being so melodramatic," Emily scolded as she dropped a piece of glass from her forceps into the rubbish bin. "Saints preserve us, lad. You look like you're at her grave. You need to stop behaving like everything that happens is your fault. We all have our own minds, you know. In fact,

I recall Finley went off and set this plan in motion without you being none the wiser. She knew what she was doing."

"I still feel responsible."

She pursed her lips as she nipped another sliver of glass. "Yes, well, I think you *like* feeling responsible. Just so ye know, it's not a terribly attractive trait in a man, this brooding and moaning."

"This, coming from the girl who thinks the sun rises and sets on Sam Morgan? Bit hypocritical, don't you think?"

She blushed, the pink obliterating her freckles. "Sam wasn't always a brooder. You, on the other hand, have always welcomed the weight of the world. There's nothing wrong with wanting to be a hero, Griffin. Just see that you don't end up a martyr in the meanwhile."

There was nothing he could say to that because she was completely right, and he felt like an arse for it. So he remained silent but not brooding.

An eternity later, Emily finished removing all the glass from Finley's back and draped a sheet over the sleeping girl. Then she took Griffin by the hand and pulled him over to the bed where the two of them sat side by side.

"You care about her, don't you?" Emily asked, nodding at Finley.

"I care about all of you."

"But you don't want to be kissing Sam or me."

"Hell, no."

Emily laughed. "I didn't t'ink so. So what's the problem, lad?"

He glanced at Finley's prone form. A little blood had soaked through the sheet that covered her. It turned his stomach, despite knowing that her wounds had already begun to mend once more. Her body had even tried to start healing around the glass fragments.

"What if it turns out that her darker nature is her true self? What if she decides she'd rather be bad than good?"

The expression on her face spoke volumes; she thought he was an idiot. "Griff, my friend, if she wanted that, she would have gone that way weeks ago. She wouldn't be with us now."

"I just don't know if I can trust her to do the right thing." He looked away. "I don't like it."

"You think I don't wonder if Sam's going to run off and get mixed up with the wrong sort again?" she asked. "You think I don't wonder if someday he's going to decide that he can't forgive me for turning him into a mandroid? Everyone has doubts, lad. What you have to decide is if the risk is worth it. Is she?"

He glanced again at Finley, thought of that sharp pain in his chest when he saw the glass in her back—how he'd actually prayed for her to be all right. If Dalton had hurt her, he would have not only brought the house down on the bounder, he would have ripped him apart—just as Sam had threatened.

"Yes," he whispered. "She is."

★ ★ ★

Jasper was very much aware of Sam watching him as he cleaned the pistol he'd managed to take back from Dalton. With any luck he'd be able to retrieve the other, as well. If not, he'd have to hire Emily to build a replacement.

"You got a problem, Morgan?" he asked, without looking up.

"Just wondering what happened to seize up that normally flapping tongue of yours."

"Maybe it's the company," he retorted coolly.

"Perhaps." The bigger fella didn't seem the least bit offended. "Or maybe something happened that's got you all holed up in your head."

"You mean like being kidnapped and forced to work for a criminal against my will?"

"No. I mean like whatever it was that made you leave your girl behind."

Jasper stilled, but he still didn't raise his head. Sam was smarter than he suspected. "She's not my girl."

"But she was. Wasn't she?"

"I thought so. Seems I was wrong."

"So what happened? She toss you over?"

Jasper's head came up, and he glared at the darker boy. "It's none of your damn business."

Sam's face lost all traces of humor. "She did, didn't she? Devil take it. I'm sorry, Renn."

He buffed the sides of the pistol with a soft, clean rag.

"Don't need your sympathy, Morgan. I was stupid, and I got played. That's how the world works."

"You want a torch or a candle, maybe? You've got your head so far up your own arse, it must be dark in there."

For a second, anger burst hard and fast inside Jasper, but then the absurdity—and the truth—of Sam's remark struck him, and he began to laugh. He laughed until it hurt and beyond. He didn't even try to stop, because he needed to let his emotions out, and he was very much afraid that if he didn't laugh, he'd humiliate himself by crying.

When his laughter stopped, he wiped at his eyes with the backs of his hands, and glanced up to find Sam watching him with a smile that wasn't exactly sympathetic or overly friendly but was one of understanding.

"You're not the first bloke to ever be played for a fool," Sam reminded him. "I almost helped get us all killed just a short while ago. Remember?"

Jasper did remember. "I thought she loved me," Jasper heard himself confess. "I guess she doesn't. I'm not sure that she ever did."

"Is she the kind of girl you would want to have love you?"

He didn't have to think about it that hard. "No. She killed a man in cold blood and let me assume the blame—told me it was in self-defense, but she was working for Dalton even then."

"Love's like being barking mad," Sam commiserated. "Makes a body do the damnedest things."

Jasper regarded him closely. "Like give a man a mechanical heart just to save his fool life."

Sam went very, very still. "That would be foolish indeed," he said quietly. "Especially if the idiot didn't appreciate the effort."

Until that moment, Jasper hadn't grasped the depth of Emily's feelings for Sam. If he had, he might not have flirted with her quite so much. Then again, he might have, if for no other reason than to get under this big brute's skin.

"Right," he said, slapping his hands against his thighs. "That's enough girly talk for me. How 'bout you?"

Sam nodded. "Yeah. Tell me about Dalton. How many men does he have with him. Any I need to worry about, other than the big one?"

Jasper shook his head. "Little Hank's a brute, but I doubt he's a match for you." Heck, he doubted Dalton's entire posse would be a match for Sam, but he didn't say that aloud. No need to cater to Morgan's confidence.

"It's the machine we need to worry about," he said. "Miss Emily could shut it down if she got close enough, but Dalton's bound to have someone guarding it, so someone would have to take out that person."

Sam looked thoughtful. "Griff found out he has something of an effect on machines that work with Aether. I didn't understand all of it, but Mr. Tesla seems to think Griffin could shut the machine down. What about the girl?"

Jasper shrugged. "I can always shoot her."

Black eyes widened. "Could you do that?"

"Nah." It wouldn't help the team to lie. "I couldn't, and the only person I know who might be able to best Mei in a fight is Finley. I want Dalton."

"Because he shot Kirby?"

Jasper nodded. Thank God his brother-in-law—tarnation, but that was a hard fact to wrap his head around—was going to be all right. He owed Emily for that. "And other things I ain't inclined to discuss."

"Understood." Sam glanced toward the door. "What the bloody Sunday is keeping them so long?"

"She had a lot of glass in her back." He felt responsible for Finley's injuries. He was the one that took them through the window, and he'd only suffered a couple of cuts—nothing like what had happened to her.

Sam shrugged. "Better that than a bullet to the head. Those are much more difficult to come back from."

"Even for you?" Jasper asked, talking just for the sake of talking.

"If one managed to penetrate my thick skull, I might be able to regenerate provided it didn't destroy anything vital. I'm not sure, and I'm not terribly anxious to find out."

Jasper grinned. "I suppose not."

A comfortable silence lapsed between them, but it only lasted a few moments because the door to Sam's room opened, and Emily and Griffin walked in.

"Success?" Sam asked the redhead.

Emily smiled when she looked at him. It was a genuine smile, and it rubbed salt that much harder in the wound of Mei's betrayal. Jasper had thought Mei looked at him with affection, but it had only been a lie. He had been blind.

"She'll be fine," Emily replied. "Left her sleeping off the ether. I'll check on her in a few moments. Have the two of you come up with any ways to defeat Dalton?"

"We could just walk right into his house and take the bloody thing," Sam suggested. "Griff could shut it down."

"That would be tricky," Griffin remarked. "It takes a lot of focus, and I would hesitate to try with such a device. If Dalton has modified it to work on humans, as well, I could kill a lot more people than just us and Dalton's gang. Who knows what sort of range the thing has. No, I'm not going to take that chance. This is for you from Kirby." He turned to Jasper and offered him an envelope.

Jasper took the letter and opened it. The sight of Whip's familiar scrawl warmed his heart. Now he wouldn't have to face his sister knowing he had brought about her husband's demise.

"He says he wants in on whatever we plan for Dalton. He wants to be able to drag the rascal back to San Francisco in chains."

"I think we can oblige him," Griffin replied with a smile. "Emily, send a note round to Tesla tomorrow morning, will you? Tell him I'm willing to let him study me if he'll let me practice on some of his machines."

★ ★ ★

She had no clothes.

This unhappy realization came to Finley shortly after she woke up on the desk in Griffin's room. The corset she had been wearing earlier was ruined. Her shirt was in even worse condition. Her pantaloons were filthy from landing on the ground and also stained with blood. The only thing she had that was reasonably clean were her stockings.

And she didn't have much in her room here at the hotel, either, as she had taken all of her clean clothes with her to Dalton's. Nothing of Emily's would fit, so that left her with one other option.

Griffin.

She held the sheet around her as she hopped off the desk. Her back itched and stung a little—like a rash or several nasty bug bites—but it wasn't anything too painful. She owed Emily a big hug for digging all the glass out and not severing her spine. Good show. Though, she had a morbid curiosity about whether or not her spine would have healed.

Tucking one end of the sheet under her arm so it wouldn't fall, she opened the wardrobe and surveyed the clothing inside. Griffin was tall, but he was lean, so his clothing should fit reasonably well. She took a pair of gray trousers, a white shirt and a waistcoat. Then she dumped her bounty onto the bed and proceeded to get dressed, keeping her ears sharp for the sounds of anyone approaching. She'd be mortified if one of the boys came in and caught her starkers.

First, she stepped into the trousers. They were way too long and a little snug in the hips, but they'd do. The shirt was also long and just fit around her chest. She tucked the tails into the pants and rolled up the sleeves before putting the waistcoat on over top. It acted like a corset, protecting her modesty and providing support—and, it looked pretty bloody sharp, if she said so herself. She tucked the long trouser legs into her boots and tightened the laces.

Finally ready, and resisting the urge to scratch at her back, Finley walked to the door and wrapped her fingers around the knob. A thought stopped her. A memory, actually.

She remembered hearing Griffin and Emily talking. Had she dreamed it, or was it real? Griffin had said he didn't know if he could trust her, and then Emily had asked if she was worth the risk. What had he said in reply? She couldn't remember.

A vaguely sick feeling squirmed in her stomach. If Griffin didn't know if he could trust her... Oh, bugger it. If Griffin was in doubt, she would just have to remove that doubt. Simple as that. Hadn't he convinced her that he was different from the other spoiled rich boys she'd encountered?

As she strode from the room, she suddenly understood why Emily liked to wear masculine garb. It was very liberating. Comfortable, too.

When she reached Sam's room, she heard multiple voices chattering. Making plans for bringing down Dalton, no doubt. Hopefully making plans to return to England, as well.

New York was lovely, but she wanted to go home. Wanted to curl up with a book in front of one of the many windows in Griffin's library. Wanted to get some decent fish and chips.

All heads turned when she entered the room. The most comical expression had to belong to Griffin, whose jaw dropped when he saw what she was wearing.

"Hope you don't mind," she said. "All my clean clothes are at Dalton's."

"Not at all," he replied with a shake of his head. There was something in his gaze that told her he liked how she looked in his clothes. It had to be a bloke thing, because she certainly wouldn't want to see him wearing hers.

"Do we have a plan yet?" she asked, sitting down next to Griffin on Sam's bed. Emily came over and gave her a gentle hug, mindful of her back. Finley squeezed her tight and murmured thanks in her ear.

"We're getting there," Griffin told her. "We know that there's close to a one hundred percent chance that Dalton will go after the treasures on display by the Historical Society at the Museum of Science and Invention. I can get us into the gathering. If Dalton brings the device in with him, Emily will shut it down if she can get to it. If not, I will, using the Aether. Then we nab him and hand him over to Whip Kirby."

"And then we're back to London?" She wasn't able to keep the hope from her voice.

Griffin smiled. "Then back to London."

Finley turned to Jasper. She had grown to know and like him even more over the past few days. "You're coming with us, right?"

He managed a smile, but she saw the sadness and betrayal in his green eyes. Poor thing. She just wanted to hug him. She'd kick Mei's tiny little arse for doing this to him. She and Dalton deserved each other.

"I might take a trip home to San Francisco first. Been a while since I last saw my family. 'Sides, Whip might need some help escorting Dalton and...the others back. I would like to return to England after that. If you have room for another." This last part was directed at Griffin.

"Have you seen my house?" Griffin asked drily. "You could bring your entire family with you, and I'd still have room. We'd be glad to have you."

"I suppose you might be useful," Sam commented, but even he was smiling.

"The lot of you are going to need suitable clothes for the event," Griffin informed them. "Sam, you and I and Jasper will go off to the tailor tomorrow. Surely there will be some ready-to-wear items that we can have altered for the pair of you, though Sam's shoulders might prove a hindrance. Finley, you and Emily should go shopping, as well. Get gowns and all the necessary accessories. Have the boutique send the bill to me here at the hotel. If they give you any grief, act like an offended aristocrat."

Emily made a face. "I have to wear a dress?"

Sam slipped his arm around her shoulders and squeezed. "If I have to wear a bloody cravat, you have to wear a dress."

She elbowed him in the ribs.

Griffin turned to Finley. "Get yourself whatever else you need, as well. We probably won't be able to retrieve the clothes you had to leave behind."

In her head, Finley swore. They were only clothes, and they were replaceable, but she hated taking advantage of his generosity.

As if reading her thoughts, Griffin rolled his eyes. "Finley, you could shop every day for the next ten years and not even come close to breaking me. Please, buy yourself whatever you need. I trust you."

Her gaze locked with his. "Not yet," she replied confidently. "But you will."

Chapter 16

Tesla met Griffin and Emily at the door with a smile peeking out from beneath his moustache. If he'd been rubbing his hands together, he would have looked just like a villain out of a penny dreadful. Griffin made a mental note to tell Sam about the comparison later.

"I am very pleased that you deigned to allow me to study you, Your Grace," Tesla said in his soft tone. "I expect to learn many wonderful things from you."

"It is no trouble, sir. I thank you for allowing me to practice Aetherically controlling the machines you've designed." If it would help him take out Dalton and his machine, it was worth being treated like an experiment. He frowned when he noticed the inventor's strange clothing. "Whatever are you wearing?"

Tesla spread his arms so that both Emily and Griffin might

admire him. He wore a bizarre one-piece suit, which enveloped him from head to toe. Valves, switches and several telephone dials covered the torso of it, while wires and coiled tubing connected to the hood, out to the arms and down the legs. He also held a mask in his hand—one that was designed to cover the face—but he had attached a hose to it, which was attached at the other end to a small metal canister.

"I call it my Aetheric Mortality Disambiguation Suit."

Griffin stared at him. Even Emily seemed at a loss for words. "Are you saying that this thing will kill you?"

"Almost," the genius replied with uncharacteristic glee. "I constructed it immediately after our last meeting. It will drop all of my body's functions to the brink of death and, therefore, fool the Aether so that I may see what you see."

Griffin nodded, still not quite believing his ears. "It makes you a ghost."

"Exactly, Your Grace! Exactly."

Griffin and Emily exchanged a glance. He didn't want to insult Tesla, but the suit was one of the most foolhardy devices he'd ever heard of. Inviting death was never the intelligent choice, no matter how bloody smart you were. "Mr. Tesla, that sounds very dangerous."

"Oh, no, it's quite safe. And we will have Miss O'Brien here to assist should any complications arise."

Emily paled just enough that her freckles stood out against her cheeks. "Of course," she said, but it was obvious she didn't want the responsibility of making certain Tesla stayed alive, though she would do everything in her power to make certain he did just that.

"Mr. Tesla, sir," Emily began. "You said a person wouldn't have to be holding your machine to work it, correct?"

"Yes. The device is designed to focus on a specific target. Your villain could do that most easily from anywhere with a clear view."

"What if there were multiple targets?" Griffin asked. "Say, if he wanted to render more than one item intangible?"

Tesla looked dismayed. "I designed it so that it could be used Aetherically using what I call radio waves. If he also has the controller or has made one, he could leave the device anywhere within range and simply activate the controller in the direction of whatever he wished to move through."

Griffin raked a hand through his hair. "Wonderful."

"However, he could not use the machine on more than one target at a time. He would have to wait at least five seconds for the charge to build once more."

If he had been standing by a wall, Griffin would have banged his head against it.

"On the bright side," Emily piped up, "is that, even if you can't pinpoint the machine itself, you may be able to disable the device by focusing on the controller."

"Very true," Tesla agreed. "Miss O'Brien, you are most certainly the most intelligent female I have ever met."

Griffin bit the inside of his cheek to keep from laughing. For a second, Emily looked as though she didn't know whether to be flattered or offended.

"Thank you, sir," she said with a tight smile. "Shall we get started?"

Poor Emily, Griffin thought. She had been so excited to meet Tesla, but the man hadn't turned out to be exactly what she had hoped for. There was no denying the inventor was brilliant, and he had been fairly polite and considerate, but there was something slightly cracked about him, and his fascination with the military applications of his various devices was...*creepy*.

Regardless of his eccentricity, he was the only person who could help them at the moment.

Tesla walked to a chair, which looked like the sort one would find at a barber's, and sat down. "Miss O'Brien, would you be so kind as to assist me?"

Griffin watched as Emily helped the inventor slip on the mask and stored the metal cylinder where it wouldn't fall. Then she strapped him to the arm and leg rests. Tesla's breathing could be heard throughout the room as he sucked the gas from the cylinder into his lungs. Emily flicked the switches and dialed a series of numbers on each of the dials. Then she took a long cable connected to what appeared to be a modified radio/etching machine, only instead of brass cylinders, the arm of the etcher held a pencil over a length of paper stretched between two rolls. She slipped the small, flexible disk at the end of the cable onto Tesla's temple, beneath the snug hood of his suit.

"What does that do?" Griffin asked.

"It monitors his heart rate," she replied. "I'm to revive him if it drops too low."

"What's too low?"

She gave him a wry smile. "If it stops completely."

"Ah." He glanced at Tesla, who was rendered deaf by his helmet and the sound of his own breathing. "Am I the only one who thinks this is quite possibly insane?"

Emily shook her head. "Not at all. Although, if this works, I may be able to modify the design so that I can also observe you in the Aether."

Griffin frowned. "Why would you want to do that?" He didn't bother to add that there was no bloody way he'd allow her to risk her life out of scientific curiosity.

She blinked—as though the answer should be obvious. "Why wouldn't I?"

He laughed. "Because it's dangerous."

A shrug of her shoulders dismissed his concerns. She consulted the etching apparatus. "All right, his heart has slowed to almost nothing. Do you see his Aetheric projection?"

What a lovely term for a living ghost. Griffin had never sought the living in the Aether before, and the last time he'd encountered such a phenomenon it hadn't gone well.

He relaxed his hold on this world and opened himself up to the Aether. Some referred to the sight as having a "third eye" and it certainly made sense. It was as though he was seeing a new layer of the world on top of what was already there, as if reality was a glass slide in a microscope and the Aether was simply another set on top.

When the Aetheric plane came into focus, its gray and washed-out gauziness settling, Tesla's spirit stood beside the chair where his body reclined. Even in this realm, he wore the suit, made slightly less ridiculous by the sheer fact that it worked.

"How very extraordinary," the inventor remarked, jaw slack in awe as he glanced about the mist.

"I suppose it is," Griffin replied. He had been able to see the Aether for most of his life, so it didn't hold the same wonder for him. "You set an Aether conductive device in motion before we arrived, correct?"

"Yes, of course. I hid it somewhere within these rooms. Can you sense it?"

"Not yet." He hadn't even tried. "Just give me a moment." First, he looked around to see if anything looked or felt wrong or out of place. There was Emily standing beside Tesla's body—the man's spirit was right beside her, and she couldn't see him, which was just as well, seeing that Tesla kept trying to poke her.

Griffin could tell him that he would never, ever make contact, but then the inventor might want to talk to him, and that would slow down this process. They didn't have that much time. The Historical Society event at the Museum of Science and Invention was in a matter of days.

He wondered what sort of gown Finley would buy. He should get her a suit. The way she looked in his clothes last evening... That wasn't the sort of thing he should let distract him, either, nor her not-so-cryptic promise that he would trust her eventually. He turned his head, and that's when he saw *it*.

Along the ceiling, there drifted a small wisp of churning energy. Its color was a little different than normal Aetheric energy. It had a slightly reddish cast to it, as though it would be hot to the touch. He knew—felt it in his gut—that this particular signature belonged to Tesla's machine, but he couldn't remember if he had seen a similar shade around the previous machine he had shut down. Of course, he had been too preoccupied with the shadow-thing that had attacked him.

He wasn't going to think about that right now, either.

He probably didn't have to actually hold up his hand, but it gave him direction and focus if he reached out toward the energy he sought to control. He pointed his fingers at the reddish wisp and willed it to come to him.

The energy came easily—it was Aether, after all. He gripped it—an intangible rope that hummed in his hand— and slowly took it as his own, letting the warmth of it seep through his skin, into his bones.

Griffin closed his eyes. It felt good, this surge of power. It was like a hot shower or lying in the sun. It filled him with peace and contentment, as though he was a well that had been allowed to run dry and was now filling with rain.

When he opened his eyes again, he knew that he held the control of Tesla's machine. He felt its location—in the wardrobe in the bedroom—and concentrated on taking the energy away from it. In a way, his mind was like one of Tesla's radio controllers, shutting the device down without touching it. He simply cut off the power running to and from it.

It hadn't been difficult at all, he thought with a smile. As he turned to comment to Tesla, he heard a cry of pain. All of his pleasure at having so easily shut down the machine fled, replaced by horror as he saw the reason for that cry.

Tesla's spirit had been slashed—ripped—by a black mass that was almost entirely shapeless, except for long black claws.

Griffin's heart froze in his chest. For a split second, he was unable to do anything as fear rendered him immobile.

He didn't want to go near that *thing*. Neither could he allow it to harm Tesla.

"Emily," he yelled. "Wake him up."

"What?" She looked up at him, then back at Tesla, just as the inventor's body began to thrash against the restraints. "Mary and Joseph!" She began working the dials and switches on the suit in an attempt to bring Tesla's soul back to his body.

It would take more time than the inventor had. Thoughts of his own mortality vanished as Griffin bolted toward the inky mass. God only knew how ridiculous he looked to

Emily, tearing across the room to deal with an unseen enemy. A potentially lethal unseen enemy.

Tesla's spirit was trying to fight the thing off while simultaneously trying to protect itself. Deep slashes marked his chest, arm and face. Much more of this and the older man would die for real.

Griffin put himself between Tesla and the mass. He just had to distract the thing until Emily succeeded in her task.

The first swipe of claws tore through his jacket and waistcoat but not his flesh. The second, he managed to duck and avoid. A low rumbling noise came from deep inside the blackness, as though coming from deep within an old well. Was that...laughter?

"What the bloody hell?" he demanded, arching back to avoid another swipe. The thing was *laughing* at him. What was it?

It was something he had to get rid of.

"Go back," he said to it. "Go back where you belong, or I swear on my father's grave, I will end you."

The mass seemed to take umbrage at that and drew itself upward. It stretched at least a foot over the top of Griffin's head. For a moment, it looked as though it almost had a face, but then it was gone.

It had to be a ghost, but how? Why? That didn't matter now.

"Go back," he said again, turning his hands palms up at his sides and extending them ever so slightly to begin calling his own power. He could feel it slowly warming up his veins, tingling in his fingertips. The mass hadn't corrupted the entire Aether, just the part it occupied.

The thick, oily strands wavered but didn't flee. Claws reformed, drawing back to deliver another blow. Griffin set his jaw and thrust both hands out, sinking them wrist deep into the entity before releasing the energy he had summoned.

The thing screamed—sounding like a cross between the caw of a crow and a rusted hinge—before blowing apart like kicked sand.

Griffin stood there for a moment, waiting to see if it came back. When it didn't, he let the Aetheric dimension slip away, leaving nothing but the world of the living around him.

"Is Tesla all right?" he demanded as he turned toward Emily.

"Quite," the older man replied. He was sitting up now, and had removed his mask and hood. He looked tired and shaky. "Thanks to you, Your Grace."

Griffin didn't bother to remind him that he wouldn't have gone into the Aether were it not for his curiosity about Griffin's abilities. Still, Tesla was a grown man and knew his own mind.

"You should rest," Griffin told him. "And perhaps avoid Aether exploration from here on. That's the second time I've encountered that thing, and both times have been here, with you."

Tesla nodded. "I've seen what you see, and that's enough."

Emily shot Griff a dubious glance at the inventor's statement but did not voice her doubts. "Do you need assistance with anything, sir?"

"No, no." The man rose to his feet, wavered slightly and then seemed to find his legs. "Please excuse my poor manners, but I believe I need to lie down. Will you excuse me?"

"Of course," Griffin answered. "We'll leave you, but I hope you will indulge us if we check in on you later?"

Tesla nodded and then slowly made his way from the room. Griffin and Emily gathered up their things and left the hotel. He wished he had a greatcoat to put on to cover his ruined jacket, but he did not.

"What happened?" Emily demanded once they were outside. "Did that thing come back?"

Griffin lifted his hand to run it through his hair and stopped. He rubbed the back of his neck instead. "Yes. It seemed bigger this time, and, Em...I'm fairly certain it was sentient."

Emily swore softly. "Saints preserve us. You have no idea what it is?"

He shook his head as he hailed a cab. "A malignant spirit, perhaps."

"A haunting?" She looked at him with huge eyes. She was a bit superstitious about such things.

"Could be." He turned to her as a cab pulled over for them. "I've never seen anything like it, and I hope to never again. Whatever it is, it's bloody dangerous."

"Well, I hope Mr. Tesla never encounters it again." She held up a small mechanical component. "I stole this from his suit."

"Smart decision," he said, opening the cab door for her to climb in. "Maybe it will keep him from doing any more Aetheric experiments." He didn't tell her his theory—his fear. Tesla wasn't the entity's targeted prey. Tesla wasn't the one who had gotten a threatening letter.

He was.

When Finley asked Emily what had happened to Griffin's clothing during their visit with Tesla, she got the story in vivid detail—to the point where her throat went dry at the thought of Griffin running into that Aether…*monster* again. She still hadn't recovered from how badly he'd been hurt the last time.

Emily, however, seemed totally oblivious to her distress as she perused the selection of ready-to-wear gowns the little shop they were in had to offer. "The fool was more concerned about his waistcoat than he was about anything else."

Part of Finley thought perhaps Emily was trying to make her feel better. Another part thought she might be telling the truth, as well. "Well, he and I have done a good job at losing our clothes here in New York."

Laughing blue eyes locked with hers over the display. "Oh, is that so? Is there something you want to tell me?"

Blushing, Finley made a face at her. "You know what

I mean. So does he have any idea what the thing is?" She shouldn't have to ask Emily for this information, but Griffin hadn't volunteered it when she'd asked back at the hotel. He probably had some absurd notion that he was protecting her by not telling her. Maybe he thought she'd worry. Of course she was going to worry about him, the lunatic.

"Not really, but the prevailing theory is that it might be an angry ghost tethered to Tesla's rooms or the hotel in general. Provided Tesla doesn't go into the Aether again, everything should be fine—including Griff."

A sigh broke free from Finley's lips. That was the best news she'd heard in a while.

Emily held up a golden-colored gown. "What do you think of this one?"

"Perfect," Finley replied. "You'll look gorgeous. Sam will slip in his own drool."

The smaller girl's nose wrinkled. "That's an attractive picture to put in a girl's head."

Laughing, Finley found a gown for herself—it was a rich purple-colored silk. "I think this is one of the most beautiful dresses I've ever seen."

"Perfect choice," Emily agreed. "What else do you need to get?"

Their gowns chosen, they then went about finding a few items for Finley, to do her until she could get the clothes she had at the hotel laundered. Right now, she was wearing more of Griffin's things but with one of her own corsets to add a feminine touch. No doubt he would be glad when she stopped wearing his clothes, given that he had lost some of his, as well.

They didn't talk about Dalton or any of their plans as they shopped. Both of them were too paranoid to talk in public— plus they knew better. One never knew who might be listening. So instead they talked a little about Sam and Griffin and a little about poor Jasper, for whom both of their hearts ached.

Finally their shopping done, they stood patiently while seamstresses pinned them in each garment for alterations. The shop was equipped with sewing automatons, and many of their selections would be ready the next morning, if not this evening.

"Please, send the bill to the Duke of Greythorne care of the Waldorf-Astoria," Finley instructed the shopgirl.

"Don't you dare," Miss Astor-Prynn interjected before Finley could tell her that she could also have the clothing delivered to the same address. "This girl is a scam artist."

The skin of Finley's neck and cheeks warmed with embarrassment. Everyone was looking at her, perhaps finding this nasty baggage's words easy to believe. "You don't know me at all," she said in a calm, even voice. "You don't know Griffin, either."

The other girl bristled. "You brazen slattern, calling him by his Christian name! Of all the arrogance. I don't know

how you managed to escape arrest, but you won't be so fortunate next time."

Finley turned to Emily, whose face was beet-red, and whispered, "If I punched her in the mouth, do you think she'd
shut up?"

Emily smiled, but it was obvious she was furious on Finley's behalf.

"I'm sorry," the shopgirl said sincerely, "but I'm afraid
given Miss Astor-Prynn's accusations, I'm going to need proof
that you are in the duke's traveling party."

Finley's narrow gaze went back to the righteous slag responsible for this. To think that she had thought this was the
kind of girl Griffin would prefer to her. No one could prefer
this nasty bag of bones.

The door opened behind her, the little bell tinkling, but
Finley ignored it. She took a step closer to the girl who, at
the moment, was making her life difficult. "What do you
think he's going to do? Propose? Take you back to England?
He's eighteen. No gentleman ever gets married so young."

"Lengthy engagements aren't unheard of," Miss Astor-
Prynn argued. A cruel smile twisted her lips. "What do you
think will happen when he tires of you and your—" she raked
Finley with a blatantly insulting gaze "—talents?"

"I cannot imagine that ever happening" came a voice from
behind them.

Finley's fingers uncurled, releasing the fist she'd been
about to drive into the witch's face. She noted how the blood

drained from that once smug face before turning her own toward her savior.

"Your Grace," she said happily. "I'm so glad you're here. Miss Astor-Prynn has doubts as to whether or not Emily and I are part of your entourage. Would you kindly disabuse her of such thoughts so that we can return to the hotel with our purchases?"

Griffin's teeth flashed as he grinned. Obviously he found her overly sweet and proper tone amusing. "I would be delighted, Miss Jayne." He shot a particularly cold glance at Miss Astor-Prynn before addressing the girl at the counter. "Please have the ladies' items delivered to the Waldorf." He handed her a crisp bill for her "trouble."

The girl scurried to do just as he asked, stammering apologies as she moved.

Griffin's smile faded as he regarded Finley's nemesis once more. "Miss Astor-Prynn, I wish you every happiness in your life. I believe you do not have many of them. But I can honestly and without regret inform you that, even if I were inclined to marry at my age, you would be the absolute *last* girl I would think of spending the rest of my days with. Good day." He bowed and then took Emily and Finley on either of his arms. "Shall we, ladies?"

If she were a better person, Finley would have kept her gaze fixed on the exit ahead of them. Instead, she gave in to temptation and craned her neck to peer back over her shoulder at Miss Astor-Prynn, whose face was as hard as marble and just as white, save for two angry red splotches on her cheeks.

Finley smiled and waved.

"Stop that," Griffin commanded under his breath as they reached the door, but there was no anger in his words, only a sparkle in his gray-blue eyes.

Finley's smile softened into a more sincere expression. "Thank you. I don't know what we would have done if you hadn't arrived."

"I do," Emily volunteered. "We would have been asked to leave, and you would have knocked that cow's teeth down her throat. I rather like to think she would have choked on them."

Griffin and Finley laughed. "The two of you are the most bloodthirsty wenches I've ever met."

"Do you like it?" Finley asked, squeezing his arm before releasing it.

He turned to her, his eyes bright. Was it just the reflection of the sun that gave them such warmth or something from within?

"I love it," he said. The sudden deepening of his voice caused a wild fluttering in her stomach. It wasn't so much what he said that thrilled her, but how he said it—and what was left unsaid, as well.

She couldn't think of a bloody thing to say in reply.

Still smiling, Griffin held open the door of the hired cab for Emily and her to climb inside. Finley had just gotten herself situated when he plopped down beside her. His leg rested against hers, warm and solid.

When he took her hand in his and gave it a light squeeze, she didn't try to pull away. For a moment, as she and Griffin stared into each other's eyes, smiling, it seemed as though everything was right and perfect with the world.

But Finley had the sinking sensation that the feeling wasn't going to last.

Chapter 17

Wildcat was absolutely the last person Jasper expected to see that evening. Not just because he thought their business concluded, but because his room was several stories up and she was smiling at him from the other side of his window.

Cat's smile had frightened more than one man senseless—girls with fangs tended to be somewhat intimidating. Jasper wasn't quite certain what she was, but his time with her had convinced him she was more than merely human. She wasn't called Wildcat just because of her attitude.

More curious than afraid, Jasper crossed the carpet of the room Griffin had secured for him and opened the window. He wasn't the least bit surprised to see Cat hanging off the side of the building without the aid of rope. Her claws could dig into the brick, and she was strong enough to support her weight with her fingers and toes.

They had enjoyed quite a bit of adventure during his brief time in New York City, given his speed and her talents.

"Evening, Cat."

Her smile grew. "Jasper. May I come in?"

He stood back so that she could slink through the window into the room. She was all muscled grace as she slipped one arm over the sill and then the other, bracing her palms on either side of the frame as she leaned back and swung both legs inside. Her knees bent toward the floor as her torso appeared, then her head. Then she rose to her feet in one fluid motion.

Jasper gave her a quick nod. "That's quite the display."

She shrugged, lilac eyes taking in the opulence of the room. "Nice place."

"It'll do," he replied drily. "What brings you here, Cat?" He wasn't trying to be rude, but he knew the gang leader wasn't there on a social call.

Gnawing on the side of her thumb, she plunked herself down on the bed and reclined there, braced back on her elbows, as if it was her own. "There's a strange rumor going round Five Points."

When she didn't immediately elaborate, Jasper raised a brow. "So far, I don't know what that has to do with me."

She crossed her feet at the ankles. The soles of her boots were dusty but not dirty enough that he worried for the quilt. "The rumor is that there's to be a riot tomorrow night. All the gangs. Word is that the cops are going to hit the area full force to contain the participants."

Jasper stared at her. He knew that Wildcat's grandfather, a freed slave, had been shot and killed during a riot back in the '60s. She had to be thinking about that right now. Had to be worried or maybe even frightened.

"You want to stay here?" he asked. "There's not a lot of room, but you're welcome to stay until it all blows over."

She bolted upright, sitting so that her legs hung over the side and her elbows rested on her knees. "There ain't no riot, Jasper. None of the gangs know anything about it, even though they're supposed to be involved."

He shook his head. "I don't understand."

"Someone started the rumor to make sure all the police are going to be in Five Points instead of someplace else."

Frowning, Jasper crossed his arms over his chest and leaned his shoulders against the wall. The Historical Society event was tomorrow night. That couldn't be a coincidence; he knew better than that. "Would that someone happen to be Reno Dalton?"

Wildcat inclined her head, a slow smile taking over her lips. "Seems to be. I had to do an awful lot of digging to find that out, otherwise I would have been here sooner. That scalawag has something planned, and he's putting my people at risk over it."

Anger glittered in her unusual eyes. Wildcat might run with a rough bunch—might be the leader of a rough bunch—

but she cared about her people and tried to make certain they had the best lives possible given the poverty of the Five Points neighborhood.

"We think he's got a job planned, Cat. I reckon he wants to make sure the law isn't around to interfere."

Her pretty face hardened. "People are going to die tomorrow night, Jasper. The cops will shoot first and 'express their remorse' later. Remorse can't raise the dead."

There was nothing Jasper could do about that. Even if he went to the police, they wouldn't believe him, and there was a very good chance they had a wanted poster with his face on it. However, Whip might be able to do something.

"I'll see what I can do, Cat. Meanwhile, tell your people to stay inside, avoid the normal fighting grounds and not to travel in packs—anything that could be mistaken for aggressive activity."

Wildcat swore, then sat there, her lips tight. "I guess that's all I can ask for."

"I wish I could do more."

Her gaze locked with his. "You can get that trash out of my town."

"I plan to. In chains."

That put a smile on her face—full of fangs. "You do that, and I'll give you that six-shooter you were always trying to talk me into giving you."

The thought of actually having that pistol cut through the

fog of depression that had surrounded him since Mei's betrayal. "You don't have to do that."

"I want you to have it." She rose to her feet. "I have to get
back and spread the word. Most of them will listen to me,
but those Dead Rabbits and Bowery Boys can be an ornery,
stubborn bunch. They might decide to taunt the cops. Idiots."

As she moved toward the window, Jasper said, "You can
use the door, you know."

Cat threw a grin at him over her shoulder as she slipped a
leg out the window. "And let the fancies see me? Nah, I have
a reputation to uphold. Take care, Jas."

He smiled. "You too, Cat."

And then she was gone. He wondered if she climbed down
the building or jumped—she had a knack for always landing
on her feet.

He consulted his pocket watch. It was almost half past
seven. He would be meeting Griffin and the others soon for
dinner; he'd relay what Cat had told him then.

For the first time since being roped back into Dalton's
circle, Jasper felt like there might actually—finally—be an
end to this chapter of his life. He would be exonerated of the
murder charges, and his family would be released from the
shame that lie had brought upon them.

He could look toward the future now and stop living in
the past. He could move on. Hopefully his heart would, too.

★ ★ ★

Finley's eyes snapped open. The room was dark save for the moonlight shining through her open window.

That window had been closed when she went to bed.

Hunkered down beneath the covers, she let her gaze move slowly from the curtains gently billowing in the breeze to survey the rest of the room. Unless she'd developed the habit of opening windows in her sleep, she was not alone. The faint creak of floorboards confirmed the suspicion.

She had been expecting Dalton to send an assassin after her and Jasper. In fact, she was surprised he'd waited this long to try to snuff them out. No doubt he wanted to foster a false sense of security in them before he struck, lovely bloke that he was.

Keeping her breathing shallow, she feigned sleep, waiting for her would-be killer to make his or her move. They would choose an up-close-and-personal method of death, of course, as firing a pistol would attract too much attention. Her eyes were open just enough to watch the shadows in the room.

One of the shadows moved, taking on a human shape as it drifted toward her. It was too big to be Mei. Disappointing, that. She'd rather hoped she would get the chance to square off against the detestable chit. It was also too small to be Little Hank. Either it was one of the other fellows, or Dalton had hired a professional. Or perhaps an amateur, given how easily she had sensed his presence.

The shadowy figure came closer, moving up the side of the

bed to hover by her head, blocking out most of the moonlight. Closer it came, bending over her, a length of rope stretched between both hands. Finley waited until that rope just barely touched her neck before reaching up, grabbing the assassin's coat and pulling him down to smash her forehead into his nose. He cried out—her assumption that her attacker was a man had been correct—but she didn't let go.

Finley came up onto her knees, still holding the man. He'd regained his wits and struggled against her hold, but he wasn't much of a threat without his rope. She coshed him with her head again—this time hard enough to knock him out.

Then—still in her unmentionables—she climbed out of bed, flipped him onto his stomach on the floor and used his own rope to tie his hands behind his back. She used the laces out of one of her corsets to secure his feet and then tied the lace to the rope, effectively "hog-tying" him.

The thought of Jasper's colloquialism made her think of the cowboy himself. If an assassin had come for her, one might have come for Jasper, as well. Or maybe hers was supposed to eliminate both of them, but she couldn't be certain.

Hastily, she threw on the trousers she had borrowed from Griffin and the shirt, as well. They hadn't been laundered, but they would do for the moment. In her bare feet, she hurried silently from her room and just down the corridor to Jasper's.

The door was locked. Bollocks.

Finley ran back to her room, hopped over the unconscious

man on her floor and leaned out the window. Jasper's room was two doors down from hers, but the only way to get there was to traverse the narrow brick ledge that ran around the building.

Good thing she wasn't afraid of heights.

Sighing, she slipped half of her body out of the window and unhooked the assassin's climbing apparatus. It landed on the sidewalk below, the attached rope muffling the crash.

She braced her toes on the ledge and got a good hold on the window frame with her right hand before easing the rest of her body out. Then she pressed her back against the rough brick and quickly moved toward Jasper's room, legs moving in wide strides.

As she approached, she spotted a rope dangling from Jasper's open window. *Don't let me be too late.* She couldn't bear to get there and find him already dead. She would have to kill Dalton herself if that happened.

Neither finesse nor silence played any part in how she launched herself through the window. Her ungraceful sprawl onto the floor was quick as she immediately sprang to her feet. Jasper was struggling with his attacker, who appeared to be a bit more skilled than hers. The cowboy couldn't use his incredible speed to hit the man because he was trying to keep the rope around his neck from cutting off his supply of oxygen.

Finley walked up behind the man and kicked him hard between his legs. As he doubled over, crying out in pain, Jasper turned and punched him hard in the jaw, sending him sprawling.

Jasper pulled the rope from around his neck, coughing and gasping. "Thank you," he said.

Finley grinned and snatched the rope from his hands. "Happy to be of service. Help me tie him up."

It was at this point that the door to the room crashed open—thanks to the sole of Sam's boot. He, Emily and Griffin all rushed in. Sam in trousers and an untucked shirt, Emily in her nightgown and Griffin in nothing but a pair of trousers.

Finley wasn't the least bit ashamed of stopping what she was doing to simply admire the view.

"What happened?" Griffin demanded.

"Assassins," she replied as she pulled the limp man's legs up so Jasper could bind them with a pair of braces and then secure them to the man's wrists. "One for me and one for Jasper. A lovely gift, courtesy of Reno Dalton if I'm not mistaken."

"You're not," Jasper replied. His voice was slightly hoarse from being strangled. "He's the only one who would know to find you and me in the same place."

Griffin offered his hand to help her to her feet. She didn't need any help, but she accepted the gesture, regardless. When she stood, he pulled her against him in a fierce hug. If he planned to do this every time someone tried to kill her, she might risk her life more often.

She returned the hug—shamefully, more so she could touch his naked back than comfort him in any way. His skin was warm and smooth. Muscles twitched beneath her palms. When he pulled back their gazes locked, and she knew—*knew*—that if they had been alone, he would have kissed her.

"Are you hurt?" he asked.

"No." Reluctantly, she released him. "But Jasper is."

Emily swept forward, her bare toes peeking out from beneath the hem of her white cotton nightdress. "Let me see." Jasper had no choice but to stand and offer her a view of his bare throat.

And of course, Sam scowled because the cowboy was wearing a robe and showing an indecent amount of collarbone.

"Sam, could you fetch my bag?" Emily asked. "I need to put some salve on these abrasions."

Sam hurried off to do as she asked and returned in a few moments. While Emily tended to Jasper, the big lad hoisted the assassin over his shoulder.

"There's one of those in my room, too," Finley informed him. "Do you want me to help?"

"I've got it" came the stern reply, and he walked from the room as though carrying nothing more than a sack of potatoes.

"You're going to have to pay for that door." Finley nodded at the splintered wood.

Griffin shrugged. "I would have had him go right through

the bloody wall if necessary." He glanced at Jasper. "Your window's seen a lot of traffic tonight."

The cowboy chuckled—a hoarse sound. "Maybe I should put in a toll."

Griffin turned back to Finley. "I feel as though I should apologize for all the trouble you've had since meeting me."

Both of her brows shot up as she looked at him. "In case you haven't noticed, I was attracting trouble long before I met you." She didn't say it in a self-pitying way, because she didn't feel the least bit sorry for herself. She felt sorry for the people who tried to harm her.

Sam appeared in the doorway, a man over each shoulder. He looked massive—like a mythical hero—standing there with his mussed long hair and fierce expression. "Oy, Finley. What's the address of Dalton's house?"

She told him. "Why?"

He shrugged, lifting each man as though the answer was clear. "I'm going to deliver a present."

"I'll come with you," she announced. "If he's waiting for them to report, he'll be watching. He might use the device on you. It will be faster if I come along. The sight of me might throw him off."

"Be careful," Griffin urged, but he didn't try to stop her. She liked that. He knew she could look after herself, and even though he worried about her, he had faith in her and her abilities.

That was something like trust, wasn't it?

"I will." And then, out of impulse, she kissed him on the cheek before following after Sam.

Since it was so very late, they had to operate the lift themselves, which was just as well. It also meant that the lobby was deserted, also a blessing. How would they ever explain why Sam had two men trussed up like Christmas geese over his shoulders? They might be able to lie about the men, but they could never, ever come up with a believable explanation of Sam's incredible strength.

For the same reason that the hotel was so quiet, Finley assumed they would have a difficult time finding a cab. She was wrong. There was one sitting just around the corner. Apparently New York, like London, was a city that rarely, if ever, slept.

Or perhaps the carriage was waiting for the assassins to finish the job and return them to Dalton.

"You waiting for these two?" Finley asked the driver.

The man's eyes grew wide, the whites clearly visible in the light of the streetlamps. Sam turned his back to the man, so he could see his captives' faces. The driver nodded. "Yes. They paid me to wait for their return."

"Well, they've returned," Sam replied glibly and proceeded to toss his burdens into the carriage.

Finley gave the driver Dalton's address and climbed into the carriage behind Sam. The large young man sat across from her on the opposite side of the coach. The two men were piled on the floor between them. It might have been her imagination, but she was fairly certain the cab leaned to one side—Sam's.

"How much do you weigh?" she inquired.

He frowned. "Plenty."

Fair enough. She leaned back against the upholstery and remained silent for the rest of the trip. Obviously Sam had woken up on the wrong side of the bed. Huh. One might think that *he* was the one who was attacked by a hired assassin.

When they pulled up in front of Dalton's abode, several windows glowed with light despite the late hour. Obviously he was expecting company.

Finley opened the cab door and stepped out onto the sidewalk. She pulled one of the men out into the night and tossed him unceremoniously onto the ground. His grunt was the only indication that he had regained consciousness.

Sam tossed the other out of the carriage. He landed with a groan next to his partner, so that both of them lay on the walkway leading to the front steps. Finley jogged toward the house. Her bare feet slapped on the cool ground—she'd have to wash them before she went back to bed.

She climbed the steps and rang the bell—several times—before turning and running back to the cab. "Get in," she commanded Sam. Then to the driver, "As soon as I give the word, you get us out of here as fast as you can."

He nodded. "Yes, miss."

The front door of the house opened just as Finley jumped

into the coach. Pivoting on her heel, she turned with a grin. Little Hank bent his head to walk out the door. It didn't take him long to see the men on the walk.

"Give Dalton my best, will you, ducks?" she called out. The behemoth looked at her in disbelief, and then she had the pleasure of seeing Dalton come to the door. His too-handsome face hardened into sheer rage. Finley waggled her fingers at him and then yelled at the driver to drive away. She didn't want to risk the poor man's life, and Dalton was sure to have a pistol nearby if not on him.

The steam carriage sped down the street, but no shots were fired. Finley was almost disappointed.

"That was a bit of fun, wasn't it?" she remarked, feeling as though she'd eaten too much sugar—her insides positively buzzed with energy.

"We could have grabbed him," Sam replied, his frown slightly deeper than usual.

"And do what with him? We can't prove he hired those men. We can't prove he means to steal anything. The only thing we could prove is that he shot at Jasper and myself, and Jasper is still considered a wanted criminal. No, we let him make his move, and then we take him."

To her surprise, a small smile tugged at his lips. "You're starting to sound like Griffin."

"I'll take that as a compliment."

"By all means, if you reckon sounding arrogant, demanding and overbearing is a good thing."

She stared at him for a second before bursting out laughing. He laughed, too. She didn't know what she'd done to warrant this friendliness, but it was nice being able to talk to him without feeling like there was bad blood between them. It was almost as though they could forget that he had tried to kill her and that she had almost killed him.

They arrived back at the hotel and had to use Sam's telegraph machine—that he had been smart enough to bring—to ask Griffin to come down and pay the driver as neither of them had any money on them. When he arrived Finley noticed, with chagrin, that he had put a shirt on.

"Did Dalton see them?" Griffin asked.

"He certainly did," she replied. "I've no doubt he wants my head so badly now, he can taste it."

His smile twisted. "Nice image."

The three of them rode the lift up to their floor, and after checking on Jasper, Griffin walked Finley back to her room. He kissed her on the forehead before she slipped through the open door. Smiling—more from the kiss than from rubbing Dalton's face in his failure—she closed the window and locked it, then pulled the drapes closed, as well. Then she climbed into bed and pulled the blankets up to her chin. There was so much to think about—so much to do and so much that had already been done—that she doubted she'd get any more rest that night.

She was sound asleep within five minutes.

Chapter 18

Finley liked dressing up, especially if the gown was also designed to give her freedom to kick arse.

The gown she had found at the shop—so pretty and dark purple—was just that sort of dress. The little puff sleeves did nothing to restrain her arms. The bodice was snug, but she wore a flexible corset beneath so she could bend and move without difficulty. But the skirts were the true masterpiece. Today's fashions were for lean skirts, which created a lovely silhouette, but were absolute rubbish for kicking or anything else that required lifting one's leg any more than a thirty degree angle. The skirt on Finley's gown was constructed of individual pieces and layers of fabric. The result looked very much like the petals of a rose. It was beautiful, and best of all she could kick as high as her head in it—it would reveal a shocking amount of her leg if she did, but the mobility was worth it.

She and Emily had helped each other with their hair and in getting dressed. Emily was beautiful in her golden gown that made her skin look like ivory. Finley had coiled the ropes of her hair on top of her head in an elegant topknot, which showed off the length of her neck. In exchange, Emily had gathered Finley's hair into a loose cloud high on the back of her head. It looked like the whole of it might fall at any moment, but it was as secure as Westminster Abbey.

Neither of them had much jewelry, just the small gold earrings they'd purchased the day Griffin made them go shopping. But with gowns like these—especially Emily's—little jewelry was better.

"The lads are going to fall all over themselves when they see us," Emily predicted, patting her hair.

"They'd better," Finley added. "It's taken hours for us to look like this. I would hope they'd appreciate it."

They were just about to meet the boys in Griffin's room when Emily hesitated. "What's wrong?" Finley asked.

"It's Jasper," the redhead replied, her pretty face all concern. "His poor heart must be broken, being used like that by a girl he loved."

"This whole mess is because of her," Finley added. "I wager she was the one who knew Jas would recover the machine to protect her. The collar was probably her idea, as well. She's a coldhearted slag."

"Maybe we could find him someone new in London."

Finley smiled. Emily seemed to have a penchant for match-making. Maybe her love of fixing machines made her want to fix people, too. "Or we could let him do that himself—when he's ready."

Emily obviously preferred her own suggestion but saw the merit in Finley's, as well. That was the end of their discussion of the brokenhearted cowboy. They had an event to get to and a villain to stop.

And then they could go home. As fantastic as the city was, Finley couldn't say that she'd be sorry to leave it. Not after the "adventure" they'd had.

Her friend had been correct in one thing, however, Finley realized as they entered Griffin's room—the boys did look as though they might fall over at the sight of them.

"Amazing what the right dress can do, isn't it?" Finley asked with a slightly embarrassed grin.

Griffin offered her his arm. "It's not the dress—it's the girl."

She blushed as she tucked her arm around his. She wasn't certain how to react when he said such things, because she knew he meant them.

Behind her, she heard Sam tell Emily how pretty she was. She could tell he meant it, too.

"I think we're all dang pretty," Jasper commented, sounding more like his former self. "Me especially."

Finley grinned at him. "Perhaps we can simply dazzle Dalton into surrendering, eh, Jas?"

He stared at her, a surprised light in his green eyes. Finley realized she had started to refer to him by the nickname a few days ago. It was a sign of how quickly she had come to think of him as a dear friend, and he knew it.

Poor thing. She really just wanted to hug him and tell him it would be all right. Bloody hell, now she was starting to think like Emily. Next, she'd probably try bringing nice girls home to meet him.

"Maybe, Miss Finley. Maybe."

Despite the gravity of their situation, their spirits were fairly high as they climbed into a shared cab that was fortunately large enough for the five of them—Sam took up the space of two people. And why shouldn't their mood be bright? They knew what they had to do, how to do it and had the confidence that they would each be able to play their roles. Sam was their physical strength and would provide muscle, as would Finley. Emily was in charge of gadgets and anything mechanical. If she was able to get close to Dalton's machine, she would be able to disarm it with a touch, but if she couldn't, then Griffin would find its Aetheric signature and do it remotely. And Jasper would do anything that required speed or accuracy. The boy could shoot a marble at a hundred yards while at a dead run—faster than any of the rest of them could ever imagine.

And she...well, she was willing to play a little dirtier than her friends.

They would not let Dalton succeed, and they would certainly not let him escape. Finley was the only one who held the same determination where Mei was concerned. She would not allow the girl to get away after all she'd done to Jasper.

The Museum of Science and Invention was located in a fashionable neighborhood near 2nd Avenue and 11th Street. It was a stately stone building, which looked as though it might have been a wealthy family's address rather than a place where art and scientific discoveries were displayed.

The area teemed with steam carriages, horses and street cars. Men and women in elegant clothes and glittering jewels streamed into the facility, their conversations a low buzz mingling with the sounds of the street and city.

Finley felt like a princess as she entered the society building on Griffin's arm. She hadn't said anything, but he looked absolutely gorgeous in his black-and-white evening clothes. Really, if she was honest with herself, she thought he'd look gorgeous in a burlap sack. Jasper and Sam looked very handsome, as well. It was odd to see Jasper in anything but his hat and casual kit.

The building was just as impressive inside as out. Pale walls showcased beautiful, colorful paintings of all sizes. Glass cases on tables and pedestals held delicate and priceless treasures.

"It's amazing," she breathed.

Griffin smiled at her. "We can go to some of these sort of events in London if you like."

For a moment, Finley's heart jumped at the idea, but then she remembered that she was not of the same social sphere as Griffin. Here, they could pretend, but back home, everyone would know she was lower-class and shun her. They might shun him, and she didn't want to be responsible for that.

"Perhaps," she replied around the fist-size lump in her throat and then glanced away before he could see the truth in her eyes—that they would never attend such an event in London.

Griffin didn't seem to notice her change in demeanor, for which Finley was thankful. He turned to the rest of their party. "Keep your eyes open for Dalton or any of his gang. Check your communication devices."

Emily offered each of them the small metal buds to put in their ears that amplified sound and voice. Each was attuned to the frequencies of their individual voices, so while they would pick up some background noise, they would amplify anything they wished to communicate with one another so that it could be heard by the rest, even in different parts of the building.

Each of them said something in a whisper and the others nodded if they heard it. When they were convinced the system was working, they split up: Finley and Griffin, Sam and Emily, and Jasper on his own. Since he would be a primary target for Dalton, the rest would make certain to keep an eye on him, as well.

Then they waited.

They mingled, ate, drank, but all the while, they were constantly on guard, waiting. It was exhausting. Mr. Tesla had recovered enough to join them but seemed uncomfortable with all the attention he garnered. He was so "twitchy" and withdrawn that Finley didn't know if he'd be any help to them if they needed it—and the machine was his bloody creation.

Finally at half past eleven, Griffin suggested the inventor go home and get some rest. Tesla didn't argue and quickly made his getaway.

"He's an odd man," Finley remarked.

Griffin stared at her as if she had just made a gross understatement. "You have no idea. Come on, let's look at the 'realistic' automaton dog in the corner."

They spent the next half hour visiting the exhibits, marveling at some, chuckling at others, all the while waiting for Dalton to strike. Finley knew she wasn't the only one wondering if he had fooled them and actually had a different target in mind. Her anxiety grew with every tick of the clock.

Then at midnight, Dalton appeared. Literally, appeared. One moment, there was a wall with a schematic on it, and the next, Dalton stood in front of that drawing, Mei at his side.

They had walked through the wall.

Finley's hand tightened on Griffin's arm. "They're here," he murmured so that the others would know. "Far east wall."

It was so tempting to jump on both of them right then, but Dalton hadn't done anything wrong just yet, other than sneak in without an invitation. Hardly the sort of thing that warranted police attention. Whip would be waiting outside to swoop in when needed, just as Jasper would now make his way to the roof, where he would be less of a target and where he had set up a rifle earlier that day. From there, he would keep watch over Dalton's carriage in case the criminal managed to escape the building.

"I'm here." Jasper's voice rang in Finley's ear. She marveled at his speed. Before Griffin announced Dalton's arrival, Jasper had been in the same room. Now he was in position on the roof.

"We see Dalton" came Emily's comment. "We're not far behind you, Griff."

Finley kept her gaze glued to the criminal. He didn't seem so pretty to her, now that she knew how evil he really was.

"He's moving," she said.

Sure enough, arm in arm, Dalton and Mei made their way through the crowd. They looked like any other influential young couple. They were gorgeous together, Mei's bright magenta gown a contrast to Dalton's black-and-white attire. They were heading straight toward the display in the center of the room—a rare diamond on loan from Mrs. Rothschild, which she had been gifted by some European royal. It was as big as a baby's palm, set in gold filigree. It sparkled under the chandelier, so brightly that at just the right angle it could blind a person. It had been cut using some new process that was apparently a technological marvel—which was why it was on display here rather than in an art museum.

The diamond wouldn't be the only prize Dalton had his eye on for the evening, but it would be the most prestigious and certainly the most illustrious. For all they knew, he might have already helped himself to other items located within different areas of the building or the vault. This was his primary objective—it made sense that he would save it for last.

Slowly, they closed in on Dalton. He hadn't noticed them yet, or perhaps he had and just didn't care. Finley watched in fascination as he pressed a switch located on a wandlike thing in his hand. The glass case holding the diamond shimmered for what might have been a second and then appeared completely normal again. That was when Dalton stuck his hand—the one Finley hadn't broken—right through it.

It caused a bit of a sensation, as there were other guests to witness his display of criminal bravado. Security approached, as well. Dalton appeared unconcerned, until Griffin said his name.

Dalton's gaze locked with hers, and that was when his face lost all trace of prettiness. An ugly snarl twisted his features. Would he be brazen enough to try to kill her right then and there?

She and Griffin lunged into action, but they weren't fast

enough. Dalton yanked his hand from the case, diamond clasped in his long, greedy fingers. He took off running, Mei at his heels. Finley and Griffin raced after them, Sam and Emily close behind.

In the corridor, Dalton pointed the wand at the opposite wall, and he and Mei ran through it. It had resolidified when Finley reached it, and she banged her fist against it in frustration.

"Split up," Griffin commanded. "We can't let them get away."

"They won't" came Jasper's voice, and Finley thought she heard him pull the hammer back on the rifle. Dalton had better hope they got to him before Jasper did, because Jas was likely to kill the bounder.

She raced down the corridor, rounded a corner and came face-to-face with Mei. That was when she noticed that Mei had one of those wands, as well. Wonderful.

The smaller girl didn't waste time being surprised. She whipped out her leg and kicked Finley hard in the chest. All the air swooshed out of her lungs, but not before she managed to land a solid punch of her own to Mei's pretty face. While Finley was bent over, gasping for air, Mei slipped through the wall and was gone.

Cursing and panting, Finley took up the chase once more. She ended up in a storage room on the outside edge of the building. All of the windows were shuttered and reinforced with bars to prevent break-ins, but they wouldn't be able to stop Dalton. If he made it through the shelf-lined walls he would be free and clear, because there were no doors through which Finley and the others could run.

Sam grabbed hold of Dalton, but the villain pointed the wand at him and slipped out of Sam's grasp. Sam cried out, clutching his arm to his chest. There was blood on it, even though it appeared to be whole. "It was like he ripped right through me," he whispered, face white. It must have brought back memories of the automaton attack that had killed him.

"Griffin!" Finley shouted. Dalton and Mei were both headed to the back wall, wands outstretched. She raced to Griffin as he stopped dead in his tracks and began to concentrate.

His hands shook. Was he afraid that the "ghost" might be waiting for him? Or was he worried that he might not be able to shut the machine down and Dalton would get away? Finley didn't know, but she did know that she was there for him. She reached down and wrapped her fingers around his arm—she knew better than to touch his hands. His gaze locked with hers for a split second, and then his eyes closed.

And then something strange happened. It was as subtle as a breeze, but Finley felt it—a shift in the Aether. When she looked, the wall looked as it had, and Dalton and Mei were gone.

"Damn!" It was Griffin who swore, not her. "I thought I had it." He raked a hand through his hair, mussing the previously perfect waves.

Finley grabbed his hand. "Come on, we need to get out-side."

"Jasper," Griffin barked. "Do you see them?"

"Not yet," he replied. "What the tarnation…? Griff, there's something going on. I'm going down."

"We'll be right there."

The four of them tore off in search of the back entrance to the building. When they found it, they raced along the side of the building until they turned the corner where Dalton's carriage supposedly waited.

Finley stopped dead in her tracks as the scene before her suddenly came together in her mind. The horror of it brought a rush of bile to the back of her throat. And the noise. That horrible noise.

"Oh, my God."

If there had been anything in his stomach to come back up, it would have. Tears filled Jasper's eyes as his heart twisted in his chest and his stomach rolled in protest. He heard the others approach and whirled to face Griffin.

"Do something!" he cried.

Griffin and the others stopped and stared, just as Jasper had done when he raced down here and arrived on the scene.

Dalton had made it through the building but not quite into his vehicle. His hand was lodged inside the newly solid carriage door, and he whimpered in pain. But it was Mei…

Mei hadn't gotten as far before Griffin shut the machine

down. Mei hadn't made it completely out of the building. Most of her upper body protruded from the brick and stone.

The rest was trapped in the wall, and she was screaming in pain.

Griffin held out his hands. There was a slight shift in reality—so subtle, like a blink—and Dalton fell to the ground by his carriage, clasping his ruined hand to his chest. Mei tumbled from the wall into Jasper's arms. He caught her and slowly lowered her to the ground as her screams gave way to a guttural, gurgling sound.

"Mei," he whispered. He thought his heart had broken when she'd betrayed him, but that hadn't hurt nearly as much as this.

Wide dark eyes gazed up at him from her pale face. Blood stained her lips. Jasper turned his gaze to Emily. "Can you help her?"

Emily shook her head, her face a study in anguish and remorse. And Griffin...Griffin looked like hell.

"Send for an ambulance," he shouted as Whip and his men came onto the scene. Jasper's brother-in-law took one look at the carnage and nodded grimly, sending one of his men to do as Griffin commanded.

Little Hank tried to escape, but Sam grabbed him, and that was all the attention Jasper bothered to give the others. He turned back to Mei, knowing full well that there was nothing anyone could do to help her now.

"I'm so sorry," he whispered, voice hoarse with the tears

he fought to hold back. He brushed a stray lock of inky-black hair back from her face. "I'm so very, very sorry."

She made a choking noise in the back of her throat. "Not… your…fault." Her fingers clutched at those he held to her face. "For…give me."

And then she was gone. Her eyes changed, and all the tension left her body, and that's how he knew that she was dead.

He couldn't hold the tears back any longer. A sob tore from his throat as he held her against his chest. He buried his face in her silky hair and, heedless of the crowd around him, wept as though his heart was breaking.

It was.

Chapter 19

"What are you doing?"

Griffin managed a small smile as the cold night air numbed his cheeks. He was on the narrow deck on the front of the airship, leaning against the rail. "Thinking."

Finley came up beside him, the lights of the *Helena* casting golden highlights on her hair as the wind tried to rip it from the knot at the back of her head. "It's not your fault," she told him.

He nodded. He had heard similar sentiments over the past two days, but none of them—not even the one from Jasper—could ease the horrible feeling of guilt and responsibility that weighed heavy on his chest. "I know, but I still did it."

Mei was dead because of him. It didn't matter that it had been her own greed that had brought her there in the first place. He had killed her and—worse—he'd had to stand there and watch her die.

It made him want to vomit every time he thought about it—which was about a thousand times a day.

Jasper didn't blame him. Jasper forgave him. He said he knew that Griffin would have done anything to save Mei. None of them knew it, but Griffin had even gone to Tesla on the wild hope that maybe the eccentric inventor had managed to construct a machine to travel back in time. But he was told that no one had yet perfected the art of time travel. Griffin would have gone back if he could. He would have even let Dalton get away if it meant that Mei might live.

But there was no going back, no matter how much he might wish for it. He hadn't killed Mei on purpose, but he just hadn't thought of timing. His only thought had been stopping them.

Well, he had certainly done that.

"Are you going to be all right?" Finley asked, a small frown pulling at her brows. "I'm worried about you."

He took her hand in his own and brought her knuckles to his lips. "Thank you. I'll be fine in time, I'm sure." But that was a lie. He didn't think he'd ever be "right" again.

Finley watched him closely, as though she could see through him. Maybe she could—she seemed to know what he was thinking at the most inconvenient times.

"How long did Jasper say he'd be in San Francisco?" she asked, turning her gaze back to the sky.

"A few weeks. He wants to spend time with his family."
He didn't need to add that he was also going to make certain
Mei had a decent funeral. He and Whip took her body with
them, as well as Dalton and the other prisoners. Personally,
he'd be surprised if Jasper returned to London afterward. If
he was the cowboy, he wouldn't want to stay under Griffin's
roof—but perhaps that was just his guilty conscience talking.

"It was good of you to give him that money," Finley remarked quietly, her voice barely audible over the thrum of
the airship's engines.

Griffin shrugged. Paying for the funeral was the least he
could do, wasn't it?

"I don't know about you." There was forced brightness
in her tone. "But I'm delighted to see the backside of Miss
Astor-Prynn."

That actually brought a small smile to his lips. "I didn't
notice her backside. Was it nice?"

She squeezed his fingers. "Ow!" he cried, but it hadn't
hurt—not really. "Bloody hell, woman."

"Take that as a warning, Your Grace. I can beat you into
shape if need be. And don't think you're going to be allowed
to wallow in guilt with me around. I won't stand for it. Do
I make myself clear?"

Griffin swallowed. She was rather…attractive when she
bossed him around. He was so used to being the boss himself that it was nice to have someone looking out for him.
"Crystal," he replied.

Finley smiled. "Good."

He gazed into her eyes, so bright when the light hit them. "Finley, I want you to know I trust you. I was a git, thinking you might prefer a life of crime instead of with me, Emily and Sam."

"No, you weren't," she corrected, surprising him. "Being part of Dalton's gang—getting his attention—was fun at first. And then Whip Kirby put those irons around my wrists, and I realized the consequences of being an idiot. I don't want that life. I want to be with you—and the others."

A grin spread across his face at her halfhearted amendment. He knew what she meant, and he meant it, too. It was all right if neither of them said it aloud. They both talked too much, anyway. Thought too much, too.

So instead of thinking about it, Griffin simply wrapped his arm around her waist, pulled her close and pressed his lips to hers. She tasted like the strawberries they'd had for dessert, and she smelled of fresh air and cinnamon. Her arms came up over his shoulders, around his neck, and she kissed him back.

Tesla might not have invented a machine for going back in time, but Griffin thought he'd just found a way to stop it.

A thousand years later, he lifted his head. Finley stared up at him. He stared back, and after a moment, they both began to smile.

"It's cold out here," she said. "We should go in."

"I suppose we should."

Then she came up on her toes and kissed him, and all thoughts of going inside and cold noses vanished for a while.

He held her hand when they returned to the inner cabin of the dirigible. Sam and Emily were waiting for them there. Griffin's heart lightened at the sight of them. They both looked concerned when they met his gaze, and their worry warmed him. They didn't think he'd done anything wrong. Maybe in time he'd agree with them.

"About time the two of you came back," Sam commented with his usual charm. He pointed at Emily. "She thinks we should all have some kind of wing contraptions so we can fly on our own."

Finley glanced at Griffin. "When we first came to New York, you asked me if I would like to know how it felt to really fly."

"Such devices would be very beneficial," Emily informed him.

"My arms would get tired," Sam countered.

"They're for gliding, Sam. You don't have to flap. How many times do I have to tell you that?"

The image of Sam flapping wings attached to his arms like a chicken caused Griffin to laugh out loud. The three of them stared at him for a second and soon joined in.

"Get whatever you need, Em." Griffin wiped his eyes. "The expense will be worth it just to see Sam flap."

They laughed some more—Sam possibly the hardest.

It was at that moment that he knew everything was going to be fine. If he could still laugh, then all was not lost.

He was going to be all right after all.

★ ★ ★ ★ ★

Author's Note

One of my favorite parts of writing a book is the research I get to do. My world might vary from the real Victorian era, but I've tried to keep many things true to history. For example, the Waldorf-Astoria really was on 5th Avenue. It was torn down early in the twentieth century to build the Empire State Building. Incidentally, it's rumored that there was to be a dirigible docking bay at the top of the Empire State! Wouldn't Finley have loved that.

The neighborhood known as Five Points had been cleared away by 1897, but in "my" world it stuck around for a little while longer. I really wanted that rough contrast to the world that Griffin is drawn into. There were a lot of gangs there, as well. A great book for more information on the area is *Gangs of New York* by Herbert Asbury. And just in case you're wondering, it was indeed the basis of the movie starring Leonardo

DiCaprio and Daniel Day-Lewis. I found it amusing that the Irish actor played an Italian character, and the Italian actor played the Irish....

Nikola Tesla did indeed live in New York City in 1897, and he worked on strange and wonderful inventions in his laboratory in the Gerlach Hotel where Griffin and Emily call upon him. What I find most fascinating about this man, other than his desire to build a death ray to use against America's enemies, was that he worked on radio waves and wireless transmissions more than a hundred years before Wi-Fi was ever invented! Few people have contributed more to the world of science than Tesla—or to the world of science fiction. There's no denying he was one of the most brilliant minds of his time, even if he did have to have a certain amount of napkins for every meal—and counted them all!

As usual, this book could not have been written without the following people: Miriam Kriss, who propped me up and cheered me on; Krista Stroever, who has always been amazing to work with and one of the truly special people in my life. Jesse, Sharie and Colleen, who listened every time I called and whined. I love you girls! The Fabulous Dr. Grymm and his lovely Mrs. Grymm, who helped with inventions, helped bring me into the steampunk community and just generally rock as people. And lastly, this book could not have been written without Steve, who helped with research (Tesla, baby!), bragged me up, helped me brainstorm, wore a top hat and tails when I asked, and basically supported my madness.

Also, I've been asked what music I listen to while I write. This book was written almost entirely to a sound track of Emilie Autumn, Amanda Palmer and My Chemical Romance.

★ ★ ★ ★ ★